DEATH BY UNNATURAL CAUSES . . .

"Quatorze, this is Laura Ireland," Theo said. "Laura, Quatorze. He's deputy sheriff on this side of the parish."

"How do you do, ma'am?" drawled the deputy. He shook her hand, then rubbed a palm over his peroxided burr haircut. Quatorze was as homely as a catfish. He had massive, muscular arms and thighs, and on his biceps was tattooed his single claim to beauty: a seraphic mermaid with huge breasts and a rounded belly.

"When'd you find him, Quatorze?" asked Theo.

"I didn't. Hot-T Daigle down the road called in this morning. He was taking his wife to Mass, and when they saw the body they just turned around and went back home."

"Any idea who did it?"

Quatorze folded his arms. "Gus thought it might be you." He eyed Theo. "You didn't do it, did you, Theophile?"

Theo walked down the road and Laura followed. They walked up to the body and Theo squatted down. He pulled back the canvas and Laura made a little noise.

Boo Guidry lay face up on the asphalt, his nose bent gently to one side. His white forehead was a scrambled mass of flesh and hair, and two oily streaks ran down his khaki shirt. Oddly, there was no blood. . . .

SNAKE DANCE

LINDA MARIZ

BANTAM BOOKS
NEW YORK • TORONTO • LONDON • SYDNEY • AUCKLAND

SNAKE DANCE

A Bantam Crime Line Book/September 1992

ISBN 0-553-29515-2

Published simultaneously in the United States and Canada

*Bantam Books are published by Bantam Books, a division of Bantam
Doubleday Dell Publishing Group, Inc. Its trademark, consisting of the
words "Bantam Books" and the portrayal of a rooster, is Registered in
U.S. Patent and Trademark Office and in other countries. Marca
Registrada. Bantam Books, 666 Fifth Avenue, New York, New
York 10103.*

PRINTED IN THE UNITED STATES OF AMERICA

RAD   0   9   8   7   6   5   4   3   2   1

For all the Annas

Redemption Parish is a fictional amalgam of places on Bayou Lafourche. The people who live in or pass through Redemption Parish are wholly the product of the author's imagination, as are the events which occur there. The Atchafalaya River, which flows west of the parish, is very real, however; the name is pronounced CHA-fa-LIE-ya.

A note to Northerners: Southerners use "y'all" only for second-person plural. "You" works perfectly well for the singular.

PROLOGUE

GRINDING SEASON, 1979

A tube led from Claiborne's neck into a covered steel canister on the floor. The skin of his legs was stitched together with coarse black sutures and his body was the color of crab bait left in the trap. Money Perrier worked with a huge hypodermic, drawing clear fluid from the abdomen.

Theo closed the back door and Money looked up. "Theophile, you can't be in here." He put down the hypodermic and pulled a drape over Claiborne's body. "Go on home now. I'll let you see him when I'm finished."

"I heard he was all torn up."

Money walked over to block his view. "Only his hipbone's bad. I told your daddy I'd have him fixed up fine for the casket. You go home. Your daddy needs you."

Theo strode over to the steel table. "No, he doesn't. He's not there." Pulling back the sheet from his brother's body, he studied the face. Claiborne's pimply cheeks looked like pork flesh cut for rendering, his mouth like new dried figs. Theo put a finger on Claiborne's winged collarbone. "Was he in a lot of pain?"

Money stood close, smelling of starched shirt and formaldehyde. "I don't think so. The pain of something like that comes if you stay alive." He touched Theo's arm. "Go on home, now, Theophile. I'll call y'all for viewing tomorrow."

Theo walked out the back door of the funeral home and drove north up the bayou highway. Speeding through the three blocks of business district, he passed Boudreaux's cane fields on the north side of town and turned off at the live oaks shading tumbled-down Wildwood Plantation. Bumping down the road to the mill, he parked next to the October mountain of sugar cane in the grinding yard and entered the massive mill door. Somewhere a radio played and Theo looked up at the lighted laboratory loft where his father had slept during grinding season for as long as he could remember.

Climbing the stairs, he lifted his hand to knock. Inside a woman laughed. Theo held stone still and listened as his father said, ". . . against my religion to put water in good liquor. That's why I always drink beer." His speech was slurred.

The woman laughed again and Theo pictured the fat face of Marie Arsenault, who worked in the Dollar Store. Turning quietly, he crept down the stairs as Marie sang along to a rock-and-roll song.

CHAPTER 1

Onstage they hung the fiddler upside down. Red hair dangling nearly to the floor, he sawed out a chorus of "Paddy on the Bayou" while a woman guitarist fed him straight lines and beer. Down in the crowd Theo walked up behind Laura and kissed the warm skin of her neck. She turned and flashed a pearly smile. "Did you find out about your sister?"

"I did. Another nun is leaving for El Salvador at the end of the week and Honorée said it wasn't a good time for her to come to a family reunion."

"That's too bad. I was looking forward to meeting her. But at least your father's in town. Can we drop by there after the dance?"

He slipped an arm around her waist and pulled her

close. "I had other ideas for after the dance. I thought we might"— he paused to make himself perfectly clear— "turn in early."

Laura smiled again. The peachy skin on her cheekbones looked like soft fruit next to her blue eyes. Gently Theo put his teeth into her bare shoulder.

"Theo! What is with you tonight?" She looked around at his eighty-odd relatives enjoying themselves on the tennis court in his Uncle Gus's front yard. "What's your family going to think?"

"They'll think I like your shoulder. Cajuns are very literal."

Laura looked up at the Christmas lights strung through the giant live oaks. "Okay," she said, "if we're going to turn in early, maybe we can see your father tomorrow before we go fishing."

"Can't do. We have to leave early for the lake."

"Today you said it was too close to dinnertime to see him."

Theo looked at the stage and applauded the fiddler, who was now back on his feet taking bows. "Hell of a way to make a living."

Laura turned to catch Theo's eyes but he resolutely stared at the makeshift stage where the Chacahoula Bon Ton Players exchanged insults and drank everclear from mason jars. "Theo, you don't actually want me to meet your father, do you?"

"It's just that Daddy's not in very good shape right now."

"I don't care."

He watched the stage.

"Theo, look at it from my perspective: I get invited to Louisiana to meet your family and when I arrive, you won't even let me meet the only immediate member who's actually in town. Now, what am I supposed to think?"

"Shh. They're announcing something."

The woman guitarist stepped up to the mike. "It's getting late and I see some little people out there who look like they need to *fais do-do*. Y'all think it's time for the 'Hokey Pokey'?"

"Yeah!" bellowed the crowd.

From the back a voice called out, "Let T-John do it!" "T-*John*!"

Instantly an adolescent male leaped onstage and took the microphone from the surprised woman. Grinning hugely at the crowd, he moved nimbly across the platform. Tossing his head, he let a shock of brown bangs fall artlessly over one dark eye.

Theo leaned forward. "This should be great. T-John's going to lead 'Hokey Pokey' the way they do in his fraternity at LSU."

"I'm not very interested at the moment."

"Sure you are." He pulled her by the hand over to the center of the court, where the relatives formed a big circle. "Old family tradition, everybody does it."

Joining hands with the rest of the Talbots, they watched as parents shuffled preschoolers into the center, where they walked around bumping into one another or spun in dizzy circles.

The band gave T-John a downbeat and into the microphone he sang, "All right, y'all, it's time for the 'Hokey Pokey.' " With a swish of his hips and a toss of his head, he vamped in the manner of a Bourbon Street female impersonator: "Right foot!" The crowd joined in: "You put your right foot in, you put your right foot out, you put your right foot in and you shake it all about." T-John blew kisses and pouted over his shoulder. Down in the circle a little girl shrieked, "T-John's acting like a *lady*!" and the crowd roared.

"Theo," called Laura, "this won't make me forget."

Theo strutted in a circle like a third-rate hula dancer. "Can't talk; I'm dancing."

"Left foot," sang T-John. Coyly he presented his left toes and quickly pulled them back. The dancers followed, working their way through "arms" and "head," then looked up to see what body part was next. Prissily, T-John turned his hindquarters to the audience. "Right buttocks," he sang, pointing to that part of his anatomy. The crowd whooped and sang along.

Next T-John turned to display the other side of his posterior and they sang through that, wondering what could possibly follow. Slowly T-John unbuttoned his shirt. The children squealed and at that moment the guitarist swooped down to retrieve the mike. "Whole self," she sang. The dancers booed but sang that too.

After the "Hokey Pokey" families with young children picked up diaper bags and began saying their good-byes. The band struck up a quiet two-step and Theo took Laura in his arms to lead her through the boxy patterns. "Now, that was fun, wasn't it?"

"Don't patronize me."

"Laura, listen. Daddy's not set up for company right now."

"But from the way you talk, this might be the last time I ev—"

"I can't believe it!" Theo stopped dancing and looked across the tennis court.

"What is it?"

On the far end of the green asphalt a crowd gathered around a woman who had just arrived. Her sculpted silver coif stood in elegant contrast to the others' casual hairdos, and her ivory cotton dress made everyone's Bermuda shorts look dowdy. She was holding hands with one of Theo's young cousins and listening attentively, as if hearing unearthly music. Although at least sixty, she was incredibly beautiful.

"Who is she?" asked Laura.

"Aunt Cecile. But she *never* comes to reunions." They watched as Cecile kissed cheeks and rolled her eyes, making children smile and putting grown-ups at ease.

"She's really electric, isn't she?"

"You should see the men."

They danced slowly in place, watching his aunt's progress through the crowd. As she passed from group to group, the women greeted her enthusiastically and the men all sucked in their bellies, staring hungry-eyed at her face.

Theo pivoted Laura and said, "She's coming over here." They stopped dancing as Cecile glided over in a rush.

"Theophile! How are you?" Standing on tiptoe, she kissed him on both cheeks.

"Cecile, what you are doing here? I thought you said reunions make you feel old."

"I *am* old." She smiled and the porcelain skin around her eyes gathered in delicate lines. Laura inhaled and caught the heady scent of a perfume that smelled like white flowers after a rain.

Cecile said, "I only came up the bayou because they kicked me off Grand Isle." She touched Laura's hand. "And I've only just heard about *this* beautiful girl. Theophile, you have to introduce us."

"Cecile, this is Laura Ireland. Laura, this is my Aunt Cecile."

"Glad to meet you," said Laura.

"But not as glad as we are to meet you, dear. We had just about given up on Theophile." Cecile leaned her silver head to him. "Theophile, don't let this one get away."

"No, ma'am."

Laura said, "I don't understand what you just said about Grand Isle."

A herd of screaming children exploded out the screen door of Uncle Gus's lumbering white farmhouse far back under the trees and Cecile said, "Hurricane Dinah is just north of Havana and they wanted us off the island in case she decided to come in tomorrow. Theophile, do you mind if I stay at y'all's house?"

"No, ma'am. You're always welcome."

"I was hoping to stay in your sister's room"—she turned to Laura—"unless you're in there, dear?"

Theo broke in, "Laura's sleeping somewhere else. You can have Honorée's."

"Then I'll try not to be a bother." Cecile looked up at the top of Laura's streaky blond head, nearly eight inches higher than her own. "Laura, someone said you were in sports."

"Off and on. Right now I teach anthropology."

"I guess Theophile told you he used to teach at Jesuit High before he became a policeman."

Laura nodded. "I get him to edit for me whenever I can."

Shifting his weight from foot to foot, Theo said, "I can already tell I'm not going to like this conversation. Anybody want a cold drink?"

Cecile shook her silver head. "No, thank you, dear."

"Nothing for me, Theo."

They watched as he trudged across the thick Saint Augustine grass to where a bar had been set under the hundred-year-old oaks. "Do you always call him Theo?" asked Cecile.

"I can't even say 'Theophile.' "

"*TOE*-feel," corrected Cecile.

"See?"

Cecile laughed a lovely note and looked out at the dancing kinfolk. "Well, how much of Bayou Lafourche have you seen so far?"

"Not much. We just got in today and I think all Theo wants to do is fish." Laura looked across the yard at Theo, who squatted next to the bar plucking out a beer from a big galvanized tub of iced drinks. He was looking up, talking to the bartender, his forelock hanging like T-John's and his dark eyes smiling as he spoke.

Cecile followed Laura's gaze. "You can't let Theophile fish the *whole* time you're here. He should at least take you up The River Road to see the plantations."

"He said he didn't know when they were open."

"Honestly. You would think they actually eat all those fish they catch." She patted Laura's hand. "If you really can't get him to go, let me know and I'll at least take you around Belle Plaisir."

"Which one is that?"

"It's up the bayou a way, on the other side. I used to live there."

"You owned it?"

"My family did. Parts of them still do. But my half was stolen out from under me when I was six."

"You're kidding?"

"Oh, no. My mother and my Uncle Charles both had half interest in Plaisir and when Momma died in 1928,

Uncle Charles bought my half from me for one new dollar bill."

"Didn't your father . . ."

"Daddy died when I was two. I was left an orphan."

"And you can't do anything about it?"

Cecile shook her head. "Everytime I mention Plaisir, everyone just smiles like I'm crazy: 'Oh, no, there goes Cecile with her heiress story again.' So mostly I just try to keep my mouth shut and be pleasant."

"That's too bad."

Suddenly there was a tense shout from near the bar and Laura turned to see two grimacing middle-aged men wrestle each other to the ground. "They're fighting!" she cried.

"Who?" Cecile rolled her eyes. "Oh, Lord. It's Billy and Bobbie again. You'd think they'd have had enough by now."

The whole crowd stopped to look at the wrestlers. Three small boys raced over and leaped up on a picnic table, faces keen with excitement.

"Come on," said Cecile. "Let's go see which one gets his dentures broken this year." She led Laura to where the crowd was gathered around the grunting red-faced men rolling in the grass. The man on top wore a neatly ironed madras shirt and appeared to be trying to separate his adversary at the neck. On the edge of the picnic table lay two sets of false teeth on clean handkerchiefs.

A woman in blue stripes hovered over the wrestlers shouting angrily. "Stop it this instant!"

"Go for his wallet, Billy," called a spectator. "That'll stop him!"

Laura turned to Cecile. "What are they fighting about?"

"Bobbie shot Billy's dog on a hunting trip three years ago and he wouldn't pay as much as Billy thought she was worth. It's a real shame because they'd been hunting buddies since they were kids."

"Bobbie, get up right now!" The blue-striped woman danced sideways to avoid the rolling men.

Laura watched as the man on the bottom groped for

the other's eyes and ended up putting fingers in his nose instead. "They're going to kill each other," said Laura. "Somebody needs to stop them."

"Men don't stop fighting until they've ripped their shirts or drawn blood. It's something to do with their glands."

From the back of the crowd came a voice: "Coming through." The crowd parted as Theo and a shorter, sandy-haired man shuffled forward carrying a heavy tub of iced drinks. Straining against the weight, they set the tub on its edge and the short man counted, "One, two, three." Tipping the contents of the tub onto the fighters, they scooted sideways, trying to avoid the icy cascade.

The wrestlers gasped in surprise. Pulling apart, they sat up and wiped their faces, staring astonished at the short man. Laura studied him too. He wore a lawman's shirt and badge, jeans and cowboy boots. Tucking his thumbs around his chunky pewter belt buckle, he narrowed his eyes at the wrestlers. "Aren't y'all a little old for this?"

Billy and Bobbie stood up sheepishly, each scooping a set of teeth off the table. The woman in blue stripes put her hand to her mouth and ran sobbing to the house. The relatives dispersed and Cecile leaned toward Laura. "Excuse me, dear. I want to make sure Bobbie's wife is okay. She just had a hysterectomy."

"Sure." Laura walked over to Theo and the lawman as the officer reached into his pocket and pulled a five-dollar bill from a money clip. Calling to the three boys on the table, he said, "Y'all come here." The boys hopped down, eager to please.

"How about y'all putting the drinks back in the tub and then bringing them over to the bar. Ask Friday what he wants to do with them."

The boys whisked away the bill and began picking up soft drinks and beer.

Theo poured water out of his Loafers and slipped them back on. "You okay, Laura?"

Laura shrugged. "All I did was watch."

"Pretty stupid, wasn't it?"

The lawman shook water off his suede boots. "I don't

know about that, Theophile. That was no more stupid than some of the things *we* used to fight about."

Laura smiled politely as the short man stepped forward with his hand extended. "Theophile was just saying he wasn't going to let me meet you when the fight broke out, but it looks like he's stuck now, doesn't it?"

"Laura," said Theo, "this is Brian Guidry, sheriff of Redemption Parish."

The sheriff pumped her hand. "You can call me Boo."

"Boo," she repeated. "Are you a Talbot, too?"

"Oh, no, ma'am. People invite me to parties because they think I won't pull in their drunks driving home." Boo turned on his thick cowboy heel. "But I don't know. Theophile, you think we might be related back there someplace?"

"God forbid."

Across the yard a male voice called, "Theophile!"

They looked up to see T-John jogging down the yard. "You have a phone call," he shouted, and then sprinted back to the lighted farmhouse under the trees.

Theo frowned. "Boo, you think you can keep Laura happy for a while?"

"Depends on how particular she is."

"Don't try to marry her or anything."

Boo snorted a surprised laugh and turned to Laura as Theo jogged off behind T-John. "Can I get you something to drink, Miss Laura?"

Laura nodded. "I saw some mineral water in the tub. A bottle of that would be nice."

Boo called to the boys dragging the galvanized tub across the the grass. "Y'all wait up." He brought back a seltzer for Laura and a beer for himself. As he opened her drink and handed it to her, she asked, "Are you really trying to get married?"

"Oh, no, ma'am. I'm about as married as you can get. That was Theophile's little joke." He opened his beer with a whoosh and took a long, thirsty drink.

"It sounds like you and Theo have known each other from way back."

"All our lives, I guess. Although I can't really remember Theophile until we started playing football in fourth grade. He ever tell you about that?"

"Not really."

Boo's eyes rested on the hollow of her neck. "Guess y'all have better things to talk about than what happened down here during the Jurassic."

Laura attempted a merry smile. "He *did* say some of his friends were pretty wild and didn't seem to be getting better with age."

Sheepishly Boo looked at his cowboy boot and laughed a flat syllable. "I'm afraid Theophile doesn't approve of the way I was brought up. We don't see eye to eye on a lot of things." He gave Laura an appraising look. "You going to be busy the whole time you're here?"

Laura took a step backward. "It sounds like we're going to spend a lot of time at the lake."

Boo nodded. "Theophile's into fishing."

"So am I, but not for my whole vacation."

"I tell you what: first time you get bored, call me and I'll drive you around the parish in a patrol car. Lots of nice things to see around here."

"I keep forgetting 'parish' doesn't refer to a church."

"A parish is a county in Louisiana." He smiled, gap-toothed, vaguely reminding her of Howdy Doody, and they stood in silence watching the band until Theo appeared from under the trees. As he approached, his face was shadowed and distracted, and when he arrived, he stood somberly at Laura's elbow.

Laura leaned close. "Who was it?"

"Daddy."

"What'd he want?"

"He'd like to see me back at the sugar house. *Just* me."

"When? Tonight?"

"Right now."

CHAPTER 2

~~~~~~~~~~~~~~~~~~~~~~~~~

Theo turned at the stand of live oaks that used to shade Wildwood Plantation. Under the trees now stood a tiny new subdivision, each rambler carefully angled around one of the great oaks, as if trying to attain dignity and elegance by proximity to the dignified and elegant.

Down the gravel road Theo's headlights caught the sign: Talbot Brothers Sugar Refinery. He parked the truck in front of the office and looked across the grinding yard to the looming mill. Paint flaked off the machine shed and there was a missing light bulb over an exit sign. In October the sugar yard would again hold a mountain of cut cane. Now it was empty.

In front of the toolshed a spigot leaked, leaving a patch of gray mud across the yard. Theo tiptoed to the spigot and found it turned off tightly and spraying a fine mist from the valve. Cursing silently, he walked over to the mill and waited in the massive doorway for his eyes to adjust to the dark.

The sugar house smelled of machine oil and tool steel, and in the dimness he could just make out the huge mill belt pyramiding two stories to the ceiling. He followed its path through the wash tables and the mesh screens, all the way down to the monstrous grinding rollers near the floor. Walking over to the toothy steel cylinders, he rubbed a hand across the cogs, intermeshed—despite their size—as exquisitely as those of a fine old watch.

As he passed the vacuum pans that cooked up the black strap and the centrifugals that spun it into sugar, he looked up at the second-floor laboratory, listening to the canned laughter of his father's TV. The curtains were closed across the loft windows and soft yellow light glowed under the door. Slowly he climbed the stairs and knocked.

"Who is it?"

"Theophile."

"Come on in."

Theo opened the door. The shrunken old man lying slack on the couch bore no resemblance to his father. This man was a beery drunk with a pink pickled face and a shaggy gray beard. The skin around his eyes was both shriveled and bloated, and despite the August heat, he wore a long-sleeved shirt and pants. Theo stayed on his side of the room.

"Hello, Daddy. How you doing?"

The man on the couch said, "Fair to middling." He tapped the TV remote to turn down the sound. "Can I offer you a beer?"

"I couldn't drink it, Daddy."

"Mind getting me a cold one?" On the table beside him stood six empty beer cans.

"Yes, sir, I do mind. You'll have to do that yourself."

"Ungrateful child."

Valmont Talbot rose slowly on unsteady feet and shuffled across the room to the old stoop-shouldered refrigerator. In spite of the long sleeves, Theo could see the malnourished thinness of his father's body. The once-strong shoulders were as fragile as a bird's, the bony legs like a starving African's. Theo watched the sad performance, biting his lip so he wouldn't cry.

Opening the refrigerator door, Valmont steadied himself in front of the fully stocked cooler of Budweiser. Clouds of chilled air poured out from the box and Valmont said, "Best part of my whole day: standing right here."

"Who buys it for you, Daddy?"

Valmont grabbed a can and glanced sharply at his son. "Never mind who buys. You don't get any ideas, you hear?" He opened the can. "I can always find me a nigger to buy it."

"Of either race."

Valmont took a long swallow and added, "I got me some mighty good friends in this parish." He shuffled back slowly to the couch and collapsed. Picking up a pack of cigarettes, he lighted one, took a drag, and put it on the end table to burn in an ashtray. On the ceiling was a brown nicotine stain two feet across. Sipping beer, Valmont asked, "How's the truck running?"

"Fine. Do you mind if I keep it while I'm in town? We don't have any other way to get around."

"Just leave the keys in the ignition so the welders can use it if they need it."

"I always do."

Valmont looked at his son again and pushed the beer to the other side of the table. "I hear you brought a girl with you to the family reunion."

"Name's Laura. She's from California."

"Heard there's not much meat on her."

"She's just tall. Plays volleyball."

"Pretty?"

"Takes your breath away."

"Ha!" Valmont slapped his thigh and reached for his beer. As he drank, his Adam's apple bobbled against the ropy sinews of his neck.

"Daddy, you look awful. You been eating okay?"

Valmont mumbled angrily to himself.

"What'd you say?"

"I said, I have to be pretty careful about what I eat now. They could be poisoning me if they want."

"Come on, Daddy. Who's going to poison you?"

Valmont took a sip and looked directly at his son. "You." He crossed his ankles in smug satisfaction and his pants leg rode up, revealing pink, splotchy flakes.

"What's that on your ankle, Daddy?"

Valmont dropped his leg. "Rash."

"That's not rash, that's malnutrition sores, just like they said you'd get."

Belligerently Valmont swallowed a reply. ". . . can't cook worth shit." Picking up the cigarette, he sucked on it deeply and put it precisely back in its groove.

"What'd you want to see me about, Daddy?"

"Wanted to show you some things while I got you in town. Just in case."

"What kinds of things?"

"Like a broken railing, like fire in a chair I don't use, like someone letting a snake loose up here. I think it all has something to do with a land deal I got going."

"Daddy, what are you talking about?"

"Theophile, somebody's trying to kill me."

Theo looked at the decrepit old drunk. "Shoot, Daddy." Slumping into a wooden chair, he pushed his bangs off his forehead. "They *told* you this was going to happen. It's called paranoia. It's from drinking too much, just like everything else in your life is from drinking too much."

"Theophile, I am not that bad off."

"You can barely stand up and you smell like week-old piss. I'd call that pretty bad off, wouldn't you?"

"I want you to go out on that landing and take a look at the railing."

Theo stood. Walking out the door, he stopped on the balcony. "Well?"

Behind him his father called, "Grab ahold. But don't put your weight on it."

Theo touched the wood railing; it swung away from the newel post at one end. "Good God." Picking up the fallen end, he found the nail holes filled with short roofing tacks. "Shoot, Daddy, who's doing your carpentry?"

"You miss my point."

Theo tucked the railing back. "Daddy, all this means is you've got to stop hiring high school kids. Nobody's trying to kill you."

"Damn." Valmont stood painfully and shuffled over to the beer cooler. "I had 'em take out the chair that caught fire—you can see the scorch on the rug—but let me show you something I've been saving." He opened the refrigerator again and pulled at the inner door of the freezer. Finding it frozen shut, he reached in his pants pocket and pulled out a Swiss Army knife. As he fumbled with the blades, Theo walked over and banged the freezer door with a fist, popping it wide open.

"Thank you," Valmont muttered. He put his knife away and slid out a bulky black trash bag onto the floor. "Open that up, Theophile." He stumbled back to the couch.

Theo untied the knotted bag and peeled back the plastic, catching his breath in surprise. Inside was the thick brown body of a frozen snake. The frosted scales curled up off the skin and the triangular head rested permanently on one of the solid coils. " 'S a rattler."

"Thirteen rattles on that mother. Shit in my pants trying to kill it." Valmont lightly squeezed his beer can just to hear the sound.

"Why's it in the freezer?"

"I already told you. I kept it as evidence, just in case something happened."

"You mean you think somebody let it loose up here on purpose?"

"Not think, *know*. It's a dumb-ass thing to do but it certainly scared the shit out of me." He laughed at his own joke.

"Daddy, you know perfectly well this snake was chased out of the field from planting."

"From an *open* dirt field?"

Theo shrugged. "Could have been something else."

"Shit. Now you're starting to *sound* like one of them." Valmont gulped greedy swallows and looked at the flickering TV. "Get out of here. I want to watch the weather."

"Not yet, it's my turn. I want to talk to you."

Valmont pressed the remote for more sound. "Hurricane Dinah swings up this way, I'm going to rent me a generator for my beer."

Theo shouted, "Daddy, will you turn that thing down? I want to ask you a question."

Valmont pressed the control. "What do you want?"

"What's the money like in this family? Do we still have any?"

"You'll get yours, if that's what you mean."

"That's *not* what I mean. I want to know what's going to happen to the mill if you don't take care of it."

"It'll go to hell. Somebody'll buy it."

Theo got up and walked to the window. Pushing back the faded curtain, he looked down to the mill floor and the shadowed grinding rollers that pressed juice from cane.

"Daddy, when did things start going so wrong around here? We were still doing okay after Momma died, weren't we?"

"I can't remember."

"I actually think we were even holding it together all the way up until Claiborne got pulled through the rollers."

"Possible."

"I remember the exact minute they came to get me in class. I could tell by their faces that something terrible was wrong, but I never thought it was going to be about my baby brother." Theo turned to look at his father. "You know, that was *my* job he was doing when he fell off the truck."

His father was silent a moment, then said, "I remember I was up here boiling syrup and when I heard the noise, I looked down and saw Claiborne's red shirt in the rollers, and a whole big piece of my brain froze up right then and there. Never did get it back. It was like walking around looking up from the bottom of a well. One point I even went up to Rapides and fucked my brains out. But it didn't do any good." The old man sipped beer and smiled with memory. "There was this one ol' gal up there who kept trying t—"

"Daddy, I don't want to hear it."

Angrily, Valmont slammed down his beer. "I'm telling you this for your own good!" With a shaking hand, he reached for his cigarette and took a deep drag.

Theo looked again at the mill floor and said, "Five years ago, when I was home, there was a stonemason working in the cemetery so I borrowed his keys and went inside the crypt."

"Who'd you see?" Valmont replaced the cigarette.

"Claiborne looked the best. His coffin was gone and he was just lying there, really lifelike. Money Perrier must have done an awfully good job embalming. But I wanted to tell you," he looked at his father, "I touched his cheek and made a hole in it."

His father smiled with brown-stained teeth. "I was wondering who did that. I did that once too: to your Papa Theophile. You'd never know by looking at 'em they're as fragile as they are."

"Yeah." Theo looked around the room at the coiled heating elements and testing equipment. On the shelves were long rows of tiny mason jars of raw sugar, all different shades of beige and brown. "What are you going to do at grinding time, Daddy?"

"I can still test sugar. Nothing wrong with me." He pressed the remote and on the screen Vanna White gracefully turned letters. Valmont said, "You finished here? This is my program."

"Yeah, I'm finished." Theo walked to the door and turned for one last look at the gaunt, starving drunk who was his father. "Well, bye, Daddy. Try not to kill yourself too fast."

His father smiled, lifting his beer can in silent salute.

CHAPTER 3

Laura lay in bed watching Theo rummage through his shaving kit. Air from the window fan pressed the sheet against the long muscles of her legs. "What did your father want?" she asked.

"Nothing."

"Theo, you don't seem to understand how awkward it is for me to be here and not be able to meet him. Even the housekeeper as—"

"Dorothy."

"Even Dorothy assumed I'd been over there. She asked me if I thought he looked healthy."

He turned away from the dresser and asked, "Do you want me to clean up or not?"

Laura looked down at the hills and valleys of her body under the sheet. "I don't know if I'm in the mood right now."

"Good." He shoved the shaving kit across the dresser. "I can show you my baseball cards."

"Now?" She sat up on her elbows.

"Just a minute, they're in Claiborne's room." He went across the hall and came back with an old shoe box. Sitting down on the bed, he opened the box and rubbed his fingertips over the edges of the colored cards. "Twelve years of my life, right here in this box."

"You shouldn't have rubber bands around them. It decreases their value."

"Only if I plan to sell." He pulled out a bound packet. "Here's the '81 Dodgers."

"Really?" Laura pulled at the brittle rubber band and it popped and flew across the room. "Did I ever tell you I saw that series?"

"Yes," he said flatly. "L.A. in six."

"Hey, I didn't know Dusty Baker played i—" A low boom rumbled across the cane fields outside. "What was *that*?"

Theo walked over to the window and looked through the invisible fan blades. "Probably an M-80 left over from the Fourth." He turned around to see Laura totally absorbed in the Dodgers, her UCLA nightshirt pressing against her body in the soft wind from the fan. Sitting behind her—very close—he busied himself with stray Expansion players who did not have permanent packets to live in.

Laura turned over beautiful blond Andy Messersmith to read his statistics. "I don't suppose you guys ever arranged your cards in order of cuteness, did you?"

"Oh, yeah, that was real big down here."

She tucked Messersmith away and from the back of the box pulled out a strip of photos made in an automatic photography booth. They were four wildly varied poses of a fourteen-year-old Theo and a gap-toothed friend. In all the photos the friend's eyes had been poked out with a pin. "Theo, who's this with you? Is this Boo?"

He reached for the photos. "Yeah. We took those in Donaldsonville."

"Why are his eyes poked out?"

"I don't know. Must have been ticked off at him for something." He tucked the photos back and handed her a single card in a glassine slip. "Here's the only one I ever bought in a store."

She turned it right side up. "Lou Boudreau?"

"BOO-drow. He used to announce for the Cubs."

Laura read the card. "But he played for Cleveland and Boston. Why'd you buy him?"

Theo looked at the fine hairs on the back of her neck glistening softly in the light. "Boudreau's a Cajun name. I figured we might be related. But look." He brushed her hand deftly. "He was born in Harvey, Illinois, 1917."

Laura's nostrils flared and she straightened her back. "Where are your Cardinal cards?"

He zipped a finger along the back half of the box. "Everything from here on back."

"Wow! You *were* loyal. Didn't your friends all follow the Braves?"

"Depends on your family. My family never got into Expansion—Daddy and Uncle Gus and all them. Said it was against their religion. So I kept up with the Cards."

"Weren't you a social outcast?"

Breathing softly on her neck, he said, "I never worried about it." He let her look a moment longer and then scooped the Cardinals out of her hand. "Well, we'd better put these away. We've got to get up early tomorrow to beat the fish."

"Wait a minute," she protested. "I'm not finished looking."

"You can see them tomorrow. We need to hit the sack."

"I thought—"

"You thought what?"

"I thought maybe you still wanted to see what's under my nightshirt."

Theo sat back on the bed smiling with half-closed eyes. "I already know what's under your nightshirt."

"Oh-ho. He's playing hard to get." Laura stood up on the bed. "Okay, I have a better idea. We'll play this game, see: You're a major league baseball player, and I'm another major league ball player, except I'm really a woman and I don't know it yet. And you have t—"

"Wait a minute." He called time-out with his hands. "If I'm in the majors, who am I?"

"Andy Messersmith."

"That weenie? He blew it in the '74 Series."

Downstairs the phone rang. Laura looked alert but Theo said, "Dorothy'll get it."

Lowering her voice, Laura said, "Andy Messersmith won twenty games one year. And anyway, he's really cute, and he's six-one, same as me."

"Oh, yeah?" Theo leaped up on the bed and unzipped his pants. "Well, I think I'll be Calvin Klein, the famous underwear designer."

Dorothy's houseslippers flapped on the stairs. Laura sat down quietly and Theo stepped off the bed, tugging at his zipper. They both looked at the door, waiting for the knock.

Dorothy pounded three times with urgency. "Theophile?"

"What is it?"

"Can I open this door?"

"Sure."

Dorothy pushed back the door and stood blinking in the hall. The housekeeper's black hair was wound around pink foam rollers, and her brown face gleamed with night cream. Clutching her housecoat to her chest, she said, "That's the hospital. There was an explosion back at the sugar house. Your daddy's been brought in hurt."

The electronic doors glided open and cool hospital air flowed out. Theo and Laura paced through the lobby, Nikes squeaking on the smooth terrazzo. Pushing open the swinging doors to the emergency room, they were met by a nurse who rose defensively behind her Formica counter.

Theo said, "I'm looking for Valmont Talbot."

The nurse was dark-haired and slightly younger than them. "Theophile?" she asked.

He looked at her uncertainly.

"I'm Renée Bergeron. I went to school with your sister." Her name tag said, "DUGAS, R.N."

"Renée, I didn't recognize you. How's Daddy?"

"Fine, considering the shape he's in."

"What happened?"

"He *said* he kicked a pipe bomb off the landing right before it went off."

The blood drained from Theo's face. Renée nodded gravely, drawing a finger across the back of her head. "He has a scalp laceration where he landed, some powder burns on his face, and what Dr. Rodrigue is calling shrapnel in his lower legs. Doctor is trying to pick that out right now."

"Come on, Laura." Theo started down the hall. "You get to see Daddy in all his glory."

Renée moved over to block the hallway. "Y'all can't go back there. They're in surgery."

"Renée, he's waiting for me. If somebody set off a pipe bomb, I've got to talk to him now, while he's still sober."

"I can't let you do that."

Theo moved a step closer, squaring his shoulders in front of the nurse. Renée looked at the center of his chest and said, "I tell you what, Theophile: you come with me and we might be able to get Doctor to slip out and talk to you for a minute." Looking pointedly at Laura, she added, "But the fewer people, the better."

Laura dropped into a vinyl chair. "No problem." Picking up a rare back issue of *Highlights for Children,* she watched as Theo and the nurse disappeared into a door down the hall. The air-conditioning whooshed on quietly from ceiling vents and she turned magazine pages, looking for jokes.

Suddenly there was a noise across the room and she looked up to see a white-coated physician stride over to a medication cabinet behind the nursing station. He was stoop-shouldered and tall, thinning at both temples so that his brown hair looked like three peninsulas of land on a sea of ivory. Moving aside medication in the cabinet, he selected a small clear bottle with a sealed rubber gasket and dropped it in his pocket. Looking amiably at Laura, he closed the cabinet and said, "They're just about finished with her cast. She'll be out in no time."

"I'm not waiting for a woman."

"You're not with Diggy Savoie?"

"I'm with Theo. Theophile Talbot. We're here about his father."

"Theophile's here?" The doctor approached in a swift bent-kneed gait that reminded her of Groucho Marx. "Where is he?"

"Talking to Dr. Rodrigue," said Laura.

"Okay." He exhaled and extended a hand. "I'm Hypo Hebert. I didn't get your name."

"Laura Ireland. I came with Theophile to his family re-union this year."

"Glad to meet you, Laura."

"Do you know if Mr. Talbot'll be all right?" she asked.

Hypo tucked his hands in his lab coat pockets. "I'm not the one to ask. I don't work ER."

She glanced at the medications cabinet. "Oh."

"I'm a urologist, honey. Your basic plumber; and when they need me, I'm the coroner."

Clomping footsteps sounded out in the hall and Boo Guidry pushed through the swinging doors. Wearing cowboy boots rimmed with black mud, he chewed gum with his mouth open. Eyeing Hypo, he stepped back warily. "He's dead?"

Hypo mouthed the word, "No."

Boo glanced at Laura. "Theophile's here."

"Yes," she agreed.

"He's not back with his father, is he?"

"No. The nurse took him to see Dr. Rodrigue."

"Good." Boo turned to Hypo. "Mr. Talbot going to be okay?"

Hypo raised his eyebrows and the undulating lines on his white forehead formed deep troughs. "As I was telling Laura, I'm not the one to ask. Even Cootsie Rodrigue probably won't want to say, it's so hard to tell with an alkie. I passed by a few minutes ago and he was cussing his head off trying to dig shrapnel out of his leg."

"Shrapnel," said Boo. "Haven't heard that word in a long time."

Laura watched as Boo moved toward the back hall, bits of black mud flying off his boots. The sheriff was the wrong age to have been in combat. He turned on his heel. "Are you sure Theophile isn't trying to see his father?"

"He might be," said Laura. "He wanted to."

"Shoot."

Boo clomped toward surgery and Hypo grabbed his arm. "You can't go back there. The nurses'll scream blue enchiladas, you track mud on their floor."

"Theophile can't talk to his father."

"Sure he can," said Hypo. "They both speak English."

"Very funny, Hypo. It's gonna look really great in the papers if later on we find out Theophile set out that pipe bomb, now won't it?"

Laura stepped forward. "Theo didn't set the bomb."

"Have you been with him since he left the party?" Boo asked.

"Yes. I mean no."

Boo clomped over and stood directly in front of her. "Look, Miss Laura, I heard Theophile say he was going to the sugar house." Exhaling deeply, he touched the frame of the bayou print on the wall behind her and said, "Now, you're a very nice person and I know you mean well, but there's a lot of things gone on in this parish that you can't possibly know about."

Laura looked at his pupils, thinking of the defaced photos in Theo's room. "I'd love for you to fill me in."

"Fine. Just fine." He stuffed his hands in his jeans pockets and looked her up and down. "Maybe you could even hitch a ride with me out to the sugar house in a little while. That way I can work and talk at the same time."

"Sure."

Hypo cleared his throat as Theo came out of the door down the hall. Laura watched as he strode toward them, eyes rimmed with red pain. Catching sight of Boo's dirty boots, Theo said, "You've been out to the sugar house."

Boo lifted a pointed cowboy toe. "Yeah. Y'all ought to get your faucet fixed."

"Find out what happened yet?"

Boo chawed his gum. "Not yet. All I know is the deputy said when he went to check out the explosion, he found your daddy upstairs lying on a door blown off the hinges. We couldn't do anything without more light so we just roped the whole place off."

Without listening to the end of Boo's summary, Theo turned to the doctor. "Maybe you could tell us, Hypo: Daddy's doped up and Cootsie Rodrigue was real vague about when I might be able to talk to him."

"That's because Cootsie don't know either. They'll have to hold your daddy at least overnight to see about internal injuries and I imagine they'll keep him in la-la land the whole time. I know for a fact they don't want to mess with an alkie in withdrawal."

Boo looked at his watch. "Theophile, listen. I got to go. I just talked to your Uncle Gus, and he and a few thousand relatives are going to show up here in about ten minutes. The last thing I want to do is have to baby-sit the Talbots, so if you'll tell me where the lights are at the sugar house, I'll get back over there and start work."

"Better than that, I'll meet you there in a few minutes. I just need to drop Laura off at the house."

Laura opened her mouth but Boo interrupted. "Theophile, I don't think you ought to be working on this. I know you and your daddy didn't see eye to eye on a lot of things."

"You what?"

"You heard, Theophile. I don't want you around for the investigation."

"Get real, Boo. You know perfectly well if I were going to kill Daddy, I'd certainly do better than set off some half-assed pipe bomb."

Laura opened her mouth again and Boo said loudly, "Even so, Theophile. I think I'm going to have to pull rank on you. I don't want you back there."

"Damn it, Boo."

Hypo interjected. "For chrissake, Guidry, let the man help with the investigation. You know perfectly well he didn't plant a pipe bomb on his daddy."

Laura spoke up, "Boo, he could stay back out of the way with me."

Theo said, "Be quiet, Laura. You're not going."

"Yes, I am. Boo said I could."

"He w—?" Theo's face contorted with rage. "Boo Guidry, what do you think this is? Some kind of dating game? She is *not* going to the sugar house—be quiet, Laura. If you let her go, she'll do exactly what you did: walk through the mud puddle, where there are *probably* prints of the last person who walked through it—whoever tried to kill Daddy. Where's your brain, man?"

High heels clicked out in the lobby and the swinging doors breezed open for Cecile. "What is going on back here? We could hear y'all all the way out at the front desk." She smiled sweetly at Theo. "How is he, dear?"

"Probably okay. The alcohol is making things difficult but Cootsie Rodrigue thinks he has it under control."

"Cootsie!" Cecile's eyes widened. "You let that man loose on him? He nearly killed me stripping my varicose veins." Cecile noticed the doctor for the first time. "How are you, Hypo?"

"Just fine, Cecile. Hurricane chase you off the island?"

"At least until tomorrow." Turning to Theo, she said, "I don't suppose your daddy's taking visitors yet?"

"No. And even when Cootsie's finished, they'll probably keep him doped up. I tell you what you could do, Cecile: About a thousand relatives are going to show up here in a few minutes. Do you think you could handle them?"

Testily Cecile raised her delicate eyebrows. "No, sir. Not me. I'll be damned if I'm going to be responsible for a roomful of Talbots." She squinted at her tiny gold watch. "It's only twelve-thirty and I bet the whole bunch is still ready to party."

Theo took Laura's hand and pulled her away from Boo's side. "In that case, could you give Laura a ride back to the house? Boo and I are going to the sugar house and I'd like to get out of here before the clan arrives."

"Now, that I can do." Cecile raised her elegant chin and smiled up at Laura. "Come on, dear. You really don't want to be here when the Talbots arrive. You have no idea what that's like in a closed space."

Defiantly Theo said to Boo, "I've got Daddy's truck. I'll follow you out to the sugar house."

"I can't stop you."

"I know." Theo turned to Laura. "See you at home."

"Don't be long."

Cecile watched them leave. Then she said to Hypo, "I can't believe those two aren't tired of fighting."

"Yeah," grunted Hypo. He walked with Laura and Cecile into the lobby and said, "Y'all take care," and disappeared down the main corridor.

Out in the parking lot Cecile stopped in front of a big silver Mercury and searched deeply in her purse for the keys. Fumbling as she unlocked the door, she said, "We don't usually lock our cars down here but I have some valuables in the backseat."

They climbed in and Cecile wrinkled her nose. "Ugh. Those boots." She reached around and pulled a pair of fishing waders from the floor in the back. "These are *not* valuables. I'll put them in the trunk."

Laura turned around to watch Cecile deposit the waders in the trunk and on the backseat noticed a gleaming full-length mink and a boxy little Louis Vuitton vanity. Climbing back into the car, Cecile said, "I'd have thrown out my husband's old waders long ago except that they come in handy during hurricanes. After Frederick last year we were slogging through two feet of water."

They drove past miles of soldier-straight cane back to Theo's house in town. As Cecile's headlights hit the long front porch, a cat scurried from behind a fern stand and ran to hide under the house. Above the upstairs windows the striped awnings looked like half-closed eyelids covering the dark dormers. Cecile pulled around to the back and, ignoring the old barn used as a garage, parked on the oyster shell gravel directly below the back porch stairs. Pulling out her vanity case and mink coat, she asked, "Could you take these, dear? I have to get my suitcase out of the trunk."

"Sure." Laura scooped up the yards of dead animal

skins and threw them over her shoulder. "There must be fifty pelts in this coat."

Cecile tugged at her suitcase. "It looks ridiculous to carry a mink in August, doesn't it? But I have to take it wherever I go because the money-grubbing insurance agent won't write it for me without putting a rider on my policy. I got so furious, I told him, 'You just never mind. Go put your greedy hands in someone else's pocket.' He *never* would have done that if Bronier were still alive."

Inside Laura draped the mink over a kitchen chair and put the vanity on the table.

"Are you hungry, Laura?"

"Probably."

The door to the dayroom opened and Dorothy poked her head out. A ribbed pattern from a corduroy pillow impressed the brown skin of her face, and her pink foam rollers were flattened on the same side. "Mr. Talbot's okay?" she asked.

Cecile opened a kitchen cabinet. "They think so. Still drunk as ever, though."

"Y'all need anything?"

"No, thank you, Dorothy. We're just going to make a little snack."

"Sally Guidry dropped off a Yamboree Cake for Theophile. Y'all can cut into that if you want."

"Thank you, Dorothy. We'll try not to make a mess. Good night."

"Good night."

Dorothy closed the door and Cecile took out two juice glasses. "I don't know about you, but I could certainly use a nightcap."

"No, thank you." Laura pulled out a chair. "Is Sally Guidry related to Boo?"

"His wife. But she and Theophile used to run together." Cecile put back one of the glasses and dropped a single large ice cube into the other. Popping open the brass locks of her vanity, she pulled out a bottle of black-labeled Johnnie Walker and poured the amber liquid over ice. Taking a long sip, she switched on the radio above the refrigerator, turning the volume low. "We have to keep up with Hurricane Dinah."

"Where is it now?"

"Last I heard she was twenty-eight north, eighty-four west. That would put her over by Tampa." Beads of moisture from Cecile's glass dripped onto the shining heaps of mink and she brushed them off with a manicured hand. "Bronier always said that if he had to die in a hurricane, he wanted to have his Scotch in one hand and a deck of cards in the other. I miss him so much during hurricanes." She put down her glass and opened a cabinet, where a creamy frosted cake sat next to a battered metal recipe box.

"Laura, how big a piece?"

"Just a taste." She watched as Cecile cut two slivers of chunky brown cake. "Are you related to Theo on his mother's side or his father's?"

Cecile brought the two plates of cake to the table. "I was married to Theophile's father's brother, although I am also a second cousin to his mother. We were both Bergerons."

"She died of breast cancer, didn't she?"

"That's right. Twelve years ago. And the very next fall poor little Claiborne got killed at the sugar mill. I suppose Theophile told you about that?"

"Yes."

Cecile took two forks from a drawer and closed it with her hip. "Those were some hard times around here."

"Is that why Mr. Talbot drinks?" asked Laura, taking a fork.

Cecile glanced at her, surprised. "I believe they say an alcoholic will find a reason to drink, no matter what. I would imagine Valmont would say he drinks because he likes the taste." She brought her Scotch to the table.

Laura waited as Cecile pulled out a chair. "Who was older, your husband or Theo's father?"

"There are—were—four children in that family." Cecile held up red-lacquered fingers. "There's Valmont, my Bronier, Augustin, and the baby, Louise. Louise lives in Paris; she was an opera singer. And Augustin you probably met at the dance: the heavy-set man whose house we were at."

"Oh, Uncle Gus. No, I didn't get to meet him; somebody just pointed him out. He's pretty important, isn't he?"

"*He* probably thinks so. Right now he's chairman of the board at the bank, president of the police jury, and I don't know what-all else. He's taken over a lot of things that Theophile's daddy used to do."

Cecile cut off a tip of cake with a fork. "I was thinking the other day about Valmont sitting up there drinking in that sugar house. Bronier would be turning over in his grave if he knew how his brother was running it into the ground."

"Did Bronier work there too?"

"All three of the boys worked there growing up, but when their father died, he gave it to Valmont because he was the oldest."

"That's not fair."

"There *was* a lot of resentment, even though the two younger ones both got cash." She chewed cake and swallowed. "I shouldn't complain. Bronier bought an oil distributorship and we lived very well."

Laura broke off an edge of cake and put it in her mouth. She swallowed, ate another mouthful quickly, then put down her fork to look at the cake. "What is this?"

"Oh, this cake is famous. Yam-pecan with cream cheese icing. Sally won first prize with it in the Houma Yamboree when she was in high school. Theophile didn't tell you about it?"

The dessert vaguely resembled a very rich carrot cake, but the yams and fresh ground pecans made Laura think of rich Southern farms: the shade of the pecan trees, the sandy loam of the yams. Eating yam cake was like tasting seduction. "He hasn't mentioned it." She picked up her fork and finished her piece.

After mashing the utensil onto the plate to get every last crumb, Laura looked yearningly at the cake plate, and Cecile said, "Have some more."

Laura leaped up to cut herself a piece twice as big as

the first and Cecile watched amusedly, smoking a cigarette. Between mouthfuls Laura said, "This is the best cake
I've ever eaten."

"It should be. Sally sells them to John Folse's restau-
rants for twenty-five dollars apiece. Y'all are very privi-
leged to be given one. But Sally and Theophile are old
friends."

"You said they used to run together."

"Actually, there was a time when we thought they
were going to get married." She smiled at Laura and
tapped ashes. "But it appears everything works out for the
best." Blowing smoke at the ceiling, she asked, "Do you
play cards, Laura?"

"Sure."

Cecile opened her vanity and pulled out a deck. "Gin?
It's what we always played during hurricanes."

Cecile shuffled like a Vegas dealer and they played gin
for an hour to the low background sound of old radio
tunes. Cecile won game after game, losing only when Laura's spirits started to flag. At two A.M. Laura stretched and
looked at the kitchen clock. "I guess Theo's not coming
anytime soon."

"And the radio's not telling us anything new about the
hurricane either."

Laura looked at the radio. "I haven't even been listening. Where is it now?"

"They're still reporting twenty-eight, eighty-four, as if
a hurricane could stand still." Cecile scooped the cards
into a pile and yawned. "Well I don't know about you, but
this old lady needs her beauty sleep." Standing up, she
picked up her mink and vanity case. "Could you get the
radio, please, and maybe my big suitcase?"

"Sure."

They climbed the winding back stairs and Laura
brought the suitcase into Cecile's bedroom and laid it on
the pink-flowered bedspread.

"Thank you, dear, you're a love. I'm *so* glad Theophile
found you."

Laura smiled. "So am I. Good night, Cecile."

"Good night, dear."

• • •

In the middle of the night Laura turned over and tugged at the sheet. Theo slipped into bed beside her. "Did you find anything?" she asked sleepily.

"Pieces of bomb case, some footprints in the mud. The prints are from a kind of fishing boot or something. We're going back in the morning to pour molds." He threw an arm over her body. "Where's Cecile?"

"She went to bed."

"Her car's not there."

Laura pulled his hand up near her face. "Maybe she went back to the island."

Gentle knocking woke them from a sound sleep. "Theophile?"

Theo sat up on an elbow and blinked in the bright morning light. Dorothy opened the door and modestly averted her eyes. "Mr. Gus is downstairs. He wants to talk to you."

"Thank you, Dorothy."

Beside him Laura stretched and opened her eyes. "What is it?"

"Uncle Gus. You can stay in bed."

"No, it's about your father." She sprung up and stripped off her nightshirt to put on clothes.

Theo slipped on pants and bounded downstairs to find his uncle sitting at the kitchen table, an untouched demitasse of coffee before him. Gus had on a blue short-sleeved jumpsuit, the waistline elastic stretched puckerless around his prodigious belly. His thinning hair was combed straight back from his forehead, and behind his gold-rimmed aviator glasses his eyes were watery and scared.

"Gus, what's the matter?"

"I don't know yet. I'm waiting for you to tell me."

"Is Daddy okay?"

"As far as I know."

Laura arrived barefoot in the kitchen and looked at the

heavy-set man at the table. "Gus," said Theo. "This is Laura Ireland. Laura, this is my Uncle Gus."

"How do you do, darlin'. I would have come over last night at the dance but I got hung up with the relatives."

"Is something wrong?" she asked.

Gus touched his coffee cup. "Theophile, I hear you and Boo Guidry went over to the sugar house last night."

"That's right."

"Anything happen between the two of you?"

"What do you mean? We covered over a muddy place with some footprints and put sawhorses down the road to keep people out. Then we both went home."

"Who did the driving?"

"We both did. He had his car, I had Daddy's truck." Theo glanced out the window but did not see his father's pickup. "What's going on, Gus?"

Gus pushed up the bridge of his glasses and dropped his hand in his lap. "Boo Guidry's dead, Theophile. They found him run over in the Canal Road this morning."

CHAPTER 4

Theo stopped on the back porch stairs. "I wonder if Daddy came and got his truck."

Gus peered down over his belly, negotiating one step at a time. "I imagine someone from the reunion took it to the lake this morning. You need to hide the keys when there's family in town."

Laura dashed out the back door carrying sunglasses and a visor. "I'm coming."

"No, you're not. There's no reason to bring you. Anyway," Theo looked at the hazy sky, "we're going to be out on the road for a long time this morning. The heat's going to lay you flat."

Pointedly Laura put on her sunglasses and visor.

He sighed. "All right. Come on."

Gus navigated his big Ford LTD out behind town, past lush fields where high cane stood in rows like bristles on a hairbrush. He turned onto the Canal Road and after a few hundred yards stopped behind a light blue sheriff's car with its trunk wide open. White plastic sawhorses had been erected across the asphalt and neon tape run between the barriers. A stocky uniformed man with a bright yellow crew cut watched their approach.

As they climbed out of the car, the officer walked up with an outstretched hand. "Theophile, am I glad to see you. I've done everything I could think of, but it still don't seem like enough." He pointed to the canvas-covered body fifteen yards down the road.

"Quatorze, how you been?" Theo, too, stared at the shroud.

Quatorze grunted a hello to Gus and let his gaze come to rest on Laura's chiseled cheekbones.

Theo said, "Quatorze, this is Laura Ireland. Laura, Quatorze. He's deputy sheriff on this side of the parish."

"How do you do, ma'am?" Quatorze's Cajun was so thick, he could have gotten a job on *Amos 'n' Andy*. He shook Laura's hand, then rubbed a palm over his peroxided burr haircut. Homely as a catfish, he had massive muscular arms and thighs, and on his biceps was tattooed his single claim to beauty: a seraphic mermaid with huge breasts and a rounded belly.

"You found him when, Quatorze?" asked Theo, slipping into thick dialect.

"I didn't. Hot-T Daigle down the road called in this morning. He was taking his wife to Mass, and when they saw the body, they just turned around and went back home."

"Any idea who did it?"

Quatorze folded his arms. "Gus thought it might be you." He eyed Gus, and then Theo. "You didn't do it, did you, Theophile?"

"No. And it doesn't sound like Hot-T did either."

"I can check if their son is home. He drives with a six-pack. The thing is, I don't know what Boo was doing here in the first place."

"Neither me," he said.

Laura blinked at the astounding sound coming from

Theo's mouth as he continued. "When Boo and I left the sugar house last night, I thought for sure he was going home." He glanced again at the white shroud. "Well, I guess I'd better go take a look."

Theo walked down the road and Laura followed. Opening his mouth to object, he said instead, "All right, but don't touch anything." They walked up to the body. Theo squatted down, pulling back the canvas shroud. Laura made a little noise and turned away a second before finally summoning the courage to look at the dead man.

Boo Guidry lay face up on the asphalt, his nose bent gently to one side. His white forehead was a scrambled mass of flesh and hair; two oily streaks ran down his khaki shirt. Oddly, there was no blood.

"How long's he been dead?" asked Laura softly.

Theo pinched a purple fingertip but could not make it blanch. "Four or five hours."

She felt her empty stomach heave. "That means he died about five this morning." She looked at Quatorze writing on a clipboard. "What time did you get in, Theo?" she whispered.

"Three, maybe."

"I could testify to that."

"Stop it, Laura." He covered the body and walked back to Quatorze and Gus. Quatorze said, "Gus says you're still in the homicide department up there in Oregon."

"Washington. I *am* the homicide department. Bellingham isn't that big."

Quatorze held up the clipboard. "Then you want to show me what else? So far what I did was take pictures and sketch the body." He pointed to his drawing of a stick figure bracketed by two parallel lines. "What you think: that look like Boo in the road?"

"Sure. But you can't just measure in one place like this." Taking a pen from Quatorze's breast pocket, Theo drew lines between the stick man's bubble head and the road edge, and between the cartoon feet and the doodle cranium. "Measure all these distances and then measure some more."

"Okay," said Quatorze, "I know they teach you that. But it don't tell me anything I don't already know by measuring in just one place. You can look at his driver's license to find out how tall he is."

"I know. But the idea is to drown them in facts so later on they can't say you screw—"

Down the road a car approached. "Oh, Lord," said Quatorze. "I thought this might happen. She's got a scanner at the house and I bet she heard me call the ambulance."

"Who is it?" asked Laura.

Theo squinted at the windshield. "Boo's wife, Sally. You'd better go sit in the car, Laura. This might be a little tense."

Laura ignored him as the car screeched to a halt behind Gus's and a pretty little dark-haired woman jumped out. She was curvy and petite, and even in her high distress her crisp peach shirt stayed smoothly tucked in at her tiny belted waist. Spotting the white canvas shroud, she ran down the road making noises like a wounded bird. Before she could reach the body, Theo scooped her up in his arms.

"Theophile," she screamed. "I want to see him!"

"Sally, you can't touch."

She fought him with her tiny hands. "I just want to see—"

"You can, but you have to promise not to touch."

"I won't! I won't! Just let me see."

"All right. But you're not going to like it." Holding her by the shoulders, Theo led the widow slowly up to the white shroud. "Quatorze, you want to come and help?" He positioned Sally over the shroud, clutching her shoulders. "Okay, Sally, he's got a broken nose and his face is a little messed up. You ready?"

"Uh-huh."

"Quatorze, little bit of the canvas."

The burly man squatted beside the body and peeled back just enough to show Boo's face.

"Boo!" Sally bent down with an outstretched hand but Theo pulled her up by the elbow. Wrapping his arms around her, he said lamely, "It's okay, Sally. Everything's going to be fine."

"Theophile, why did they have to kill him?"

"I'm sure it was an accident, Sally."

"He wasn't that bad, Theophile. They didn't have to kill—" She choked.

Theo rubbed her softly on the back. "It's okay. It's okay." Suddenly she stiffened and pulled away, her face contorted like a tragic mask. "Gumby doesn't have a daddy! Theophile, what am I going to tell Gumby?" Her banshee shrieks echoed against the leaden sky.

Helplessly Theo patted Sally's back and glanced at Laura. "I need you and Gus to take her home. Quatorze and I have to stay here."

Laura nodded.

"Gus!" Theo called. "We want your car." He walked Sally slowly to the backseat of the LTD and helped her in. Gus opened the driver's door. "Laura, honey, you sit in back with Sally."

Laura climbed in and looked at Sally cautiously. "I'm really sorry about your husband." Sally darted a glance at her but did not speak. As Gus turned the car around, Sally leaned forward, her eyes crazy with pain. "Gus, I want to go to my sister's. Gumby's there."

"Or we could take you home and call Father LeBlanc."

"I want Gumby."

They drove into town and crossed the bayou bridge. Cruising a short distance down the other side of the sluggish stream, Gus pulled into the driveway of a little brick rambler backing against the bayou. A rusty swing set stood in the side yard and a fishing boat was trailered in the single carport.

Gus honked the horn and Sally pushed her way out of the backseat. A woman in black spandex shorts and a hot pink T-shirt opened the screen door and Sally ran hysterically up the walk. "LouAnn, they killed Boo. Boo's dead."

"No!" LouAnn grabbed Sally by the shoulders, flexing arm muscles firm from aerobics. "Why'd they kill him?"

"I don't know."

The women hugged and cried, rocking back and forth, barely able to keep their balance. Sally stumbled and stepped on LouAnn's hot pink aerobic shoes, and as LouAnn caught herself, she spluttered, "What are you going to do?"

"I don't know," wailed Sally. Her high round breasts heaved on her rib cage.

"Did you do that insurance thingie?"

"Yes," she blubbered. "But he's dead!"

The realization provoked a fresh chorus of sobs, and neighbors from next door came out to look. Gus motioned for Laura to hold open the front door and gently he shuffled the sisters into the house. "Come on, ladies. Y'all don't need to be out here."

Inside two wild-eyed little boys in underpants stood on the couch hugging toy cars to their chests. "Gumby!" cried Sally. Gumby ran away.

Instead of chasing him, Sally sat on the couch and cried in loud wheezes, as if playing two notes on broken bagpipes. The sound made Laura clench her hands into tight fists, and she stood in the corner watching neighbors creep up the front walk and let themselves in. In a few minutes the little living room was filled with people, all talking and weeping at once. The noise was so intense that Laura went outside.

Standing on the walk, she took a deep breath and looked across the road at the silent cane moving languidly in the heated air. Red ants trailed from a dead dragonfly on the sidewalk all the way up to a grainy mound at the base of the house. Holding up her palms, Laura saw that she had drawn blood with her fingernails. A minute later a black Dodge pulled up and a handsome man in clerical dress climbed out.

"Good morning," said the priest.

"Hi."

"Are you a member of the family?"

"No. They're inside."

A loud wail came through the screen door and the priest said, "Well, sounds like I better go to work."

Laura smiled weakly and watched the priest enter the

house. In a few minutes Gus came out and Laura hopped into the car. Aiming the air-conditioning vents at her face, she tried to wash away the raw emotion from the little house. As they pulled up to the back steps behind the Talbots' house, Gus asked, "You going to be all right?"

"Sure. I'll just wait here for Theo." She went inside and poured herself iced tea from the refrigerator. Neither Dorothy or Cecile was home so she walked through the vacant house, out to the front porch. Brushing past the fern stands, she lay down in the hammock, the intensity of the morning hitting her suddenly in a wave. Putting her tea glass on the thickly painted floorboards, she closed her eyes.

Inside the house someone was playing the piano. Laura sat up in the hammock and looked at her watch. She had fallen asleep. It was nearly noon and Theo hadn't come home yet. In the living room the piano player sang a snatch of gospel: she had a very good voice.

Rising quietly, Laura crept past the fern stands and opened the double screen door. She peeked around a wooden foyer column and spied a reedy black teenager who played with the piano bench tilted back on two legs. In a rich contralto she was working an arrangement of "Jesus Loves Me" that turned it into a blues song.

Unseen, Laura watched as the girl threw back her head and sang: "Jesus. Loves me. This"—she scaled three octaves on the piano—"I-I-I know." There was a long arpeggio. "For. The Bible. Tells me so-ho-ho-ho." She stretched out the word to four beats, enjoying the deliciously long last note. She had Jesus sounding like some dude who played sax in a smoky club.

Laura padded into the living room, and the girl jumped off the piano bench. She was dark chocolate brown, shading toward black at her elbows and knees. Her hair was in a shaved-neck Afro and she held her hands like limp handkerchiefs falling away from her wrists. She blinked at Laura with big doe eyes; she couldn't have been more than seventeen.

Laura smiled. "I really liked what you were doing with 'Jesus Loves Me.' "

Sullenly, the girl looked at the music stand and mumbled thanks.

Taking a step forward, Laura put a hand on her chest. "I'm Laura Ireland."

"I know."

"I-I didn't get your name."

"Reba Pugh. My momma takes care of this house."

"Dorothy's daughter. Glad to meet you." Laura looked back through the dining room. "Is Theo home yet?"

Reba's mouth crinkled, amused: "Momma said you call him that."

"Is Theophile home?"

"No, ma'am." Reba stared at the piano with affected boredom. "Theophile stay down at the courthouse."

"Can I call him there?" Laura craned for eye contact. To the piano, Reba answered, "Yes, ma'am." She sat on the bench again.

Laura went to the back hall and used the pamphlet-size phone book to look up the number of the Redemption Parish courthouse. She punched at the dial pad and found the line busy. After pouring herself some iced tea, she stood under the ceiling fan a few minutes, then dialed again. It was still busy.

Walking back to the living room, she said to Reba, "I can't get through."

Reba shrugged.

"Is the courthouse the building with the clock tower?"

"Yes, ma'am."

"What would happen if I went over there?"

Reba shrugged again, uninterested.

Laura put on her sunglasses and visor and went outside. Padding down the steamy front walk, she stopped at the street and looked up and down. Not a soul was stirring in the noonday heat. The only sound was the whir of heat pumps and air conditioners. Laura took a deep breath and felt as if she'd suffocate.

Trudging the two blocks up to the business district, she stopped under a store awning to recover from the heat.

There were no buildings on the other side of the road, only a grassy slope rolling down to olive green Bayou Lafourche. The bayou was half-covered with vegetation and looked as still as a pond. Laura watched as a purple water hyacinth broke off from a clump and moved almost imperceptibly downstream.

Walking in the shade of the awnings, she passed several storefronts and the bank. Stopping suddenly, she hesitated before going on: midway down the next block a group of black men stood listening to a boom box in front of a place called the Sportsmen's Club.

The men were intensely black and wore knotted kerchiefs on their heads. As they talked, they gestured extravagantly with their bodies, dancing across the sidewalk to make a point. Making the quick decision to walk through the group rather than cross to the other side, Laura approached, and the men became silent. Several moved out of the way to let her pass and Laura stretched her mouth into a polite smile. Behind her, the comments came.

"Umm-umm."

"Something else."

She paced straight to the corner and crossed against the light. Trudging across the courthouse lawn, she pushed open the front door. Inside, the air was blissfully cold.

The courthouse foyer led into an old tiled hallway with elaborate hanging signs jutting from both sides. Records, District Attorney, Assessor, and Sheriff were on this floor, District Court and Police Jury upstairs. Laura walked past open office doors framing scenes of women at work.

Back in the sheriff's office a young woman in a navy jacket talked on the phone. She had dark Spanish eyes and wore her brown hair pulled back in a ponytail. The sign on her desk said Daubie Crochet, Notary Public. Daubie looked up and said into the phone, "Just a minute, Momma, somebody's come in." To Laura she said, "May I help you?"

Laura's eyes strayed to a huge horned deer head mounted on the wall. As she stared, Daubie said, "Ridiculous, isn't it? The sheriff bagged it in Mexico. May I *help* you?"

"I'm looking for Theophile Talbot."

"Oh." Daubie gestured even farther down the hall. "They're all back there."

"In the assessor's office?"

"No, ma'am, in the jail. Push hard; the door's heavy." She went back to the phone.

At the end of the hall Laura pushed the painted steel door. As it opened, the smell of disinfectant hit her like a blow. The odor was so strong, she opened her mouth to breathe.

In the jail anteroom she found a desk with no one attending, and behind it, a door of formidable steel bars. The door was ajar and from it the disinfectant smell picked up middle and bottom notes to its bouquet—urine, BO, and fumigant.

Through the barred door Laura heard the sound of hearty laughter and men having a good time. Peeking through, she saw a short hall with cells along one side. The cells had three painted green walls and, along the hallway side, a fourth wall of steel bars. The door to the last cell was open. Down the hall she called, "Theo?"

"Back here, darlin'."

Laura pushed open the door. The first cell was empty and in the second, a black man stood with his arms on the bars, listening to the roaring good time around the wall. As she walked by, he pulled away, avoiding her eyes.

In the last cell, Theo was sitting on the far side of a card table playing poker with Quatorze and the priest she had seen that morning. The priest was showing his cards and counting: "*Un, deux, trois.* Gimme that pot." The men laughed uproariously. Theo looked at her and smiled but made no effort to get up. Brushing his brown forelock off his face, he tried for jocularity: "Laura, you've come to visit me in my time of need." To the men he said, "Y'all think we ought to deal her in?"

Quatorze pushed away his cards. "No way. She might beat us."

The priest smiled up at her amiably. "You were at LouAnn's this morning. Theophile, you got to introduce us."

"Excuse me." Theo stood. "Laura, you know Quatorze. And this handsome gentleman is Father LeBlanc, best known for yelling at his altar boys."

"Only when they steal the burgundy, Talbot." Father LeBlanc looked more like a movie idol than a priest. With thick black hair and a jutting Hollywood jaw he would have had no trouble winning a Clark Gable look-alike contest. He wore his collar jauntily, almost like a playboy's turtleneck, and the pleasant lines around his eyes said he spent a lot of time smiling.

Theo sat down again. "We've been having a good old time, Laura. I'm glad you joined the party. Quatorze, tell Laura what you just said about the earth being flat."

Quatorze readjusted himself in his chair. "Well, I just said that I don't think the people in Australia are really hanging there upside down, and I know for a fact that if you drive east, you will *never* get to Texas."

Laura looked at Quatorze's mermaid, not knowing what to say. "Your name means fourteen, doesn't it?"

Theo guffawed. "Go ahead, Quatorze, tell her why they call you Fourteen."

Quatorze looked modestly at his kitty.

Desperately Laura asked, "Theo, will you be coming home soon?"

Across the table he grew sober and looked at Quatorze.

Quatorze said, "Theophile can't leave just now, Miss Laura. The district attorney is having me hold him on probable cause while he decides what to do. Hell, it's the most fun we've had around here in a long time. Isn't that right, Theophile?"

Laura caught her breath. "You mean you're in jail?"

"You got it."

Father LeBlanc shuffled the cards. "Come on, y'all, you're going to upset her. Don't worry, Miss Laura, Theophile'll be out before you know it. Actually, I'm glad you came by. It gives us time for a little talk. We wanted to make sure you know all about Theophile's shady past before you get involved with him."

"What shady past is that?" asked Theo.

"Why, as an altar boy, of course. Did you know that

besides stealing the burgundy, this boy used to rub his feet on the carpet at Communion time and give people a shock when he held the plate against their throats?"

"I did not! That was Michael Cyr."

Father LeBlanc kept shuffling. "And I bet he never told you he was planning to be a priest, did he? Yessiree, Laura, there was a time when Theophile was a very serious young man; he didn't even *like* women."

Theo fingered his change. "I never recall that time."

"Like I said, here we have a former altar boy, former seminarian, and look what happens: I'm visiting him in jail." The priest slapped the deck onto the table. "Cut the cards, boy."

Laura blurted, "Quatorze, why are you holding Theo? He didn't kill Boo."

Quatorze watched the priest deal cards. "We found Mr. Valmont's pickup down in the cane fields a little while after you left. A half dozen people called in and said they saw it down on the Canal Road last night. We're keeping Theophile in custody until we get it all cleared up."

"You found it? Well, just because it was back there doesn't mean it was the vehicle that hit Boo, does it? And anyway, how do you know Theo did it?"

"Laura." Theo fanned his cards. "Remember those grease streaks on Boo's shirt this morning?"

"Yes."

"They match up perfectly with clean streaks on the oil pan of Daddy's truck. In addition, there's tissue and hair on the bumper and U-joint. It's pretty clear Daddy's truck was the murder vehicle."

"You didn't do it."

"I know that. But they don't yet."

Laura flew at Quatorze. "Well, do something. Why don't you fingerprint the truck instead of wasting time here?"

Quatorze dropped two quarters into the pot. "Calm down, girl. Truck's been wiped clean. There's not a print on it. Not even Theophile's."

"But you can't possibly think Theo would kill Boo and not say so."

"Let me tell you what our late sheriff used to say: 'I'm not paid to have opinions, I'm paid to keep my prisoners happy.' Two cards, please."

The door opened out in the anteroom and Quatorze tipped back his chair to see. "Gus," he called, "come on back. Your nephew needs some help keeping the money in the family."

Red-faced and sweating, Gus waddled back to the cell. There were sweat patches under his arms and a wet triangle on the front of his blue jumpsuit. Pulling irritably at the stretched elastic around his waist, he caught sight of Father LeBlanc. "Afternoon, Henry."

"Good afternoon, Augustin."

Gus looked up at the frosted pane of glass in the cell. "Can't y'all open that window, air the place out a little?"

"Air-conditioning," said Quatorze.

Next Gus looked for a place to sit. There were only three chairs and no one from the card game was getting up. He looked at the two frail cots, then decided to stand. Scratching again at his elastic, he said, "Theophile, this is a fine mess. What am I supposed to do, send you a file?"

"You're not supposed to do anything, Gus. I'll be out in a while and Quatorze says I can act as his consultant while he runs the investigation. Ain't that right, Quatorze?"

"Damn right."

Gus leaned his backside against the steel bars. "I went over to the hospital to see your daddy, and they were all asking if you and Boo had been drinking."

"Gus, for the last time: I didn't kill Boo."

"Well, of course you didn't. But we can only move as fast as the professionals in this matter. If the DA thinks you need to be held until he finds another suspect, then we'll just have to wait until something turns up."

"There's a quicker way."

"Which is?"

Theo looked up at his uncle. "That's what I need to talk to you about. Quatorze says that as president of the police jury, you're the one who okays autopsies around here."

Gus pushed up the bridge of his glasses. "Yes, he mentioned that on the phone. I was just now looking at the budget and I don't see a way in the world we can appropriate extra money for something as expensive as a Baton Rouge autopsy."

"So what are you going to do, just have Hypo Hebert sign the death certificate?"

"I was."

"Gus! You can't tell for certain Boo was actually killed by the truck. How do you know he wasn't poisoned or something and then made to look run over?"

"Because that's too stupid to even think about."

"I beg to differ."

Gus raised a hand. "Listen to me, Theophile: I know up there in Oregon you're used to doing things with all the money and all the supplies you want, but we don't have taxpayers worth diddley down here. An autopsy is an expense I can't justify. Now, I talked to the DA and it appears the only reason he asked you to stay is that he's covering his fanny in case something turns up later."

"Or in case he's too lazy to find out whoever really did it."

"Theophile, there's no reason to be hateful."

"Gus, it doesn't matter about me right now. The important thing is to get Boo's body up to Baton Rouge before his blood chemistry changes too much more. That's the only way you're going to find out what happened."

"Listen to me, Theophile: We all know Boo was drinking. All an autopsy would tell us is how drunk he really was. Now who really cares?"

"I care."

"Read my lips, boy: we can't afford it."

"How much is an autopsy?"

"Eight hundred dollars."

"Okay." Theo scooted in his chair. "Send Boo up to Baton Rouge and send me the bill."

Gus stared at his nephew.

"I'm serious, Gus. That body's got to have an autopsy. Boo didn't die in a bayou drive-over. Quatorze, tell him what we found."

Quatorze said, "That's right. There wasn't any injuries around the legs or knees, and Theophile was wondering why, if Boo was standing up or walking, he only got hit in the head."

Gus waved away the objection. "I don't know. It's you boys' job to figure those things out. Maybe he stumbled just before the truck hit him."

Theo stood and yelled at his uncle. "Gus, where is your brain? We can't tell what happened until we get Boo autopsied."

"My brain is in my head, trying to make do with a budget of rubber bands and paper clips!"

The two men glared at one another, and Father Le-Blanc lifted his voice to the ceiling. "You see, Lord? You see what I got to put up with?"

Theo sat down and Laura gently asked, "Quatorze, may I be alone with Theophile for a while? I haven't seen him all day."

The deputy dropped his cards on the table and stood. "I guess. You got a file hidden away anyplace?" He said it kiddingly but patted her shorts in an unpleasant way. "Come on, y'all. We've got to let these two lovebirds talk."

The three men walked out and as Uncle Gus passed by the second cell, he addressed the man inside. "Good afternoon, Zachary."

"Yes, sir," came the reply.

Theo sat back down and motioned to Laura to take the chair across from him. The outer door clanked shut and he slowly gathered the cards and shuffled. Laura watched as he laid out a game of solitaire. "Are you okay, Theo?"

He avoided her eyes. "Fine."

"Can I do anything for you?"

"No."

She tried to touch his hand but he moved it quickly, turning over three cards from the stack and putting an ace above the line.

"Theo, when are you getting out?"

He looked at her watch. "I still haven't heard from the

lawyer I want. His secretary says he'll be in Baton Rouge until four this afternoon."

"Get another lawyer." She nestled her foot in the arch of his and he moved his foot away.

"No. I'm getting out on personal recognizance and this man is the nephew of a judge."

"Not the same judge wh—"

"His golf partner."

"Theo, I know you would have told me, but what they said about finding your father's truck, you didn't really kill Boo, did you?"

"I won't even dignify that with a reply." He slapped a black queen on a red king.

Laura burst out, "It would be much easier if you wouldn't act like this."

Glancing at her quickly, he moved a long line of cards. "Laura, if I'm acting a little strange, it's because I'm highly embarrassed to be here. Now please cut me some slack."

She exhaled. "That's a relief. I thought maybe you were mad at me." She watched him turn over three more cards. "Do you think somebody will come forward and confess?"

"No."

"But it will only be manslaughter, won't it? Manslaughter's not *so* bad."

"It wasn't an accident."

"Sure it was. Nobody could have known Boo'd be walking down the road at exactly that time. You just think everything is homicide because that's your job."

"Laura, think about it. Why would Boo be wandering around in the middle of nowhere at that time of night— morning, rather?"

"I don't know."

"Neither does anyone else. Have you ever tried walking in cowboy boots? Boo never walked anywhere he couldn't drive." He laid down cards and continued. "The problem now is figuring out why Gus won't ask himself the same question."

"Oh, dear. You don't think—" She peeked out into the

hall to see if Gus was gone. Leaning forward, she whispered, "You don't think your uncle had anything to do with it, do you?"

"I've already checked. Gus was at the *fais do-do* most of the night and then played cards until six this morning."

"He was at the what?"

"The *fais do-do*. The dance."

"Oh." She watched his game a moment and then said slowly, "I have a question, and please don't get mad. You said you didn't kill Boo, and I really believe you, but how are you going to explain to your lawyer and everybody about your father's truck? You were driving it last night."

Shuffling cards, he said, "Laura, somebody took the truck from the backyard after I went to bed."

"Were the keys in the ignition?"

"Of course."

Her eyebrows formed a troubled line. "But I don't get it. Does that mean somebody's trying to set you up?"

"I would say it looks that way, wouldn't you?"

CHAPTER 5

Out in the anteroom Cecile's rich voice echoed off concrete walls. "... shouldn't have even let her in here. The smell alone would suffocate a fish." Down the hall she called, "Laura?"

"Back here."

They listened to Cecile's heels and the accompanying shuffle of whomever she spoke to. Laura leaned her chair back to see Cecile smartly dressed in a black linen skirt and jade silk blouse. She was followed by Gus.

"You're safe," beamed Cecile. "I couldn't believe it when Reba said you came to the jail." She blew a kiss across the card table to Theo. "Hello, dear boy. Are you all right?"

"Yes, ma'am."

"Can I do anything for you? Food? Magazines?"

Theo pointed to the tattered stack of *Sports Illustrated*s on the cot. "No, thank you. I'll be out in a while."

Gesturing to Gus, she said, "I hope you can forgive your uncle for letting this happen. Gus, remind me never to let you take care of me in my old age."

Gus looked sheepishly at her black patent belt. "I already explained to Theophile why he had to stay."

Theo sat forward, "Cecile, actually there is something you could do: Laura needs a ride home."

Laura reached across the table. "But I want to . . ."

"You're much better off waiting at home. Matter of fact, I need you to wait there, in case my lawyer calls."

Cecile smoothed her skirt and slipped her purse strap to the crook of her elbow. "Don't worry, Theophile, I'll take care of her. I've got some errands to run and Laura can help. Then we'll go home and take out a deck of cards." She took Laura by the arm. "You need to learn *bourrée*, child."

Laura turned to Theo. "Hurry and get out."

He stretched across the table to kiss her. "I'm doing the best I can."

Cecile, Gus, and Laura walked out to the main hall, where Cecile stopped to shake the odor from her clothes. "Did you smell that urine they were trying to cover up? Gus, if Theophile isn't out by tonight, I'm *taking* him out."

"Cecile, now don't you start in on me. I have important company tomorrow and I don't have time to go wiping noses for the family right now."

"Listen to you: T-Harry Meacham is coming to town and you think you can let everybody else go to hell in a handbasket. As if Meacham did anything other than fleece our pockets when he was in office." She touched Laura's arm. "Come on, dear. Let's go run our errands."

Cecile's black patent pumps clicked smartly down the hall and Laura took long strides to stay abreast. "Who's T-Harry Meacham?"

"An odious little lawyer from Abita Springs who used to be our governor. He let the chemical companies turn the

Mississippi into a sewer and helped steal Louisiana's oil money back when we had some."

"He's coming here?"

"Something about the parish. Gus is president of the police jury. I told you that, didn't I?" Cecile pushed open the door and heat blasted in their faces.

Laura squinted in the bright light and put on her sunglasses. "Where are we going?"

"I want you to meet my friend Sister Elizabeth. She runs a training program at the activity center south of town. But before we go there, we have to stop by the Dollar Store and buy her a present."

They crossed the shimmering asphalt and jumped in Cecile's Mercury. Cecile pulled away from the curb without even looking. And before she could even get the air-conditioning cold, she stopped the car and announced, "Here we are."

"That was half a block," Laura said.

Cecile gestured at the storefront out Laura's window. "Yes. The Dollar Store. It's a pharmacy. Let's hope Paul Theriot doesn't need his loading zone right now."

They went into the chilled interior and Cecile raised her chin to smile charmingly at the man behind the prescription counter. "Paul," she said, "I hope you don't mind letting an old lady park in your loading zone. I need disposable diapers again."

"No, ma'am, Ms. Cecile. Anytime." The druggist came out with a handcart and wheeled it to Infant Supplies. He watched Cecile from the corner of his eyes, rubbing his pointed chin with clean, tapered fingertips. The sky blue of his pharmacy jacket matched the color framing the cute baby clones on the "boy" Pampers box. "How many you need?" he asked.

"How many are there?"

"Ultras?" He did a quick count. "Eight boys' and six girls'."

"Do you mind if I take them all?"

"No, ma'am." Paul began loading them on the handcart. "That's what they're here for."

Cecile paid with a credit card and followed the druggist out to her car, where he loaded the diapers into her spacious trunk. After thanking him profusely, Cecile climbed in and started the car. On the passenger side, Laura clicked her seat belt and asked, "What does Sister Elizabeth train the babies to do?"

Cecile let out a low musical laugh. "She doesn't train the babies to do anything. She has a federal grant to teach minority women to be office workers. The *women* have the babies."

They followed the bayou highway down to a modern red brick building on the south side of town. Cecile released the lock on her trunk and climbed out. "Help me with the diapers, will you, dear?"

Carrying diapers to the cool inside, they found themselves instantly surrounded by a flock of babbling black toddlers. A sturdy white woman with a child on each hip stood shepherdlike in the center of the group while a black woman in a rocking chair read a stiff cardboard book to two squirmers in her lap. Behind a wall of plate glass windows a typing class rolled paper into machines at the direction of a heavy-breasted black woman with a yellow cardigan over her shoulders.

The white woman beamed as they walked in. "Cecile! How did you know we were almost out of diapers?"

Cecile put her box down on the table. "The only thing I ever learned about babies is that you're *always* almost out of diapers." She gestured to Laura. "This is my nephew's friend, Sister. Let us get these all inside and I'll introduce y'all."

Laura and Cecile brought in the Pampers and stacked them next to cribs in which tiny babies slept serenely through the noise. When they finished, Cecile tucked in her silk blouse and smoothed her hair. Taking Laura over to the white woman, she said, "Sister Elizabeth, I'd like you to meet Laura Ireland. Laura, this is Sister Elizabeth Reilly. She's in the same order as Theophile's sister, Sisters of the Holy Name."

"Really? How do you do," said Laura.

"Fine, thank you, dear. And I'd like you to meet someone too." The nun turned to the black woman in the rocking chair. "Mrs. Cullen? This is Cecile Talbot and her friend. Cecile is one of our patrons." Mrs. Cullen nodded and went back to her picture book.

Sister Elizabeth dipped her head to pull her cropped gray hair from the fist of a toddler. "Will you be visiting long, Laura?" she asked. The nun was a vigorous fifty with the ruddy, healthy complexion of a skier. She wore a yellow button-down shirt and navy chino A-line. On her collar was a Holy Name pin in sterling.

"Actually I don't know how long we'll be here. Theo—my friend—was put in jail this morning for murdering the sheriff."

Sister Elizabeth's eyes grew steely. "I heard that. It was his truck that was used, wasn't it?"

"His father's. But he was the last one driving it."

On the other side of the plate glass the teacher called, "Hands high. And. Begin." Twenty-five typewriters jackhammered in unison. The nun listened for a moment, then asked, "Have they any other suspects, Laura?" She pulled the children up her hip to get a better grip and Cecile put out her hands to take one of the toddlers from her. "Thank you, Cecile."

"Not that I know of," answered Laura. "And I didn't get the impression that anyone was looking too hard, since the sheriff is the one who's gone."

"Well, that's a relief. I know your friend couldn't be guilty, but I'm *so* afraid they might go accusing the wrong person." The nun scanned the room mildly.

Cecile watched her toddler rub his nose into her silk shirt and asked, "How are things going here, Sister?"

The nun rested her gray eyes on Cecile's beautiful face. "Actually, we're in violation today. The only childcare worker who could make it this morning was Mrs. Cullen and I was frantic the sheriff would come by and make trouble."

Laura asked, "Boo Guidry was bothering *you*?"

The nun raised her wiry eyebrows. "We prefer to say Boo was just keeping us on our toes."

Laura's brow furrowed and the nun quickly explained, "Boo first visited in May and then sent a deputy over to

point out that the state mandates a six-to-one child/
caregiver ratio in day-care programs. That had us scram-
bling around for extra helpers and then, after we got Mrs.
Cullen and two more volunteers, he threatened to close us
down because we had six more people in the building than
the fire code allows." She sighed. "That was unfortunate,
because I had to ask three women to quit the program."

"The jerk."

The nun lowered her eyes. "I'm just praying we make
it through 'til five o'clock today. I have to go in and teach
in a while, leaving only Mrs. Cullen out here. The last
time we were in violation they said they would close us
down if it happened again."

Cecile looked down at the baby snot on her blouse.
"Laura and I weren't doing anything today, were we,
Laura? We could stay and baby-sit." She tilted her head
charmingly. "Do you mind, Laura?"

"Ah, not at all." Laura picked up a little boy who was
using her leg to pull himself up.

"Meanwhile," said Cecile. "I'll sniff around to see
who it is that's so fragrant."

"Bless you," Elizabeth said.

As Cecile deftly changed the offending child, Elizabeth
and Laura stood swaying with toddlers on their hips.
"Who's that teaching typing?" asked Laura.

"That's Mrs. Roberts. She's secretary of the Baptist
church." The nun's eyes went to the wall clock. "When
she finishes, I go in and teach Office Etiquette. I would
ask her to stay with the children but she has very bad arthritis."

"This is a great program. Do all the women find jobs?"

Lowering her voice, the nun said, "Actually, I doubt
twenty percent of them will find employment. Most of
them have no idea how to interact well with whites in a
business situation, and very few white business owners are
prepared to hire them anyway."

"That's too bad." Scanning the students' heads, Laura
spied a tall woman with a neat Afro. "Is that Reba Pugh?"
The nun jerked her head violently. "What?" She let out a

sigh. "Oh, I see: you know Reba because her mother works for the Talbots."

"Is anything wrong?"

"No, nothing. It's just that Reba was so upset about the sheriff this morning. I thought for a second maybe they had sent you from the courthouse."

"Reba?" Laura stared at the nun. "You mean *she* was close to the sheriff?"

"Reba and her mother live next door to the Guidrys out in the cane fields back of town. She knows them quite well, as I understand."

"Oh."

The nun shifted the toddler to her other hip and exhaled deeply. "It really is too bad about Boo Guidry. I know he didn't mean to be as destructive as he was and I'm sure whomever Gus Talbot sends over next will no doubt be worse."

"Gus? Theo's uncle? He's after you too?"

"Oh, I thought Cecile might have filled you in on all of this. Gus is the one chiefly to blame for the sheriff's aggressiveness. He and his sugar cane friends are desperately afraid someone might come in and change the status quo." Her eyes flared and she shook her head. "I shouldn't talk about it; I get too angry. Go over and read that clipping on the bulletin board. It explains the situation much more objectively than I could do."

Laura went to the corkboard and read a brittle column clipped from a July issue of *The Redemption Creole.*

FEDERALLY FUNDED ORGANIZATION
REFUSES TO REVEAL
HOW FUNDS ARE SPENT

The refusal by a federally funded organization, the Southern Mutual Help Association (SMHA), led by Sister Elizabeth Reilly, OHN, to disclose any information regarding how federal funds granted to it are spent, has shocked taxpayers in South Louisiana.

Laura looked up. "There's something really tinny about this writing style but I can't tell exactly what."

"Oh, yes. When I taught journalism, we called that grandstanding. Read the whole thing; it gets better."

Laura patted the bottom of the child on her hip and went on reading the article.

> In a letter dated July 22, Augustin "Gus" Talbot, vice president and general manager of the American Sugar Cane League, urged the SMHA of St. Lô to reconsider its earlier decision not to provide the public with any information on its use of federal funds. Talbot termed the "stonewalling" by the SMHA disturbing.
>
> "The public is sick and tired of secrecy in government and government-funded programs," Talbot's letter declared. "We may be talking about over one million dollars in federal grants to this one organization. I requested information on their federal funding in May of this year. Over a month later, Sister Elizabeth Reilly, executive director of the SMHA, flatly refused my request for the funding information."

Laura looked up. "What does the American Sugar Cane League want with your books?"

"They want our books to harass us. What they really want is a list of our students. Keep reading. You'll understand when you finish."

> "The membership of the American Sugar Cane League includes farmers who produce more than 97 percent of the sugar cane grown in Louisiana," Talbot continued.
>
> "Our concern stems from the observation that one of the principal activities of the SMHA appears to be making unfounded derogatory comments about the sugar cane farmers of Louisiana. We find this both disturbing and potentially libelous."

Laura looked up. "But I don't get it. How does your program harm sugar cane farmers?"

The nun patted her baby's back in the rhythm of a heartbeat. "A lot of the women in our program live with cane field workers, or *are* cane workers themselves. We're instilling ambitions to be other things, and some people find that very disturbing. I'm from Chicago, and nothing infuriates folks like Gus more than Northerners coming down to work with blacks. I think if we hadn't had the good fortune to make contact with Cecile, Gus would have kicked us out months ago."

On the other side of the glass the typing class scraped back their chairs and stood. "Here they come," said the nun. She handed Laura her child. "Could you take Lashona, please? I need to get the snacks and prepare for Etiquette."

The women came streaming in, each making a beeline for a child. Laura gave up her children to their mothers and watched as the twenty-odd toddlers were laid on the floor like overturned turtles to get their diapers changed. Reba glanced quickly at Laura and went straight to the snack table, where she joined the few other women without babies.

After snacks the women returned to the classroom, this time with Sister Elizabeth. Laura sat on the floor and played peek-a-boo with a little boy who could never figure out where she was disappearing to, and after peek-a-boo she played roll-the-ball and hide-the-bunny. Running out of hyphenated games, she helped Cecile and Mrs. Cullen change more diapers and then tag-teamed babies in and out of cribs. By the time the mothers pushed back their chairs at five o'clock, Laura had already considered getting her tubes tied.

As the last young mother walked out with her child, Cecile padded stocking-footed across the room. The pleated shoulders of her jade silk blouse were stained with drool, and her sleek linen skirt looked like a costume for the California Raisins. "Come on, Laura. We're going home to put our feet up."

They said good-bye quickly and climbed in the car. As Cecile backed out, she turned on the air conditioner and said, "I am exhausted."

Laura aimed a vent at her face. "I think that was the second hardest work I've ever done in my life."

"Really? What was the hardest?"

"Wind sprints."

Cecile turned on the radio and reached into her purse. "Do you mind terribly if I smoke?"

"Go ahead."

On the radio the Neville Brothers effused about a pretty bayou woman they knew. Laura asked, "What happened to the hurricane?"

Cecile punched in the lighter and tucked a cigarette between her lips. "Hit Pensacola at noon. We're in for some serious rain." As Laura watched her touch the lighter to her cigarette and take a deep drag, Cecile continued, "I hate this nasty habit. When Bronier was dying of lung cancer, I used to drive around and smoke into the air conditioner so I didn't have to smoke up the house." She rested her cigarette in the ashtray and said, "Thank you so much for baby-sitting with me. I was hoping to take you up to Belle Plaisir afterward as a treat but it doesn't look like we'll have time."

"That reminds me. In the courthouse today I saw the records office and wondered if the documents for the sale of Belle Plaisir would be there."

"Would they?" Cecile glanced excitedly at her passenger.

"Should be," said Laura. "Land sale records have to be kept in perpetuity for title searches."

"That would be incredible. I'd love to go look."

"And maybe you'd find that the recorded price looks so awful the people at Belle Plaisir feel sorry for you and want to renegotiate."

"Ha. Don't hold your breath." Cecile tapped ashes and added, "But we could drop by the courthouse, just for a peek."

"Now?" Anxiously Laura looked at her watch. "Don't you think Theo might be out?"

"You poor child. Of course he is. We'll go straight home."

"It's past five," said Laura. "The courthouse is probably closed anyway. If you go tomorrow, all you have to do is ask for the 1928 land records. I'm sure you won't have any problem."

Cecile pressed her lips together and drove silently to the Talbots'. As they climbed the wooden back steps, she said wearily, "I don't know about you, Laura, but I'm going to kick my shoes off and pour a Scotch."

Inside, the kitchen smelled like Cajun heaven. Peppers, onion, garlic, and thyme mingled in a cloud over the stove, where Dorothy presided as reigning goddess. She had her shirtsleeves rolled up, and her pomaded hair was smoothed into a neat beehive. Laura filled her nostrils and spotted a red Cardinals cap on the kitchen table. "Theo's home!"

Dorothy grinned and Theo came bounding down the back stairs. Laura wrapped her arms around him, nestling her face in his neck. "Theo."

"Where have you been?" he asked.

"Taking care of babies at the activity center. How are you?"

"Cleaner than I was two hours ago."

"You smell nice."

Cecile dropped an ice cube in a glass and poured from her bottle. "You would have been proud of her, Theophile. She had all the babies thinking she was Big Bird."

"Did things go all right for you?" asked Laura.

"As well as could be expected," he said. "My lawyer showed up early and got me into chambers just after four. He says he doesn't think we'll have any problem getting the charges dropped after Boo's autopsy tomorrow. But until then I'm not supposed to drink, leave town, or associate with people of bad moral character."

"Damn," said Cecile. "I guess that means I can't take y'all to bet on big-screen horse racing."

Theo looked fondly at his aunt. "Nice offer, Cecile, but we couldn't anyway. Laura and I are working tonight."

Laura groaned and sat down. "No, Theo. I'm bushed."

"Then go upstairs and take a nap before dinner. We're going to a nightclub."

CHAPTER 6

Theo stood at the bottom of the stairs and watched her descend. Laura was wearing a black cotton tank top and matching miniskirt. She wore black strappy sandals, and her pale ivory arms and legs were long enough to die for.

"Spiderwoman," he said in a low voice. "Wrap those arms around me, Spiderwoman."

Laura circled his head with her arms and kissed the warm skin of his neck. "We look nice in our party clothes."

"*You* look nice. I get by on association." Holding open the kitchen door, he escorted her down the steps to Cecile's silver Mercury.

Laura sniffed the air. Although it was still hot, a cool scent lingered somewhere around her head, smelling like the odor from hotel air conditioners. "When's the rain coming?"

"Radio said around midnight."

She climbed into the plush car and buckled her seat belt. "How long are they keeping your father's truck?"

"Long as they want. It's evidence."

They drove two blocks and turned north to follow the bayou highway. "You still haven't told me where we're going," she said.

"A place called Willie Cox's High Life Lounge. It's up in Paincourtville."

Laura grabbed the dash. "Wait a minute. If this is anything like the Sportsmen's Club, I'm not going."

"Sure you are. Willie runs a nice place, and anyway, somebody you already met is singing there tonight."

"Who?"

"Reba Pugh."

"She can't do that, she's too young. What's the drinking age in this state?"

"Twenty-one."

"Then how does she even get in?"

Theo exhaled. "That's one of the delicate subjects we need to explore tonight."

"I saw her at the typing program today. Where'd you hear she sings at a club?"

"Remember the black guy in the cell next to mine? His name's Zachary. And Zachary had some very interesting things to say about Reba's relationship with the sheriff."

"You don't mean—" Laura turned to examine his face. "You mean: Boo Guidry and Reba Pugh? Excuse me, but that's too weird."

Theo shook his head. "Not as weird as you might think. Reba and Dorothy have a little house next to the Guidrys' back of town. Reba baby-sits over there and helps with the snakes."

"The snakes?"

"Boo raises snakes, or rather, *raised* snakes. I don't know what Sally'll do with them."

"I thought Dorothy slept at your house."

"Depends on who's there. When we're not home, all she does is open up and cook for Daddy."

In Paincourtville they parked the car on a side street in front of a tar-papered building. Young black men loitered outside, smoking skinny brown cigarettes and practicing dance moves. A homemade sign announced that inside would be found The Original Willie Cox's High Life Lounge.

Laura got out of the car. "Who's Willie Cox?"

Taking her elbow, Theo said, "One of the Coxes. They all played football." To the men out front he said, "Gentlemen. Good evening." He led her up the rickety front steps into the dark interior. Inside, the club smelled of cigarettes and stale beer. Squinting to see in the dim light, Laura whispered, "Theo, we're the only white people here."

"Be a nice guest." He went over to a huge bald-headed man perched on a stool. The man wore a Michael Jackson World Tour T-shirt that barely covered his soft belly, and in his hand he clutched a pile of one-dollar bills. Theo took out a twenty and looked at the bouncer earnestly. "Is Reba Pugh singing tonight?"

The man grunted and took the bill. Pointing to an isolated table near the stage, he mysteriously lost the twenty near his jeans. Theo thanked him and guided Laura through the darkened room. Seating her facing the stage, he said, "I'll get us some Cokes," and went off to the bar.

Laura looked around the room as her eyes adjusted to the light. Sitting at tables made from painted plywood rounds, small groups of patrons sipped beer and talked in low tones, competing with piped-in rap music. Hanging on the plywood walls were posters of black rock stars and all the brown-skinned New Orleans Saints.

Theo came back with the drinks and positioned himself against the wall. With one eye on the door, he sipped his Coke and said, "You really do look nice tonight."

"Thank you. I feel a little vulnerable wearing such skimpy clothing."

"Nonsense. You do some of your best work in skimpy clothing."

Laura raised her eyebrows. "Sounds like we're going to have to take care of you tonight."

"I could stand it. But remind me to call Quatorze when we get home to see if he needs us tomorrow."

"He's the deputy, isn't he? Is he the one keeping your father's truck?"

"Kind of. He's taking orders from Tutoo."

"Who?"

"Tutoo Landry, the DA."

"I didn't meet Tutoo, did I?"

He shook his head.

"What an odd name. I'm never going to be able to keep everybody straight." She inhaled and continued. "And what was the deal today about Quatorze? Why did you all laugh when I asked if it meant fourteen?"

Theo looked down and sipped his Coke. "His name is an anatomical reference."

"A what?"

"In inches, Laura."

Her eyes grew wide and she started to spread her hands apart to see how long fourteen inches actually was. Theo stopped her in midair. "Not here. We're in public."

"Oops. Sorry." She looked around to see if anyone had noticed.

"Anyway, remind me also to ask Quatorze how soon they can ship Boo's body up. I halfway wondered today if they didn't keep me in jail just so I couldn't see about that getting done."

"You don't really think they'd do that, do you?"

"The way Gus was acting, I don't know what I think right now."

"You know, Theo, in a way, I think I almost agree with Gus: all you'll find out from an autopsy is how drunk Boo really was. I mean, at this point, who cares? And won't having that fact public just make it harder on Sally?"

Fixing the full force of his liquid brown gaze on her, Theo said, "You still don't get it, do you?"

"Get what?"

"Laura, you saw the body this morning. Did that look like someone who'd been run over by a truck?"

"I think so. I guess."

"Where was the blood? Did you see any blood?"

"Do people *not* bleed sometimes wh—"

"No. People always bleed when you break their heads open. Unless they're already dead. Then they don't bleed at all."

Laura was silent a moment. "*That's* what you were getting at in jail today. You're saying somebody killed Boo first and then tried to make it *look* like a hit-and-run." She clutched her glass and whispered, "Were there any bullet holes in the body?"

"Not as far as I could tell." He maneuvered a small ice cube into his mouth. "But then, we won't know anything for sure until after the autopsy."

"Theo, I know you don't run from trouble, but if someone's smart enough to fake a hit-and-run, they also might be smart enough to make it really stick on you. What if we just packed our bags and left before there's any more trouble? You could let your lawyer take care of everything."

"And what am I supposed to do about my father?"

"They said he'll be fine."

"Sure. Until the next time somebody tries to blow him up. Or had you forgotten?"

Laura closed her eyes to shut out all the complications. "Theo, this is too scary. Why don't you just hire your father a bodyguard? Or better yet, do an alcoholic intervention on him, put him in dry-out."

"We've tried that." His voice had an edge. "He won't stay."

"Sorry."

They both looked away, focusing on the stage, where a guitarist came out to tinker with the sound equipment. In a few seconds he was joined by a drummer who spread a towel over his throne and put a filled plastic stadium cup on an overturned milk crate beside his drums. The guitarist thunked a few notes, brought the sound up to a squeal, and turned it back down again. Then both men sauntered off-stage.

A minute later the musicians jogged back onstage to

the sound of scattered applause. As they took up their in-
struments, the guitarist tapped to three with his foot, laid
down some chords, and looked at the drummer. The drummer joined in and turned to stage right, where a nattily
dressed man in a bow tie leaped out of the wings. The man
was wiry and small, and his only instrument was his smile.
He stood with his hands in his baggy pockets, grinning his
way through the entire musical introduction.

As the music crescendoed and died, the smiler spoke
into the microphone: "Good evening, ladies and gentlemen. Welcome to The Original Willie Cox's High Life
Lounge."

The audience cheered.

"Will-lay!" encouraged a voice from the back.

Willie grinned and raised his hands for quiet. "For
your pleasure this evening we have, as always, only the
best in fine musical entertainment." The drums rolled.
"We have for you. Paincourtville's own Diana Ross. The
one . . . the only . . . Reba Pugh!"

The crowd roared, the music rose, and Reba Pugh
sauntered out, wearing a skinny red satin dress with spa-
ghetti straps. The teenager's doe eyes were made up with
silver shadow and her woolly hair was bound in a silver
hairband with a baby-doll bow.

The dress clung to every curve. One tiny strap had
fallen off her bony shoulder and peeled back a petal of
material nearly to her nipple. It was quite clear that Reba
had on no underwear, neither top nor bottom.

Laura sat with her mouth open, unable to take her eyes
off Reba. Theo crossed his legs and said, "She didn't used
to look like that."

Laura smiled. "She's gorgeous."

Shifting uncomfortably Theo said, "Promise me you'll
never wear a dress like that in public."

"Theo, I didn't know you were such a prude."

"Neither did I."

For her first number Reba hid in the dark at the back
of the stage. The downbeat started, the spotlight hit her
face, and she commanded musically, "Stop, in the name of
love." The audience hung on every phrase and feasted on

her Motown moves. They called "righteous" when she purred and batted her eyes, and they applauded wildly at the end.

For the second song Reba snuggled up to the mike and cooed "Baby Love" in a cotton candy voice. And by the end of the song she had the audience ready to attack the fickle lover who had treated her so badly. As they applauded, Laura leaned over to Theo's ear. "She really does sound like Diana Ross."

"That's what you're supposed to say."

For the third number the guitarist began with a throbbing rhythm that Reba picked up in her hips. Grabbing a tambourine from the drummer, she bumped it against her thigh as she strutted across the stage telling the audience, "You can't hurry love."

When the music stopped, the applause was deafening. As the floorboards vibrated with praise, Reba went over to the drummer and drank from his cup. Slinking back to the microphone, she broke into an easy grin and announced, "And now, ladies and gentlemen, guitarist Ewell McNiece will assist me in my favorite Diana Ross number, 'Someday We'll Be Together.' "

The audience applauded in anticipation.

The guitarist moved close to Reba. Laying down a long twisting introduction, he finally stepped up to the mike and purred a mellow backup. Reba responded as if singing to a lover, "Someda-a-ay. We'll be together. Someda-a-ay. We'll be together."

They sang all four verses and then began passing the song back and forth between his guitar and Reba's honeyed voice, alternating backup and melody. After five minutes they looked over to the drummer to pass him a solo. On his hat and snare he laid out a mellow, syncopated chorus in which the rhythm was always on the verge of getting lost. Looking up when he was finished, the two at the microphone stepped forward again as Ewell picked out the melody on his strings and Reba purred into the microphone, "Someda-a-ay. We'll be together."

All in all, the trio kept it up for eleven minutes. Finally, when the drummer slacked off the pace and all three musicians were exhausted and glistening with sweat, Reba took the mike out of the stand, walked forward, and repeated slowly one last time, "Someda-a-ay. We'll be together."

The audience rose to their feet. They beat on the tables and clapped their hands. Reba and the musicians smiled and folded themselves in deep bows. Laura stood clapping until her palms stung. As she watched Reba leave the stage, she leaned over and said, "Theo, she's dynamite."

"So's Diana Ross." He pushed backs his chair. "Come on, we need to get her before she leaves."

They followed Reba and found themselves in a storage room lined with metal shelving for paper products and cleaning supplies. Reba was slumped in a folding chair at the far end of the room, drinking from a plastic cup. Up close her face was clownish in the silver makeup.

Theo grinned appreciatively. "Good stuff, Reba."

"Thank you, Theophile."

"Can we go someplace to talk?"

She stood up wearily. "I didn't figure y'all came just to hear me sing."

Pushing open the alley door, she led them out behind the lounge. A handful of kids, much too young to go inside, stood about posturing with cigarettes.

"Y'all go away," said Reba. "I gotta talk to the man."

As the boys went around the corner to spy, Reba positioned herself against the building and leaned on her hands.

Theo kept his eyes off Reba's expanse of chocolate skin. "Reba, Zachary Bruton was in the jail cell next to me. He told me about you and Boo."

"He say Mr. Boo and I been together?"

Theo nodded.

Reba looked annoyed. "That's what everybody says. I'm so tired of it, I don't even listen anymore."

The man in the bow tie peeked out the door. Reba leaned forward. "It's okay, Willie. These are home folks." Willie nodded and withdrew. As the door closed, Theo looked at the brown penciled line around Reba's mouth and said, "Reba, why would Zachary Bruton tell me something like that if it weren't true?"

Reba shrugged. "To look like the big man, make you think he knows something. They all think Mr. Boo couldn't be nice to a black girl without her putting out, but the Guidrys lived beside us ever since their house was built. I been helping out with Gumby ever since he was three days old. Miss Sally—" She paused and began again. "They like family."

"How homey."

"No, Theophile. Don't talk like that," she pleaded. "Mr. Boo always like my singing, and now he's dead." Her voice suddenly caught in her throat. "Theophile, he's the one told me I sound like Diana Ross. He the one gave me my first tapes."

"Jesus, Reba. I'm sorry." Theo pushed his forelock off his face. "I didn't knows it was like that."

"Well, it is." Reba sighed deeply, determined not to cry.

Gently Theo probed: "Well, if you were over there so much, you must have known what was going on."

"No I didn't." Reba put a hand up to scratch her eye and smudged her silver makeup. "Know about what?"

"You know about what: about Boo getting killed in that really stupid way."

"I do not. I don't know nothing about it." She looked at Laura in mute appeal and Laura stepped back helplessly, folding her guilty arms.

Theo moved in close, close enough to see the fine beads of sweat on Reba's upper lip. "Why is it I don't believe you when you say you don't know anything?"

"That's your problem, not mine."

"Reba, we can stay here all night if we have to."

"You can't make me."

"You ever heard of the laws about withholding evidence? Tutoo Landry would love to sit down with you tonight in front of a camcorder." He reached for her arm. "Maybe we should go there now."

Reba pulled back, the scarlet shoulder strap falling once more off her shoulder. Tugging it back up, she said offhandedly, "Only thing I can think of about Boo is maybe that thing about the Atchafalaya."

"What about it?"

Reba frowned. "That thing about the engineers letting the Mississippi flow there. Boo said he was going to do a job for somebody on it."

"The Corps of Engineers?"

"Uh-huh."

"Then you've got it backwards. The Corps of Engineers keeps the Mississippi *out* of the Atchafalaya with the dam at Simmesport."

"Uh." Reba slapped at a mosquito.

"What kind of job was Boo going to do back there?"

"He didn't say."

"How much were they going to pay him?"

She looked at her silver shoes.

"How much, Reba?"

With a great heaving breath, she answered, "A million dollars."

"Reba!"

"That's what he said!"

"Reba, how could you possibly believe that?"

She shouted, "I could believe that because he already gave me a shoe—" She faltered. "A pair of shoes."

"A *what*? What for?"

"Cause I helped him." She pulled away and knocked on the back door. "Theophile, I'm not talking to you no more."

Theo stared at her a moment and touched Laura's elbow as a signal to go. "Okay, Reba, we'll leave you alone now, but I want you to think about something: somebody out there wasn't afraid to take down the Redemption Parish sheriff, and if push ever comes to shove, they certainly aren't going to be afraid of one skinny little black girl; I don't care *who* she sings like."

CHAPTER 7

Laura watched angry clouds move swiftly across the night sky. A full moon gleamed and disappeared, leaving a glowing aureole around the edge of a cumulus. "Reba's not telling all she knows," said Laura.

"I would say."

"And what in heaven's name is the Atchafalaya?"

Theo checked his mirror and passed a pickup with four teenage boys squeezed into the cab. "It's a river that flows back of the parish, a *dis*tributary of the Mississippi. The Corps of Engineers has the job of keeping the Atchafalaya from becoming the main channel of the Mississippi."

"You mean the Mississippi is trying to jump its bed?"

"Uh-huh. River's been looking for a shorter way to the Gulf ever since the 1940's. The present main channel is really slow, all these big old meander bends. The

Atchafalaya, on the other hand, runs a straight line due south."

They pulled up behind the house and Theo came around to open the car door for her. Laura looked up at the porch light, where pale moths darted in frantic circles, nervous barometers of the changing weather. At the top of the stairs she turned back to look: Theo had not followed her, but was standing by the car door watching her progress up the steps. "Aren't you coming?" she asked.

He stuffed his hands in his pockets. "I need to go to a place called the Cookshack and find out what Boo was up to."

A rustling breeze lifted Laura's bangs and laid them down again. "Couldn't you do it tomorrow?"

"The people I need won't be there tomorrow." He opened the car door. "I might be late. Don't wait up."

"Nonsense." And she smiled as if she meant it.

He drove out into the cane fields back of town and turned onto a gravel road cut out between two sections. On both sides of the road sugar cane moved languorously in the thick breeze. With the air conditioner blasting noisily in his face, he watched the cane purl and surge in the blustery air. Pools of light from his headlamps confined his vision to two realities: sugar cane and oyster shell road, both under an angry sky.

Nearly a mile into the cane he pulled into a little parking lot where half a dozen pickups were parked in front of a homemade plywood shack. Next to the pickups Cecile's silver Mercury looked like a wallowing effete-mobile. Theo got out and stood by the car, listening to the soft sighs of the cane field. Yellow light streamed out of the shabby little building, and since his last visit, someone had painted the door trim and window sash a color that—in this light—looked turquoise. Theo smiled in spite of himself: turquoise was Quatorze's favorite color.

Gus came to the doorway and squinted into the dark. "Theophile," he said. "Come on in and rest your weary bones. We got something we want you to try."

Theo walked in and looked around. Besides Uncle Gus there was Hypo Hebert and Paul Theriot from the Dollar

Store, both huddled over the Formica table against the wall. Next to them Quatorze stood on a dinette chair looking down into the innards of a 7-Eleven Slurpee machine. Over in the corner, cousin Potch Talbot sat playing portable solitaire as he had for the last fifteen years.

Theo asked, "Nothing on the stove tonight, Potch?"

"Too hot to cook. Come back in October." Gesturing to Quatorze, he said, "If you can wait a minute, we'll give you something cold to drink."

Theo looked up at Quatorze on the chair. "What in hell's name are you doing with that Slurpee machine?"

Quatorze bent over and adjusted the insides with a screwdriver. "We *were* going to use it for our hurricane party but it don't look like we get to have one now, does it?"

"Party's in Pensacola tonight."

"That's a fact."

Theo turned to his uncle. "Gus, why's the Slurpee *here*? You closed down your 7-Eleven in Morgan City?"

"Had to," said Gus. "No business since the oil slump."

"That's too bad. Y'all carried one of my favorite baseball caps in that store." Theo raised his hand and pointed to imaginary words on his crown: " 'Oil Patch Trash, and Proud of It.' "

"Shoot," said Gus. "Don't let your Aunt Bess see you wearin' something like that. Quatorze, hurry up and put that lid back on. We need to give this boy some of our special brew."

Theo said, "I can't drink that shit."

Hoots of laughter filled the room. Gus smiled and said, "Don't worry, Theophile, this is a new kind of Slurpee, a Bayou Lafourche Slurpee. We have a special arrangement with Mr. Seven and Mr. Eleven. Ain't that right, Quatorze?"

"Damn right."

As Quatorze screwed on the lid, Gus put a big plastic cup under the spigot and twisted the handle. Lime ooze filled the cup, and Gus handed it to his nephew and waited. Cautiously Theo sipped, and smiled.

"What you think that is, Theophile?"

"A margarita?"

"That's good, huh?"

Theo raised his eyebrows. "Strong enough."

"Too strong?"

"No, no, it's fine. I just can't drink like y'all any-more."

A cat whined and Theo looked over to Hypo and Paul Theriot. On the table in front of them a brown tabby lay wrapped in a plaid cotton blanket. Paul Theriot held the cat immobile by pinning the blanket corners onto the table, and stoop-shouldered Hypo pressed the cat's head down with his left hand. In his right he held up a tiny hypodermic needle and squirted a thin stream into the air.

"Hypo, what you doing to that cat?"

The doctor grunted, meaning he was too busy to answer.

"Hypo's got some lidocaine," said Paul. "He's going to try sewing this ear back on."

Theo peeked over Hypo's shoulder. The cat's muzzle was bloodied and covered with dirt. His left ear was ripped half off and lay drooping in the cavity. Hypo worked the needle slowly into the ear skin, and the cat struggled and whined. Paul Theriot held the blanket tightly. Under his breath Hypo murmured, "No wonder vets always put 'em under."

"Yeah."

Persisting with the needle, Hypo repeated the procedure with a second hypodermic. Finally he stood upright and stretched his back. "Worst part's over now, kitty. It's downhill from here." Reaching into his pocket, he unfolded a plastic sterile pack containing plastic hemostats, a curved needle, and floss. "What you think, Paul, another minute before the lidocaine plugs in?"

"You start sewing too soon, he'll let you know."

Theo asked, "Where'd you find it, Hypo?"

"The cat, or the lidocaine?"

"Both."

"The cat was behind the hospital dumpster. The lidocaine I got on the barter system from an unnamed dentist."

They all snickered: Peetie Savoie was the only dentist in town.

As they waited for the anesthetic to take effect, Potch Talbot turned to Theo. "Where's that good-looking gal of yours?"

Spying a kitchen chair in the corner, Theo turned it around to straddle. "I left that beautiful woman at home tonight to come here and ask y'all a question about my good friend Boo."

The men sobered and Hypo glanced up from his cat. "That hit you pretty hard this morning?"

Theo shrugged. "Boo and I played football every year since Pop Warner."

Gus took off his glasses and wiped them methodically with a handkerchief. Staring myopically at his nephew, he said, "Boy did have a good arm."

"Yes he did. But my problem now is about something he told me before he died."

"What's that?" Gus put on his glasses.

"Last night Boo said he was going to do something for somebody and they were going to give him a million dollars."

Gus snorted. "The boy was sicker than I thought."

"I'll say," agreed Hypo.

"What'd you mean?" asked Theo.

The men looked around the room uncertainly and Gus finally said, "Why don't you tell him, Paul."

Still pressing tightly on the corners of the blanket, the druggist looked up from the table. "I'm afraid your friend Boo'd been treating drugstores like they were supermarkets lately. He was buying regularly from me, and then a few weeks ago I talked to a friend with a Rexall in Thibodaux and he told me what-all Boo'd been buying from him. By the time we called up everybody else and found out all the shit he'd been pulling in, we nearly fell dead on the floor. That man was a walking pharmacy."

"What *was* he buying?"

"He was partial to the benzodiazepenes. Ativan, Valium, Xanax, Tranxene."

"They lay you out, don't they?"

"That's right. Way we figure, our sheriff must have been so laid back, he wouldn'na been able to get it up for Madonna."

"But those are prescription. Who wrote them for him?"

They all looked at Hypo, who finally said, "All right. I wrote him Ativan once or twice, but it was nothing near like what Paul's talking about."

"Was he shopping docs in Thibodaux?"

"*And* Donaldsonville. *And* Morgan City."

Theo shook his head. "I can't believe he was taking all that. Boo's drug of choice was Miller Lite."

Gus sat forward. "He wanted us to believe it was for the prisoners in the jail, to keep them happy. But you know as well as I do that a man doesn't go walking down the middle of the road at four in the morning unless he's got some pretty serious mental problems." Gus pushed up the bridge of his glasses. "And if you please, Theophile, we would rather the rest of the world not know that the Redemption Parish sheriff was a druggie."

"Well, they're going to find out anyway."

"Say what?"

Theo looked at Hypo. "You'll have to tell them in Baton Rogue about all Boo's drugs so they can test for them at the autopsy, won't you?"

"Guess you're right." Hypo pinched the cat's ear and the animal flinched under the blanket.

Sipping his margarita, Theo continued, "But getting back to Boo's million dollars. Where do you suppose he thought he would run into that?"

Potch said, "Shoot. Maybe he saw my fifty-nine-dollar check for gas royalties and got confused."

Theo sighed. "Or how about this: Boo thought if he kept quiet for whoever was trying to kill Daddy, he'd ask for a million in hush money."

"No, Theophile." The men disagreed noisily. "No one's trying to kill your daddy."

Gus rested his margarita on his knee. "We were just talking about your daddy before you came in. When I was over at the hospital last night, the doctors told me Valmont is so paranoid at this point, he probably bought dynamite to protect himself and it blew up in his face."

"That's *not* what happened."

Gus looked at him kindly. "He's your father, Theophile. It's right that you should think well of him."

Theo closed his eyes and wet his lips with the heady margarita. "Okay, then. Back to Boo. Why did he think somebody would give him a million dollars?"

"We keep telling you," said Gus. "The boy was just plain sick." He twisted his ample rear on the cushioned dinette chair and began again. "Theophile, think about it: there's nothing going on in this parish worth a million dollars." He held up his fingers. "We've got sugar cane, we've got bait packing, and we've got piss-poor oil and gas. Now, *who* would give somebody like Boo a million dollars for anything? Hell, you wouldn't have to pay that much for a hit in New Orleans. Quatorze, how much you think it costs to have someone taken out down there?"

"Ten, twenty thousand?"

Theo sloshed the icy green liquid around in his cup. "Okay, I have one more idea: figure there wasn't actually a million dollars laying around for Boo, but he just *thought* he could squeeze a million out of somebody, and that's what got him killed."

Hypo leaned against the table. "Theophile, you're beginning to sound like something on television. This is Bayou Lafourche and you know perfectly well what happened to Boo. One of those high school kids back there by y'all's house took your truck out joyriding and got the wee-wee scared out of him when he ran over Boo. I predict the kid shows up at the courthouse with a lawyer before Mass on Sunday. I'd bet money on it." Hypo pinched the cat's ear again.

"That doesn't tell me why Boo was walking in the road in the first place."

"I'd call that a drug-induced psychosis." Hypo scooted a chair up to the table. "Okay, Paul, that's better. Press hard on the blanket."

Sitting on the edge of his chair, Hypo clipped away cat fur with surgical scissors. Shaving the ear with a plastic razor, he ripped open the sterile pack and swabbed the area with orange disinfectant. Stitching and tying sutures in the soft flesh, he worked with deft hands as a wall of concentration formed around him. In the shadows men sipped margaritas in admiring silence.

Laura turned in her sleep and woke up. In front of the window fan Theo stood in his Jockey shorts humming a meterless tune. Vibrating air from the fan caused his voice to waver and break, and as she watched, she wondered how old he was when he had first hummed into the fan.

"Theo?"

"I woke you up."

"I was trying to wait up for you." She rubbed her eyes and moved over to make room for him on the bed. "What did they say at the Cookshack?"

He sat down on the edge. "That Boo was zonked out on tranquilizers."

"Oh, no! Maybe whoever killed him gave them to him."

"That's not it. He'd been buying a lot of tranquilizers lately and everybody at the Cookshack just assumed that's why he was in the road." Theo followed the long line of her body up to where the neck of her nightshirt framed a triangle of pale skin. "I told them the autopsy would show whether that was true or not."

"That's right! Did you see the phone message I left on the kitchen table?"

"No. What'd it say?"

"It was the hospital. They said your father was restless and they wanted to know if they should advise you if he became out of control."

"What'd you tell them?" He reached for her wrist with his forefinger and thumb, and circled the beautiful little dip between her wristbone and hand.

Watching their hands together in the air, Laura said, "I told them you probably wanted it handled the way they thought best."

"Sounds good to me."

Laura's stomach growled and she pulled her hand away and sat up on her elbows. "I had my fourth piece of Yamboree Cake when I came in."

"Hey, go easy on that stuff. Sally says it clocks in at seven hundred calories a slice."

Laura looked at her long feet and rubbed them together. "Cecile said you and Sally Guidry used to be very close."

Theo's face flashed dismay and he lay down beside her, crossing his arms over his face. "I used to have a crush on Sally. In second grade she had these pink chubby cheeks, and I would sit there wondering what it would be like to bite one of them."

"Cecile said you and Sally were going to get married."

"Laura, this is a terrible time to bring this up."

"There's a good time?"

"Do I ask you about your past?"

"Theo, I don't mean to pry. It's just that, well, if you were going to marry Sally, I'm about a hundred-eighty degrees different from her. She cooks, I microwave. She's cute and little, I can pass for Big Bird." Laura shrugged. "You know what I mean."

"And? What am I supposed to say?"

Laura turned over on her stomach. "Well, what happened? Why didn't you marry her?"

"Let me see. I went back to college, she started dating Matt Theriot. I went into the seminary. She married Boo."

"Oh." Laura let out a sigh. "Sounds like real life." Turning on her side, she followed the molded curve of his chest muscles as they dipped into his sternum. "Cecile really admires Sally."

"We're being a bit self-involved here, aren't we?"

"What do you mean?"

"You haven't figured out why you want to talk about Sally yet?"

"Because I'm jealous."

"Give her some space, Laura. Her husband died this morning."

She watched the long stretch of abdominal muscle rise

and fall with his breathing. "But you still really like her, don't you?"

He exhaled deeply. "Laura, Sally exists in a part of me I have no control over. If I tried to pretend I never cared about her, I'd end up not knowing how much past I'm really allowed to own. It's already complicated enough, so please don't do that to me."

"I won't. It's just that she's so competent and perfect. And she's such a wonderful little shape too. Even I couldn't take my eyes off her, so I know what it must be like for you."

In the cavern of his arms, she heard his voice as if from far away. "Funny you should say that. I was standing there watching you sleep and I got tears in my eyes because something so beautiful could actually be here in my bed. I stood there thinking: this is what I used to lie here and dream about."

"Oh."

After a moment Laura sat up and peeled off her night-shirt. Leaning over his warm chest, she let the shirt drop to the floor.

It was either the rain or the telephone that woke them in the middle of the night. A fine mist blew in through the fan blades, and downstairs the ringing drilled on and on.

"Why isn't anyone answering the phone?" Laura pulled the sheet up around her shoulders and tucked it over Theo for good measure.

Theo got up and turned off the fan before starting for the phone. "Dorothy's sleeping at home," he said. Without the noise of the fan the rain sounded like a waterfall. Downstairs the phone jangled again and again, refusing to give up without a fight. Theo reached for his pants as across the hall a door opened.

"I'll get it," Cecile called.

"Thank you, Cecile." Theo lay down again, naked on top the covers.

"Get under the sheet, Theo. It's cold out there."

"Phone'll be for me."

"You don't know that." She tugged at the sheet under him and he lifted up, allowing her to cover him and then nestle her long body against his side.

"Ugh." Laura stiffened. "I'm in the wet spot."

Without a word he nudged her sideways until the cold circle of sheet was in the center of his back.

"We can move over farther if you want."

"That's okay," he said. "I like it when you feel sorry for me."

"Theophile?" Cecile was at the door, tapping softly. "Yes?"

His aunt opened the door an inch. "That was the hospital. Your father's out of control and they want to advise the family members."

"Advise?"

"I don't know what it means either."

"Damn." He sat up on his elbows and shared an anxious silence with his aunt at the door. Outside the window the rain made white noise.

Cautiously Cecile asked, "Do you think we ought to go over there?"

"Do you mind?"

"Of course not. I'll call and say we're coming." Cecile closed the door.

Laura sat up, holding the sheet in front of her. "May I go?"

He reached again for his pants. "It's not going to be something I'd like you to see."

"I know." She lay back down.

The umbrella made no difference. Rain bounced up from the hospital sidewalk and soaked them to the knees. The thick mist swirled under the umbrella spokes and clung to their faces and clothes. Theo opened the lobby door for his aunt and they dripped and stamped in front of the receptionist, who didn't drop a stitch on the afghan she worked in her lap.

Leaving the umbrella to drip under the brass plaque on

the wall, Theo approached the desk and asked, "Valmont Talbot's room?"

The receptionist nodded sympathetically. "One-sixteen. Through these doors."

"Thank you."

Cecile's heels sounded smartly against the terrazzo. Theo heard his father's angry voice from a room down the hall and the low, insistent tones of a nurse. The nurse emerged from the room, ruffled and breathing hard. Glancing at Theo and Cecile, she said, "Are you for Mr. Talbot?"

"Yes."

The nurse's name tag read, "CROCHET, R.N." She was feisty and short-legged, wearing white jeans and running shoes. Stuffing her hands in her jacket pockets, she summarized for them: "He's pulled out his IVs and he says he's leaving as soon as he gets his clothes on. If I can't get him under control, I'll have to call a restraint team."

"Theophile?" From the sick room his father's desperate voice called.

"I'm here, Daddy." Theo pushed through the door and his father's grateful eyes drank in the son, leaving him awash in happiness and feeling. The eyes immediately hardened, reading the growing repulsion in Theo's face.

Theo stayed at the foot of the bed, protecting himself with the enameled footboard from the gnarled old troll in the bed. On the pillow his father's unkempt hair was entirely gray, a fact that he had not noticed at the sugar house. The old man's cheek pads blazed scarlet and his drooping lower eyelids hung deep as a hound dog's. Above the bed the blood pressure cuff had been knocked off the wall and on the floor a Bible lay splayed open, gilt edges bright as liquid gold.

"Daddy," Theo said. "What's the deal? They don't have time to baby-sit with you." He noticed the IV stand in the middle of the room, its supple tubing hanging to the floor. Behind him Cecile and Nurse Crochet slipped into the room.

Valmont's eyes darted to the women and then back to

his son. "Theophile, you've got to help me. I need to go home."

"You can't, Daddy. They need to keep you here overnight. Why don't you just let them plug the IVs back in and go to sleep?"

With barely controlled fury, Valmont spat out, "This place is hell." He eyed the nurse. "That woman's been filling me full of shit ever since she got here. How do I know what they're pumping in me?"

Nurse Crochet stepped forward and rolled the IV stand over to its place by the bed. "I already told you, Mr. Talbot. These are simple solutions of glucose and saline: sugar and salt."

Valmont growled. "Don't you glucose and saline me, bitch."

"Daddy! Hush."

Calmly, Nurse Crochet locked the stand with her foot. "I don't appreciate that kind of talk, Mr. Talbot."

"Then get the hell out of here, you self-righteous little bitch. Theophile, get her out. She's making me mad."

"Daddy, the nurse will go as soon as you get your IVs back in and settle down. They have to keep you overnight for observation in case you have internal bleeding."

"This bitch wouldn't know internal bleeding from a mess of piles."

Theo glanced at the nurse and motioned for her to join him in the hall. When they were out of earshot, he whispered, "Can't you dope him up?"

She looked at the nursing station down the hall, where a second nurse was using the phone. "He's already on Librium and we're calling the doctor to get his dosage increased. Dr. Toupe is covering for Dr. Melançon and we're not sure the dosage is as high as . . ." She shrugged and started over. "Anyway, as soon as we get the okay, I'll *try* to get him to take his meds orally, but as it stands, it looks like we'll have to do it IM." She patted her thigh. "In the hip. And he's not going to like that."

From the lighted room, his father called, "Theophile, I need you."

Theo walked in to find Valmont sitting with his scaly

pink legs over the edge of the bed and Cecile holding him back by the shoulders. "Get me my clothes, please, son."

"You can't go, Daddy." Theo helped Cecile press him back down on the bed and scoop his legs up onto the sheet. His worn blue hospital gown looked like a costume for the insane.

Wrestling unseen demons, Valmont growled, "Like *hell* I'm going to stay!" His eyes raged lime green. "I helped build this hospital, I'll fucking leave it when I fucking like."

"Daddy, you've got to *stop* this."

"Damn it, Theophile, I can't! I got to get back to the mill."

"To your beer."

"Fucking right, to my beer."

Cecile clutched the brown-striped privacy curtain and held it for protection. "Valmont, you have to stop. Don't you see what you're doing to your family?"

"Cecile, stay the fuck out of this."

"I will not! I won't let you stand here and rip Theophile's heart out this way. And Camille, what would Camille have thought?"

Valmont growled under his breath. "Don't you dare use her name on me, Cecile Bergeron. She might have been your cousin, but we both know what you used to be when you started out: you're nothing but illiterate bayou trash."

Cecile gasped.

Valmont grunted with satisfaction. "I don't want you ever mentioning my family again, Cecile. Hadn't been for my family, you would have stayed just where you were, out in the cane fields cooking beans."

"*Your* family?" Purple fury flashed across her face. "How *dare* you talk about my husband that way. You're not even worth Bronier's"—she looked angrily around the room—"dirty handkerchief."

"Oh, shut up, Cecile. Bronier was a lush. You're a lush, too. How about a Scotch, Cecile? Could you use a Scotch right now?"

Cecile's mouth contorted with rage and then she

squared her shoulders, elegantly outlined in bias-cut linen. "I just realized something about you, Valmont. You're such garbage right now, you're not even worth wasting my breath on." She pivoted gracefully and disappeared.

"Good riddance, bitch," muttered Valmont.

Theo looked at the empty doorway. "Daddy, now, why'd you go and do that? She's just about all we have left. You know Momma would have told you the same thing."

"Leave your mother out of this."

"I can't. I just saw y'all's names on the donors plaque in the lobby: Valmont and Camille Talbot. I realized I don't even remember when this place was built."

"Broke ground in 1964. You were five years old, your mother was just pregnant with Claiborne."

"And what do you think she'd do if she knew you were in here like this?"

"Theophile, I said to quit it!" His father snarled, vicious as a cur. "You used that trick on me last time to put me in the hospital and you're not going to do it again. Now, back off!"

Theo looked at the polished stone floor. "Place still looks new, doesn't it, Daddy?"

"Terrazzo and brick. Theophile." He writhed again with the dancing demons. "I'm *not* going to stay here; I need to get out."

"You can't, Daddy." Theo softened his eyes. "That's all there is to it."

Nurse Crochet came in smiling brightly and holding a little pill cup. "We got a hold of Dr. Melançon. He suggested some new medication."

"I'm not taking it. I'm leaving as soon as my son goes."

"I'd really like for you to swallow these pills, Mr. Talbot. It would be much easier for everyone if you did."

Theo broke in, "Daddy, if you don't take the pills, she's going to call in orderlies to hold you down so she can give it to you in the ass."

Nurse Crochet agreed. "The sooner you take your meds, Mr. Talbot, the sooner you'll settle down."

"Take the pills, Daddy. They're not going to let you leave."

Hatefully Valmont eyed the two of them and then peered into the paper cup. "What's in it?"

Guarding the fluted cup in case he tried to knock it out of her hand, Nurse Crochet said, "Two white Libriums, like you had before, and some new little blue pills that will help you sleep."

"I don't need Librium. I need Budweiser."

"We're not allowed to give you alcohol."

"Go ahead, Daddy. The pills'll put you out." Theo poured water from a thermos pitcher on the nightstand and handed the glass to his father.

Picking out the tablets two at a time, Valmont put them in his mouth, sipped water, and swallowed. As Theo watched anxiously, Nurse Crochet purred soothingly, "That's the way." She crushed the cup and threw it in the trash, then leaned over Valmont's head to adjust his pillows. "Now, if you'll lay back and get comfortable, the next thing you'll know, someone will be coming to wake you up for breakfast, and after that, the doctor will be here to tell you if you can leave."

"Damn right I can leave. Theophile, I'm not staying here another day."

"Nobody can make you, Daddy." In the quiet, Theo became again aware of the wild rain outside.

"I'm calling Bert first thing in the morning."

"No need for a lawyer, Daddy. The doctor'll let you go." Theo watched his father from the corner of his eye as Nurse Crochet took his pulse and dabbed ointment on his singed cheeks.

"Unh," grunted Valmont. "Pills work fast."

"They're in your blood now," soothed the nurse.

"Unh."

Quietly Theo walked to the window and brushed back the rubberized curtain to look at the silver droplets smeared sideways across the pane. He thought of the mill and of the sugar farmers all over the parish doing exactly what he was doing now: looking out the window, hoping that no one would lose much cane tonight. Glancing back at the bed, he watched his father, knobby and gnome-like, turn on his side and curl into a fetal position. There was a thick gauze bandage on the back of Valmont's skull he had not seen before.

Nurse Crochet put a hand on the light switch and beckoned Theo silently. As he left the room, she took one last look at her patient, hit the switch, and checked her watch. In the hall she looked up at Theo and smiled professionally. "He should be fine until morning. I'm just sorry we can't do more for him."

Theo looked up and down the hall, wondering where Cecile had gone for her cigarette. "Yeah, thank you. I'm sorry too."

CHAPTER 8

~~~~~~~~~~~~~~~~~~~~~~~~~~~

Cecile stood over the kitchen table sprinkling cornmeal on her mink coat. Beside her she had a toothbrush and the Dustbuster. "Theophile's still sleeping?" she asked.

Laura looked out the window at the morning rain. "I think last night was pretty hard on him."

Working in the cornmeal with her fingertips, Cecile said, "I can imagine. I don't see how you young people live this way. I've never been so ready to get back to Grand Isle in my life."

"Is it going to rain like this all day?"

"Hard to say. But be happy. The alternative is the whole damned hurricane." Cecile picked up the Dustbuster. "What do you want for breakfast, dear?"

"Oh, I can fix it." Laura poured orange juice and leaned against the counter, watching Cecile.

"I'll be out of your way in a few minutes. I just needed to clean the oil out of this collar."

"I didn't know you could do that to a mink. Does cornmeal absorb the oil?"

"It's supposed to. The furrier would spit frogs if she saw me, but I'm not about to drive to New Orleans just for a coat." She vacuumed the yellow grit. "One more good pass and you can have the whole kitchen. Oh, fudge. The powder's not coming out." Cecile ground the toothbrush into the thick collar, working in silence. After a moment she said casually, "A rainy morning might be just the time to go through old records at the courthouse. What do you think?"

"I'd better not say yes. I know Theo has a lot planned for us. He wants to make sure Boo's body gets up to Baton Rouge and—if we can still do it with all this rain—he wants to make footprint molds at the sugar house."

Cecile's groomed eyebrows fell a polite quarter of an inch.

"I don't think looking up land sales would be that hard, Cecile. Just ask at the records office; they'll help you." Laura spooned canned figs out of a mason jar from the refrigerator.

Concentrating on her coat, Cecile asked, "Laura, in your experience as an anthropologist, have you ever met intelligent people who have never learned how to read?"

"Oh, sure. There are whole pre- and protoliterate societies that don't read. Intelligence actually has nothing to do with literacy. In fact, most preliterates have vast stores of oral knowl—"

"No, no. I mean, have you ever come across Americans who for one reason or another learned everything they know from listening and watching?"

Laura frowned. "I can't imagine that happening in a college situation."

"Do you know what dyslexia is?"

"Oh, sure. They even had an international anthropology congress on it. Somebody estimated that as much as ten percent of the population worldwide may suffer from some form of it."

"Then you know it's not a form of mental illness?"

"Oh, no. It's just some little glitch in the synaptic firing or, as one guy thinks, maybe an imbalance in the middle ear." She put her figs on the table. "Who do you know with dyslexia?"

"Me."

"You're kidding?"

Cecile blew on her coat collar. "I'm pretty sure that's what I have. But back when I was in school, everyone just assumed little Cecile was slow."

"That's so sad!"

"I always thought maybe I was stupid until I heard about dyslexia from the talk shows. I cried when I saw Donahue that time."

"Can't you read at all?"

"Some things. It has a lot to do with size of letters and typeface. If it hadn't been for my ability to memorize, I wouldn't have made it through school. Memory and mathematics. For everything else I'd get somebody to read me my assignments and I'd memorize them on the spot."

"And *that's* why you want me to go to the courthouse with you."

Cecile nodded. "If you don't mind. If I tried going myself, I wouldn't be able to make heads or tails of those old records."

"I'd be glad to go. Just let me find out from Theo when I'm free."

The phone rang and Cecile gestured to the mink in her lap. "Can you get that?"

Laura went out to the back hall and picked up the receiver. "Hello?"

"Who's this?"

"My name's Laura Ireland, I'm a friend of Th—"

"Yeah, Laura. This is Hypo Hebert. We met the other night at the hospital."

"The urologist."

"Also the coroner. Tell Theophile that Boo Guidry's body is gone from the morgue."

"What? Oh, no! Just a minute. Let me get Theo. He'll want—"

"Don't do that. I don't want Theophile giving me hell like everybody else. The DA is on the phone right now trying to figure out exactly what kind of doo-doo we're in. Just tell Theophile I'll be at the hospital for another hour or so if he wants to talk to me."

"I will." She slammed down the phone and bolted up the back stairs two at a time. Hopping on the bed, she woke Theo from a sound sleep. "Hypo Hebert just called. Boo's body is missing from the hospital."

Theo mumbled. ". . . sleep."

She leaned over his ear. "Boo's body is gone. Somebody took it from the hospital. Theo, it's *disappeared*."

He was out of bed instantly, pulling on his pants. "What else did Hypo say?"

"That he'll be at the hospital for another hour if you want to talk to him and that the DA thinks they're in big trouble. Is the DA the one named Tutoo?"

"Yes."

They clambered down the back stairs and Cecile looked up, alarmed, as they burst into the kitchen. "What's the matter?"

"Cecile, Boo's body was stolen from the morgue and we need to use your car."

"Oh, Lord. Oh, Lord." She clutched her velvety coat. "Theophile, I just can't stand all this. And I'll be damned if I'm going to start pouring Scotch at this hour of the morning."

"Pour coffee. Your car, may we have it?"

"Take it. Take it."

He kissed her hair, and he and Laura drove to the hospital watching the wipers clear fans of vision through the windshield. Parking in the empty visitors lot, they padded across the polished lobby, turned left at the emergency room, and followed the long corridor to the end.

The morgue was a boxy little anteroom with two chest-high stainless doors along one wall. Theo opened one of

the doors by pulling up the tip of the handle with one finger. Inside, a blue-and-white elderly gentleman reposed on
a steel gurney, a folded sheet across his midsection.
"That's Tuffie Boudreaux," said Theo. "I didn't know *he*
was still alive."

"He's not."

Theo closed Tuffie's door and opened the other one.
This side of the cooler was empty. They stood in the chill
looking at Tuffie's chalky body through the open space between the compartments. "What was Boo's body doing
here in the first place?" asked Laura. "Isn't this a private
hospital?"

"The parish rents space when they need it."

Hypo appeared in the doorway. "Theophile, thanks for
coming down. I feel like shit." He watched Theo close the
door without touching the handle. "I'm afraid you won't
find much on the cooler: everybody and his uncle's been
all over it. Come on into postmortem; it's too crowded in
here."

Hypo led them into a slightly bigger room, windowless
and brightly lit, with a stainless steel table in the center.
Steel counters and deep sinks lined one wall, and on another, shiny black rubber aprons hung on hooks. In front
of the aprons was a second gurney.

Hypo leaned against the counter and stretched his neck
as if trying to relieve pain in his hunched shoulders.

"When'd they realize Boo was gone?" asked Theo.

Hypo nodded to the coolers in the outer room. "Tuffie
Boudreaux died of pneumonia last night in ICU . . ."

"I saw."

"And when they brought him in, they saw Boo's cart
was empty. That was about five A.M."

"So nobody knows how or when?"

"I grilled the hell out of last night's orderlies, but it
looks like all they did was play cards all night and are trying to cover for each other. I don't even have the nerve to
call Sally. Tutoo's doing that for me."

Theo crossed him arms. "Don't they lock this place?
Who was the supervisor last night?"

"Listen, I can't even get them to lock up the medications. It's like dealing with a bunch of children."

"Who was the last person to see the body?"

"Couldn't tell you." He shifted positions. "Or maybe I could. Sally asked Father LeBlanc to come by last night and do extreme unction. If he actually came in, he would have been the last."

Over the intercom a pinging chime introduced a pleasant female voice: "Dr. Hebert, Dr. Hypo Hebert. Dr. Hebert, Dr. Hypo Hebert."

Hypo looked up. "That's Tutoo calling back." He raised his eyebrows apprehensively, making three deep furrows in his ivory forehead. "Well, wish me luck, y'all."

"Sure, Hypo. Catch you later."

"And Theophile, I'm damned sorry. I know you were putting a lot of stock in those results."

"Yeah."

Theo watched Hypo glide out, Groucho style, and then crossed the room to study the empty gurney rolled up against the wall.

"Is that the one Boo was on?" asked Laura.

"Probably. I can't imagine they'd have more than two of these."

Laura watched as he silently examined it, looking closely at the handles, the top, and the undershelf. Next he stooped over and scrutinized the floor all the way from the gurney out to the anteroom. At the hallway door he straightened and looked both ways down the hall. Laura poked her head out too. At the far end was an emergency exit: Alarm Will Sound. Do Not Use. Theo padded down the hall and flung open the door. No alarm sounded.

"It's been turned off!" Laura jogged down the hall to join him outside and found him duck-walking around the service lot, squinting at rain puddles.

"Finding anything?" she asked.

"Good asphalt. Probably came from Thibodaux."

The warm rain beat on her shoulders and dripped down the sides of her face. "Theo, somebody really doesn't want Boo autopsied."

"That's right. It means we were on the right track to

begin with. An autopsy *is* going to show who killed Boo when it tells us how."

She walked behind him until her shirt was soaked through. "I'm going in. It's too wet out here."

"Good. Go back to the morgue and make sure no one touches Boo's gurney. Stand *guard* over it. What we're looking for is black gravel in the tire treads."

"Gotcha."

She squished down the empty hall and as she turned into the morgue, a blast of chilled air hit her in the face. The door to the second cooler was open, its caged light fuming a white fog. She put a hand on the door to close it, and looked inside, spying a folded sheet of yellow paper taped to the back wall.

Hunching over, Laura walked to the back of the cooler, skimming her head against the four-foot ceiling. The icy air chilled her wet shirt and turned her skin to goose flesh.

Suddenly the light went out and behind her the door slammed shut. Laura turned, catching her hair in the metal ceiling trim. "Ow!" Blackness twinkled in front of her eyes. Tugging her hair loose, she ran to the door and banged it with her fists. "I'm in here!" She banged until her hand hurt and then began to kick. "Open up!" A blast of arctic air blew in from the ceiling as the thermostat kicked in.

Laura inhaled the cold air. Her wet shirt clung to her shoulders and the chill invaded her body all the way to the bottom of her lungs. Even her armpits were cold. She beat the door in earnest. "Let me out! Hello?" Taking off her shoe, she used it as a hammer in the black air. "Theo," she cried. "Help!"

Next she put her ear against the door and listened. The only sound was the refrigeration unit pumping air into the cooler. Again she beat the door with her shoe. "Theo!" she called, weakly this time. She put her shoe back on to protect her foot from the steel floor and as she bent down, she felt her frozen shirt crisping at the shoulders.

Standing up, she banged her head against the stainless ceiling. "Damn *it*!" She fought down a fearful wave of claustrophobia. Through the steel door she heard the remote pinging sound of someone being paged. Reaching blindly in the blackness for Tuffie Boudreaux's gurney, she tried to move him away from his side of the cooler so she could bang on the wall next to the hallway.

Touching Tuffie's fleshy arm, she groped to find the edge of his cart. Grasping the lip of the gurney, she rolled his feet into her compartment, banging the cart into a separating bar on the back wall. "Sorry." She guided the gurney forward, toward the door, then again pulled his feet into her side of the cooler. With a jolt the gurney hit the separating bar once more and Tuffie's arm fell off the gurney, obscenely caressing her thigh.

"Aack!"

Laura jumped back, bumping her head painfully on the ceiling. Suddenly she had the frantic, violent need to stand up straight. Fighting panic, she pulled the sheet off Tuffie and wrapped it around her shoulders, then sat by the door. The floor was too cold for her bottom so she squatted on her heels, pulling the sheet over her head like a tent and breathing into the little space between her chest and knees.

Wintery cold pressed against the back of her neck and radiated up from the floor. One more time, she banged on the door with her fist.

Ten minutes went by, or maybe twenty. Periodically Laura banged with her fist, each time with less enthusiasm. She listened to the faraway intercom and the rich woman's voice—coming from someplace warm—paging people who had no idea someone would very soon freeze to death in their hospital. Numbness crept up her ankles. She tried sitting on the floor and found it still too cold. Swaying back and forth on her thighs, it became harder and harder to keep the air warm in her little tent. She banged on the door.

Suddenly without warning the light came on and Tuffie Boudreaux's gurney was pulled out from beside her. Laura fell over into Tuffie's compartment. "I'm in here!" she sobbed. Her hand buckled under her and she fell headfirst onto the cold steel, smacking her face on the floor. Struggling up, she saw a black orderly gawking at her as if she were something from hyperspace.

"Lawd!"

Laura scrambled out, warm air tickling her face. The orderly helped her stand and asked solicitously, "Are you okay, missy? Whatcha doing in there?"

Laura coughed a reply and looked for a place to sit. The orderly pushed Tuffie ahead into postmortem and pulled out a lab stool for Laura. "Sit here, I'll go get help. You gonna be okay?"

Laura nodded gamely, trying to look alert and perky. Across the room, chalk-colored Tuffie Boudreaux lay stone naked, entirely oblivious to her worldly problems.

In a moment Theo rushed in from the hall. "Laura!" He examined her without touching and from behind him Hypo pushed his way in and leaned over her, staring deep into her eyes. "How do you feel, honey?"

"Better."

Ignoring the stethoscope around his neck, Hypo took her wrist and felt her pulse. Looking around the room, he said, "Let's see if we can get your temp."

Shaking her head, Laura said, "No, I'll be fine, really." Her skin flashed deliciously chill and she looked up at Theo, tears welling in her eyes. "Didn't you hear me banging?"

He shook his head regretfully. "Laura, we didn't hear a thing. I looked for you in the lobby, paged you over the intercom. We didn't know where you had gone."

Behind Theo the orderly took a sheet from the cabinet and discreetly covered Tuffie Boudreaux before rolling him back into the cooler.

"How long was I in there?"

"Fifteen minutes, maybe twenty. Why'd you go in in the first place?"

"There was a note pinned to the back wall so I went back to get it, and somebody slammed the door behind me."

Hypo said, "Nobody'd do that deliberately."

"Yes, they did. It was a trap." Laura got up unsteadily and wobbled out to the anteroom. The orderly had disappeared and she opened the door next to Tuffie. On the back wall the yellow paper still hung limply, but the cold air was more than she could bear. "That's what I went in to see. Could you go get it, Theo? I *can't* go in there again. Watch your head."

Crouched nearly in half, Theo walked to the back of the cooler and, after studying the note for a second, snatched it off the wall. Stepping out into the room, he slammed the cooler door and handed the paper to Laura.

Opening the note, Laura said, "There's nothing on it. Why would somebody tape an empty piece of paper back there?"

"I don't know." Theo stared the question at her: *Why would you go into the cooler to look at an empty piece of paper?*

"Theo," she protested. "You don't understand. Somebody left the door open, they wanted me—or somebody—to go in there. Maybe it was meant for you."

Hypo crossed his arms over his lab coat. "Well, if this is some kind of bad joke, I don't care for it at all. I'll check with the orderlies." Jerking his head toward the hall to indicate the orderly who had just left, he said, "Maybe Wiley knows something about this."

"Would you ask?" said Theo. "We'd appreciate it."

"I will. I will." Hypo shuffled his feet and put the back of his hand on Laura's cheek. "But first I want to know what you're going to do right now. How about going home for a rest?"

"I can't. Theo and I have too much to do today."

Theo took her hands to help her stand. "Sorry, Laura, but I'm going to drop you off at the house so you can at least get into dry clothes."

"But where are you going?"

Theo looked at the clock on the wall. "I think it's time to visit the priest."

He pressed the old-fashioned button, and a bell rang from somewhere deep inside the rectory. After waiting a moment, Theo let himself in. "Hello?" he called to the empty house. "Father LeBlanc? Henry?"

The big old house smelled of dried eucalyptus from the scattered arrangements used to keep musty smells away. In the darkened living room the old wood furniture was polished to a high gloss and the Belgian carpets were worn thin in the traffic paths.

"Hello?" he called up the stairs.

Poking his head into a side parlor used as the winter chapel, he looked at the bare wooden altar and Victorian parlor chairs. Here he had served Mass on rainy November mornings. The chapel looked half the size it used to.

Glancing down the main hall back to the kitchen, Theo saw Father LeBlanc walking up the porch steps with an umbrella and a bag of groceries. The priest spied Theo through the glass in the door and, with a broad smile, waited on the porch so that Theo could let him into the kitchen.

"I'm glad you came to see me." The priest set his groceries down on the counter. "I thought we might not get to talk while you were in town." Propping the closed umbrella in the sink to dry, he fumbled through his bags and put his milk in the refrigerator. "Mrs. Gaudet is off today. Can I get you some iced tea?"

"Yes, Father. That'd be nice."

"Call me Henry, son. You make me feel old."

Father LeBlanc took out a sun tea jar from the milk shelf and filled two glasses. Handing one to Theo, he said, "Let's go to the living room. Air-conditioning's better. This is some rain."

"Reminds me of winter rain, except it's too muggy."

"Say, that reminds *me*. I got an invitation for you. My jubilee is December eighteenth. I want you to come."

"What is this for you? Twenty years?"

"Twenty-five."

"Come on, you haven't been a priest that long. What'd you do, take your vows when you were twelve?"

Father LeBlanc nestled into one of the worn needlepoint armchairs. His fine dark eyes flashed enjoyment as he nonchalantly scratched his movie-star jaw. "It's all this clean living. You ought to try it sometime."

"I did, if you'll remember. All I learned was that I was

better at speaking the vernacular. But send us an invitation; maybe Laura and I can fly down."

The priest sipped his tea and nodded. "Now that Laura, that's a nice girl. I heard she does sports."

Theo brightened. "You should see her. Have you noticed how graceful she is? It just about blows me away every time she moves."

Looking down, Father LeBlanc picked at unseen nits on his navy shirt. "I suppose this is the grace in her soul we're talking about, isn't it? I'm much better at talking about souls."

Theo grinned and rubbed moisture beads off his glass. Outside rain slapped the ragged leaves of the okra plants in the kitchen garden. Taking another sip of tea, he said, "Father, I need to ask you a question. Hypo said you gave extreme unction to Boo last night."

"That's right. Is something wrong?"

"Boo's body is missing. And you were the last one to see it."

"Oh, dear." The priest clutched the arm of his chair. "And you're thinking I might be responsible?"

"No, no. Not at all. I just need to know when you were at the hospital."

"Around eight o'clock. I was there for about fifteen minutes. This is getting more serious by the day, isn't it?"

Theo nodded. "Someone might have just tried to lock Laura into the morgue cooler. Or maybe it was an accident."

The priest sat forward. "Might have? Theophile, you can't let that happen. You have a responsibility. You have to get that girl out of here."

"She wouldn't go. Not without me, and if I leave town, I would say my father's chances of staying alive are about as good as those of the tomato worms in your garden."

Bumping his glass down on a crocheted doily, the priest said, "I have to tell you something, Theophile. It's something that's got me a little scared. Usually in this parish, I know what's going to happen *days* before it actually does. I'll be sitting here saying my office and look up and think, 'Oh, God, she's going to try to kill him,' or, 'Dear Lord, those people are getting a divorce.' You're not going to like me for saying this, but when I saw you in the hallway, I thought: 'Theophile's come here to tell me what he did to his daddy the other night.' But we've been sitting here fifteen minutes and you haven't even mentioned the awful state you two are in."

Theo forced a laugh. "If *I* ever try to kill Daddy, I know better than to do it with a pipe bomb."

"Theophile, that's not funny."

"I know. I'm sorry, I thought—You and Daddy have never gotten along, have you?"

The priest clenched his fist on the chair arm. "Valmont has always been very generous. There's not much more I can say."

"I think Daddy always resented that Momma spent so much time at the church."

Father LeBlanc sighed deeply. "Your mother was a very beautiful woman, Theophile, and I don't just mean physically. Her spiritual life was the core of her existence. I mean, that level of serenity—the Carmelites work years on that."

Theo shrugged. "She just seemed like Momma to me." He finished his tea and put the empty glass on the drum table next to the priest's.

"What are you going to do now, son? If you think it would help, I'll talk to Laura myself and ask her to leave."

"Wouldn't do any good. She won't go without me, and technically I can't leave town anyway; I'm only out of jail on personal recognizance."

"Well, at least that business about Boo's drugs takes some of the heat off you for that. I guess you heard about his tranquilizers and all?"

"I did." Theo arched his body to reach into his pants pocket. "And I don't believe a word of it." In his hand he held out a yellow tablet with a hollow *V* pressed through the center.

The priest picked it up gingerly and rolled it between his fingers. "What's this?"

"Valium. 'Vitamin V.' Zachary Bruton was in the cell

beside me yesterday. He handed it through the bars. He said Sheriff Guidry would give you anything you wanted to help you mellow out or to sleep. I don't think Boo was really doing this stuff himself."

"Maybe not." The priest gave the tablet back to Theo. "I know this is a terrible thing to say, but it's already astonishing how much better off this parish is with Boo Guidry out of it. The air's even kinder. I can't believe how one mean-spirited person in a position like that can make life so miserable for so many others."

"What was he doing?"

"Oh." Father LeBlanc drummed his fingers on the chair arm. "Maybe it wasn't all his fault: the car dealers didn't help by giving him kickbacks for repossessing cars, but Boo sure seemed to enjoy doing it. People can't get to work without their cars, you know."

"I'm sure he had his reas—"

"Then there was that business last summer when he jailed Mrs. Gaudet's grandson for half an ounce of marijuana. It's the attitude, Theophile. You think he was helping that boy?"

"That's too bad."

Loud footsteps sounded on the porch. The bell rang and Father LeBlanc rose to open the door. From his chair in the living room, Theo watched as his Uncle Gus stood in the foyer tugging at his elastic waistband and shaking rain off his shoes. Looking apprehensively at his nephew, Gus took off his steamy glasses and stared into the living room. "I believe the rain is letting up."

"Anybody lose cane last night?"

Gus slipped his glasses back on as the priest escorted him into the living room. "Not that I've heard. Winds only got up to forty."

Father LeBlanc touched Gus's elbow. "Would you like some iced tea? We've just had a glass."

"Yes, please. This rain is like a steam bath."

The priest left the room and Gus waddled over to sit on the edge of the piano bench. Waiting a moment, he said abruptly, "We're going to have to see about hiring a new sheriff soon, Theophile. I don't suppose you want to help us read applications, do you?"

"No, sir."

"You know, there were people down at the courthouse who were wondering if maybe *you* wanted Boo's job."

"They will wonder, won't they?"

They fell into silence until the priest returned with a tea glass, and Gus refreshed himself with hearty gulps. "Father," he said, "I know this is rude as can be, but I really need to talk to Theophile privately."

"I can let you have the living room." The priest rose to leave.

"Stay, Father," said Theo. "You know everything that's going on anyway. Gus, go ahead and talk. I want Father to hear our sins now; it'll save time later."

The priest sat down again, holding himself motionless in the chair.

Gus took another gulp of tea and, resting his glass on his plump thigh, attempted a riveting gaze. "Baton Rouge just called, Theophile."

"What's that supposed to mean?"

Gus hesitated. "The attorney general just called. We have a problem."

"What does he want?"

"He said that Boo was holding a large sum of money for them and they'd like it returned."

"Then return it."

"Theophile, if I knew where it was, do you think I'd be here?"

"You mean you want me to find it?"

"If you please."

"Nope. Can't do. I'm too busy."

"Theophile, please."

"Listen, Gus, somebody stole Boo's body this morning and now I figure that same person might have just tried to lock Laura in the morgue freezer. Counting Daddy, that makes three people I cared about who have had 'accidents' in the last two days. Whatever's going on around here is too big for us. We need to call in state troopers."

Gus's dyspeptic face crumpled. He looked like a cross between a bulldog and a baby. "Theophile, just stop it. I know three accidents in two days seems like a lot and all I can say is, people are going to have to be more careful."

"A pipe bomb, Gus!"

"I know. I know how you feel about your daddy's problems, Theophile, but please don't start making up conspiracy theories. You're starting to sound like the Klan."

Theo crossed his leg at the knee and examined his running shoe. "Why was Boo holding money for the AG?"

"It was from a drug bust, I believe. Or maybe a drug buy."

"How much?"

"He said something in the fives."

"Does that mean five thousand?"

"No, nephew, it means five figures. I would assume twenty-five-thousand or thirty-five; he didn't say the high fives." Gus stretched the elastic in his jumpsuit. "It would be ideal if you could find it in the next little while. Governor Meacham'll be in town later this afternoon and I'd love to have it for him."

"*Ex*-governor Meacham. And I thought you said the AG wanted it."

Gus blinked. "Meacham can bring it up to Baton Rouge for him."

Standing up, Theo smoothed his pants. "Gus, you're a mess."

Gus rose too. "Theophile, this whole town's a mess. That still doesn't help me find that money."

"I need some wheels; I can't keep borrowing Cecile's car to get around. Do you still have your pickup?"

"In the barn. I can have somebody bring it over."

Theo walked to the door. "Father, thank you for the tea."

"Theophile," Gus whined. He took two waddling steps toward Theo and stopped suddenly, straightening his back with dignity. "You're going to look for the money, aren't you?"

Theo glanced at his uncle, red-faced and anxious in the dark serenity of the priest's living room. "Yes, Gus, I'll look for your money. But only because the next thing I'm going to do is call the AG and tell him we need some troopers down here."

CHAPTER 9

Sally Guidry sat on an overturned milk crate in her backyard crying in front of the king snakes. In her lap she cuddled a Ball's python. Bending over, Theo kissed the top of her head, and Sally held up the python so that he could pet it. She made no attempt to stop her tears. "Theophile, they're not going to find his body, are they?"

"They're working on it, Sally. Don't worry." Slowly he put a finger up to the huge russet snake and stroked the back of its head. "Is this Monty?"

Her voice cracking with emotion, she said, "Boo's had Monty since he was sixteen."

"I know. He saved his grinding money for this snake. Jeez, he's gotten big."

A warm wind blew over the cane field at the end of the yard. Wet diamonds of light slipped off the blades and the field sighed with a low rustling sound. Ignoring the lush verdancy around her, Sally looked at the dozen dry aquaria on picnic tables against the house. "Theophile, what am I going to do with the snakes? The corn snakes have mouth rot, and I don't have time to fool with sulfa and all that."

"That looks like a couple thousand dollars worth of California kings right in front of you." They both admired the tangle of brightly banded orange-and-gray-flannel serpents sunning themselves in the glass cage.

"The kings are no problem. But what about everything else? And I could *never* sell Monty." Standing up, she walked with Monty over to the small aquaria. Several appeared to be empty, the snakes hiding under rocks in the shade. In one, there was a curdling knot of tiny black racers in the corner. "The momma racer had a litter," said Sally. "She's been such a good producer."

Theo looked at the roiling lump of snakes, none bigger than a large fishing worm. "Was Boo still selling to that place in Mississippi—what's the name: Bob's Monkey Jungle?"

Sally's pixie face brightened at the joke. "Robert Lee's Exotic Kingdom."

"They'd buy this whole litter, wouldn't they?"

"I guess." Sally slipped Monty around her shoulders to relieve the weight and the sinuous brown serpent rested its tail in the V of her creamy neck. Theo put a hand between Monty and Sally's neck and pulled the snake's body, just to let him know there were more hands available. "Sally," Theo asked, "did Boo keep anything poisonous anymore?"

Sally shook her head. "He gave up coral snakes because they kept getting out. And I made him give away the rattlers when Gumby was born." Holding the python's head against her cheek, she said, "He was such a good father. He really was."

"I'm glad to hear that, Sally."

"Boo's snakes were the first thing that really made me like him. I remember he took me to his parents' backyard and showed me Monty, and how to hold him and all. Boo was so gentle with his snakes. That's what made me think he'd be a good husband." Her chest heaved and her voice broke. "Theophile, I'm going to miss him so much. I don't care about the things he did, nothing's worth losing your husband."

Theo looked across the expanse of lush zoysia to Reba and Dorothy's green shingled shanty. "What's he done now, Sally?"

"I didn't mean to say that."

"But you did. I thought he had stopped beating on you."

"He *had*. After that last time, I swear he had."

"He been fooling around again?"

The python held out its head and Sally covered her eyes with its snout. "I got a case of chlamydia last time he came back from hunting in Mexico. I wouldn't even have known if the doctor hadn't found it at my check-up. He put me on tetracycline."

"I'm damned sorry to hear that."

Sagging under the weight of the python Sally walked to the milk crate and sat down. "It's the first time I ever felt like killing anybody. I mean, what if Gumby caught it or something? It made me so *mad*." She looked tearfully at the python. "Now, all I am is sorry."

"Sally, something happened that I need to ask you about. Gus said a large sum of money is missing from Boo's office. Did he ever say anything about it?"

"Check his safe."

"We already tried that."

"He *did* mention some drug money last week, but I imagine it's at the bank now."

"No. Boo hadn't used the vault in a long time. Is it possible he hid money in the house?"

"Not without telling me."

"You sure?"

"You can go search if you want. But I'd have seen a shoe box if it were in my house."

"It was in a shoe box?"

"I believe that's what he said."

Theophile saw that the king snakes' water dish was dry and their AstroTurf floor littered with droppings. "Sally, you don't have time to take care of the snakes.

Why don't you get on the phone and call Bob's Monkey Jungle? I bet if you named a price, they'd be down here tomorrow."

Sally shook her head. "I think I want to keep them for a while, Theophile. I can get Reba to help." She walked over to the plywood and chicken-wire cage that was Monty's home and Theo followed. He lifted the lid for her, and she put the snake inside and locked the door with a tiny brass padlock. Looking up, she inhaled the wet, earthy air. "Don't you love it after the rain when the sun heats up? You can just feel everything start growing again."

Theo inhaled. "Always meant more grass to mow for me."

Her eyes brightened, forgetting the pain. "You want to come inside for a drink? Gumby's at LouAnn's."

Theo took a step back. "Maybe another time, Sally. I need to get back to town."

"Oh." She tugged at the little brass padlock. "I hope you really do come. It was so lonely last night, I ended up putting Gumby in the bed with me."

"Hang in there."

"Theophile." She avoided his eyes. "Do you think you could hold me a little bit before you go?"

"Sure." Theo put his arms around her small, curvy body and rested his head on her mop of curly hair. Her breasts pressed warmly against his ribs and her black curls glinted blue in the sunlight. She took a great heaving breath and asked, "Do you ever wonder what would have happened if you hadn't gone into the seminary?"

"Sometimes."

"I always thought you were such an interesting person."

"You're pretty interesting yourself." He held her a few more seconds, gave her a squeeze, and let go. Searching her dark eyes, he asked, "You going to be okay?"

"I don't know. LouAnn's taking Gumby and me up to Baton Rouge to stay at Momma's."

"Good plan." Stuffing his hands in his pockets, he leaned down to kiss her cheek. "You be good to yourself, you hear? You've got some rough stuff to go through."

"Will you come see me?"

Without speaking, he turned and looked intently at Gus's truck. Sally let out a little laugh.

"What's so funny?"

"I bet you don't even know that all the people in your family look away when they don't want to answer a question."

"You're right. I didn't know that."

"Good-bye, Theophile. And tell your new girlfriend I think she's really nice."

"Thank you. I will."

Theo parked Gus's pickup in front of the activity center and went inside. On the floor a flock of toddlers sat scribbling with cone-shaped infant crayons on paper laid under their plump bottoms. Beyond the plate glass windows a typing class hammered the machines. Theo spotted a sturdy graying white woman busy at a table. "Nun-in-Charge" might as well have been written on her crisp oxford shirt.

The nun looked up from her calculator and printed forms. "May I help you?"

"Sister Elizabeth? I'm Theophile Talbot. May I sit down?"

"Cecile's nephew," she said brightly, gesturing to the chair across from her. As Theo sat, he glanced at the IRS-style forms the nun was filling out.

"Looks like tax time around here."

"It's your Uncle Gus's latest attempt at harassment. Federal auditing forms." Looking down, she read: " 'What percentage of the gross annual budget has been used for goods, supplies, or services that are not regulated under the provisions of the Interstate Commerce Act?' " She gestured to the babies on the floor. "Is drawing paper regulated by the Interstate Commerce Commission? Are crayons?"

Theo pushed his chair back and propped a foot across his leg. "Hey, cheer up, Sister. The great martyrs would envy you."

The nun put down her pencil. "You've come for a reason."

"I need to talk to Reba Pugh."

"May I ask why?"

"Reba knows more about Boo Guidry than is good for her right now. If I don't get to her first, she could be in a lot of trouble."

"She didn't kill Boo, if that's what you came to find out."

"She told you that?"

Sister Elizabeth's pencil rolled off the table and she stooped to pick it up. "I simply overheard her when the other women asked."

"What I need to know has to do with some lost money."

"Indeed?" Sister Elizabeth examined the pencil in her hand. "And you think Reba knows something about it."

"It's possible. She helped out at the Guidrys' a lot."

"And I suppose you intend to coerce this information from her in your best—forgive me—aggressive male fashion."

"I never—" Theo put down his leg. "Sister, I've known Reba since she was born."

"So that when you talk to her, it's with a generous spirit, it's the dialogue of equal minds?"

"Sister, I didn't come here to be your whipping boy."

"I know that. You're a policeman. You came here for information: bluntly, abruptly, with no regard for how disruptive your presence might be. Our program caters to some vulnerable young women and we're trying to make a safe place for them."

"One question, and then I'll leave her alone."

"Perhaps if you tell me specifically what you need from her, I can relay the information to Reba."

"I need Reba."

"You can't have her. We need all the women in attendance to qualify for funds."

Theo pushed back his chair and stood. "We're not hitting it off very well, are we?"

The nun looked down at her forms. "A gentle heart is always welcome here."

"I'm sorry. I can't help you with that one today." He strode toward the door.

"Mr. Talbot, wait."

"What is it?"

The nun gestured to the chair again and Theo returned and sat down. Sister Elizabeth put down her pencil and folded her hands in her lap. "It's a shame that law enforcement professionals are taught that aggressiveness is their highest tool. It rarely is, you know. I do have some information that might be useful, if you can use it with the proper spirit."

"Sister, all I can do is try."

The nun sighed. "Boo often came to pick up Reba. Ostensibly she was their baby-sitter, but it was not uncommon to look out the window and see his hands on her breasts, her face, all of that." The nun looked at her hands.

"Thank you for telling me. That makes my job a whole lot easier." He glanced into the typing class. "May I talk to her now?"

"No."

Uncertainly Theo stood. "Then I guess I'd better go."

"Good-bye, Mr. Talbot."

"This is a nice program, Sister. Y'all take care."

A little before noon Theo parked the pickup under a shade tree near the courthouse. Padding down the quiet hall, he glanced into the records office and saw Laura standing at the work counter. "Laura." He backpedaled a step. "You're supposed to be resting."

"Theo, hi!" She put a huge ledger on the counter. "I felt fine so we decided to come down here and look up Cecile's plantation sale. Want to help?"

Theo spotted his aunt and smiled. She sat on a high stool with her legs crossed, clearly delighted to have been caught researching in the records office. "Hi, Cecile." Turning back to Laura, he said, "Sorry, I can't. I've got work to do." He wandered into the room and peered at the record books on the table. "Y'all finding anything?"

Laura pulled over a fading blue ledger. "Not yet. We've just done January–February 1928, but Cecile thinks she remembers that the sale was in the spring. Actually, these things are sort of interesting."

"Sure. And so's the phone book." Theo slid out the volume from 1903 and opened it on the counter. The smell of moldy paper rose up like antique memory and across the mottled pages black script swirled in a blizzard of soaring loops and random capitalization. "I don't see how y'all make heads or tails of this stuff. 'Before me, Ulgere Préjean, a Notary Public . . . therein residing and in the presence of the witnesses hereinafter . . .' "

"Don't read it. Just scan for nouns and verbs."

"Laura's a wiz at all this," said Cecile.

"Hey, here's one." Theo transferred his weight to the other foot. " 'Succession of Octavie Boudreaux, deceased wife of Jules Landry.' Cecile, that wouldn't be Sticky Landry's father, would it?"

"No. His name was Beauclerke Landry. He's the one they called Beaucoup."

"Oh, yeah, I remember him. He wouldn't have been around in 1903 anyway." Theo closed the ledger with a thud.

"What are you doing now?" asked Laura.

"I'm on my way down to Boo's office to pick up a fingerprint kit. I want to dust the sugar house before Daddy gets back."

Cecile smoothed a ledger page with her hand. "I thought they were going to discharge your father this morning."

"I called. Cootsie Rodrigue is making him take a physical first."

"That's like a bad joke," Cecile sniffed. "I can't imagine what they'll find *right* with him."

Laura rubbed her nose as the scent of moldy paper tingled her nostrils. "Do you think you can still take footprints today?"

Theo leaned against the counter. "Let's just say I'm not holding my breath."

Cecile looked down her nose at the old ledger, apparently scanning the page for names. "That's too bad, Theophile. I heard the criminal used some very distinctive rubber boots, or some such."

Theo narrowed his eyes. "Where'd you hear that, Cecile?"

"Laura told me, didn't you, dear?"

"I don't think so. Did I?"

"Yes, you did. Yesterday in the car."

Theo walked around the counter and stood close to his aunt. "That reminds me, Cecile. I have a question for you."

Cecile raised a delicate eyebrow. "I'll be glad to answer, Theophile, but only when you change your tone of voice."

Theo didn't move. "The night Boo was killed, your car wasn't in the backyard. Where were you?"

"I'm afraid that's a little hard to explain."

"Try."

"Only if you'll give me some breathing space."

Theo stepped back.

"Thank you," she said placidly. "Well, back during the time when Bronier was dying, I got into the habit of driving around at night, smoking into the air-conditioning and listening to the radio." She blinked wistfully. "The hurricane brought that all back the other night. I just couldn't sleep."

"Did you see anybody while you were out that night?"

Cecile leveled him with her gaze. "I'm sure I didn't *look*. Now, may I get back to work? Laura and I have many volumes to go through."

"Sure." He padded to the door and Laura called behind him, "When will you be home, Theo?"

"Not too long."

"Okay. See you there."

Striding down the tiled hallway, Theo found a sign on Daubie's desk saying she was out to lunch. Inside the storage closet he rummaged through typing supplies and ragged back issues of *Louisiana Sheriff*. There was no fingerprint kit, only half a dozen jars of white fingerprint dust and a cheap synthetic brush. He sniffed disdainfully: at home they used camel hair.

After leaving a note for Daubie, Theo walked down the courthouse hall, where voices from above floated down the stairwell. Gus's sympathetic chuckle played off the plaster walls and Theo leaned against a door molding to listen. Gus was negotiating one stair at a time as the other man finished his story. ". . . and I'd been practically killing myself to get a nibble from him that whole week. Finally he just looks over with those bug eyes of his and says, 'Governor, I never invest in anything I can't pronounce.'"

"Ha! What'd you say then? Did you tell him the first two letters were silent?'"

"I didn't tell him anything. By that time the banker had called back and said the man was in receivership. So I just sent a note around to my boys and we got out of there as fast as possible."

Gus chuckled. "Well, for mercy's sake."

Theo tucked his hands in his back jeans pockets and walked resolutely past the stairwell.

"Theophile! Wait a minute. I want you to meet somebody."

Theo feigned surprise as he watched Gus work his way slowly down the last few stairs, his companion amiably keeping pace.

At the bottom Gus tucked his legal folders under his arm and said, "Governor Meacham, I'd like you to meet my nephew, Theophile Talbot. You might remember his father, Valmont, from the campaigns. He's the one hurt with the pipe bomb Tuesday night."

"Oh, yes." Meacham put out a hand. "How is your father?"

Meacham was short and sixtyish with expressive blue eyes. He wore a pearl gray business suit and on his feet were expensive gray suede Loafers. His unlined face said that he hadn't had a worry in the world since winning his first primary twenty years before.

Theo looked into the former governor's concerned eyes. "Daddy's fine. He's giving them hell over at the hospital."

Meacham laughed a flat syllable. "Valmont would. You're probably too young to remember this, but there was a time when you wanted anything in this parish, your daddy was the first person to talk to."

"That's right," agreed Gus. "I don't know whether you realize it or not, Theophile, but when that mill used to get going full out, it was the largest employer in the parish. Your daddy did more hiring and firing than the school board."

Theo attempted his bored look. "I never paid much attention. But say, I heard y'all talking on the stairs. Is there really something going on back on the Atchafalaya?"

Gus clutched his file folders. "You must have misunderstood. The Atchafalaya belongs to the state."

"No, I heard you: some guy didn't want to invest in a place where the first two letters are silent."

Smoothly Gus said, "The development's not really on the Atchafalaya. It's in an area just south of there. There are some people from Baton Rouge who want to put in a boat dock, or maybe a marina."

"Yes," added Meacham, his eyes crinkling in a smile, "that's why I came down. To coordinate things from that end."

"Well that's great. We're always looking for a good place to put in the boat." Theo looked at his watch. "Hey, it's getting late. I'm supposed to meet somebody." He extended his hand. "Nice meeting you, Mr. Meacham. Gus, see you later."

"Good-bye, Theophile."

Theo climbed into the steaming truck cab and drove down the bayou to the activity center, where he parked behind a ragged thicket of banana trees. At twelve-thirty the women streamed out the door, crossing the highway to the gas station. He spotted Reba at the soft drink machine, wearing a red shirt tied at the waist and an armload of plastic bracelets. Starting the truck, he drove across the street and hopped out before she had a chance to drop her quarters in. Grabbing her elbow, he growled, "Get in, Reba."

She pulled free. "What you want?"

"You've been holding out on me, Reba."

"I have not. What that means?"

"Get in the truck and I'll tell you."

Fearfully Reba eyed him, then climbed in. Driving up the highway, he turned to her and said, "Reba, the state attorney general just called. He's missing a lot of money. He wants it back."

The teenager looked ahead. "I don't got no money."

"Boo didn't give you a pair of shoes. He gave you a shoe box full of money. Now, where is it?"

"I don't have it."

"I know you don't *have* it; you hid it somewhere."

Reba pressed her lips together.

"Reba, state troopers can make things awfully tough on somebody they're mad at. When I have to call back and tell them where their money is, they're not going to be real happy having to come down and talk to you."

"I . . . It's at the church."

Theo pulled onto the shoulder. "Yours or mine?"

"Mine."

Making a tight U-turn, he took the highway back south past town to a road leading into the cane. A quarter mile down the road he turned the pickup into the crushed oyster shell lot of a white clapboard chapel. Out front the readerboard said: BRIGHT MORNING STAR BAPTIST CHURCH. SERVICES WEDNESDAY NIGHT, SUNDAY MORNING. The sea of cane stretched slowly in the sun.

"In the cemetery?" he asked.

"No, inside. Go 'round to the back."

He pulled up by the vestry stairs and followed Reba onto the frame porch. Reaching on tiptoe above the molding, she brought down a brass key and unlocked the door. Inside the air was like a sauna.

Theo sucked in a breath. "I hope y'all have air-conditioning for services."

"You gonna pay for it?" Reba walked out into the sacristy, down the aisle to the back of the church. Tagging close behind, Theo followed her up the steep stairs of the choir loft. The treads squeaked under their feet and as they reached the loft, Theo asked, "Did I ever tell you my grandfather donated this organ?"

"About a thousand times."

He wiped a finger on the dusty organ cover. "It still work?"

"I don't know. We never play it." Reba plopped down in front of the organ pipe cabinet. "Momma and me take turns for services. We use the piano down front." She slipped her red fingernails around one of the cloth-covered organ panels and lifted it out. Plastic bracelets clacking, she reached far into the dark pipes and groped around. She found nothing, and her face showed her panic. Then she smiled and grunted, pulling out a red Italian shoe box circled by a thick blue rubber band. "Here. I don't know nothing about it. All I did was, Boo asked me keep it for him."

Theo peeled off the rubber band and looked inside. The box was filled with new packets of twenty-dollar bills bound in bands from the East Ascension National Bank. "My Lord, Reba, how much is this?"

"Thirty-two thousand dollars. Boo said."

"How much did you take?"

Reba fidgeted. "I put a twenty in my purse, but I didn't spend it."

"You'll have to give it back." Theo put the lid back on and stretched the rubber band around the box. Dropping onto the organ bench, he said, "Okay, Reba. Why not make this easy on yourself."

"Make what?"

"You know I'm going to have to keep you here until I find out what Boo was up to."

She eyed the stairs. "You can't keep me. I can go anytime I want."

"Don't try me, Reba."

"I already told you. I don't know *what* Boo was doing. He just asked me to keep the money for him."

"That's because you're the good little baby-sitter, aren't you, Reba?"

Reba didn't answer.

"How long you and Boo been sleeping together?"

"We didn't sleep!"

"God, Reba, do you know how dumb it is to fuck the sheriff?"

Reba blinked angrily. "Shit. You wouldn't know dumb if it ate your face. You know what the calamities is?"

"The what?"

"'S a venereal disease. Boo gave 'em to me and I gave them to Willie, and now Willie won't *be* with me no more."

"You been to the doctor?"

"I been. But that still don't get me Willie back."

"Willie's married."

"I'm glad Boo's dead. He got what was coming."

Theo sighed and took the box into his lap. "Okay, just one more question and I'll let you go: the million dollars Boo thought he was getting, what was that for?"

"I don't—It was supposed to be hush-up money for keeping quiet."

"About what?"

She pressed her lips together.

"About blowing up my daddy?"

"I can't remember."

"Reba, the people in Baton Rouge are going to ask questions about a hundred times harder than mine."

Reba put her hands to her face. "Theophile, don't push on me like that. I told you everything I know: about the shoebox, and the Atchafalaya. And now you even know about me and Boo. You gonna tell my momma?"

He stood and walked to the stairs. "I'm sure she already knows." Cradling the box under his arm, he looked at the dark, skinny teenager who had grown up in his house while he hadn't been looking. "Come on, Reba, I'll drive you back to town. But I want to tell you one thing: if you were as dumb as you're pretending to be, you'd have been dead a long time ago."

CHAPTER 10

Theo walked into the sheriff's office and put the shoe box on the desk. In front of a glowing computer screen Gus—in a state of high agitation—was reading an instruction manual.

"Meacham gone?" Theo asked. He pushed the shoe box toward his uncle.

Gus put a hand on the monitor. "Theophile, come here and tell me what to do with this."

"What you got, Gus?" Theo walked over and looked at the lighted screen.

Gravely Gus announced, "Sister Elizabeth is a Communist."

On the monitor glowed the FBI dossier of one Elizabeth Reilly, 844-A Wheaton Avenue, Chicago, Illinois. Gus moved his finger across the abbreviated information: "She was in the NAACP in 1966, and SDS from 1967 to

1968 in Chicago. SDS is Students for a Democratic Society." Crossing his arms thoughtfully over his massive belly, he said, "I wonder if her superiors know about her double life."

Theo read the screen. Quite possibly it was their own Sister Elizabeth Reilly. The height, weight, and eye color were the same. Under aliases it identified her as " 'Elizabeth Reilly, OHN,' and 'Sister Elizabeth.' " Theo smiled.

"What's so funny?" Gus demanded.

"All this says is that she belonged to the NAACP and SDS for a while in the 1960's. If I remember my textbook correctly, the only ones the FBI were really interested in was a splinter group called the Weathermen who wanted to blow up buildings. The rest were just supposed to be harassed by Nixon under something called COINTELPRO."

"What's that?"

"Counter-Intelligence Program."

"Theophile, if the woman wasn't a criminal, the FBI wouldn't have a file on her."

"Nonsense." Theo sat on the edge of Boo's desk with a hand on the shoe box. "The feds have all kinds of files they have no business keeping. Sixteen million of them, in fact. They were supposed to have destroyed all that stuff after somebody sued the pants off them a few years ago."

"I'm calling her superiors."

"Gus, calm down. I've got something to show you." Theo peeled back the rubber band and took off the box top.

Gus's eyes grew wide with pleasure and he smiled as if sedated. "How much is it?"

"Thirty-two thousand dollars."

"You count it?"

"Not me. Takes too long."

Taking out a packet of twenties, Gus fanned it in front of his face, intoxicated by the smell of the ink. Satisfied that the box was entirely what he expected, he laid his packet inside and put the lid back on. "I wish Meacham hadn'ta just left."

"I thought you said it belonged to the AG."

"It does. You better tell me how you found it. He'll want to know."

"No, he won't." Theo took the box on his lap and stretched the rubber band around it. "Nobody gets to ask questions about dirty cash. Different set of rules for that game." He handed the box to Gus.

Spying a zippered sweatshirt hanging on Boo's coatrack, Gus swaddled the box in the navy fleece and tucked it under his arm.

"What are you going to do with it, Gus?"

"Put it in the bank vault, then call Baton Rouge."

"Will the AG be coming down to pick it up?"

"I imagine he'll send some troo—"

Laura appeared breathless in the doorway and Gus pulled the fleece more tightly over the box. Brightly he said, "Well, hello, gal. What can we do for you?"

"I need to see Theophile."

"Come right in, honey. He's here, having just performed a magnificent feat."

"Did he? We just performed a magnificent feat ourselves." She grabbed Theo's arm, dragging him into the hall, and he called over his shoulder. "You can thank me later, Gus. Laura, what is it?"

"Wait until you see what we found in the records office."

"Cecile still owns Belle Plaisir."

"Almost as good."

In the records office Cecile stood at the work counter, a wadded handkerchief in her hand and her eyes brimming with tears. "Theophile," she said, "come look at this. Uncle Charles didn't steal Plaisir. He paid me good money for it." She pointed to a brown foxed page covered with letters from a primitive typewriter: "Transaction No. 1223, Cecile Bergeron to Charles Lefleur Bergeron and Ondine Mouton Bergeron."

Out loud Theo read, " 'Before me, Louis Ulysse Folse, a Notary Public duly commissioned, sworn and qualified in and for the Parish of Redemption . . .' " He skimmed a bit. " 'Personally came and appeared:

"Mistress Cecile Bergeron, a minor child, orphan

daughter of the late Eloi F. X. Bergeron and Sydonia Le-Blanc.' "

"Momma," sighed Cecile.

Theo continued, " 'Who declared that she does for and in consideration of the price and terms and conditions hereinafter set forth and expressed, sell, convey, transfer, assign . . .' " His voice petered off and he began again, " 'A certain tract of land situated in this Parish on the left descending bank of Bayou Lafourche about four and one half miles north of the town of St. Lô and forming part of the "Belle Plaisir Plantation," measuring one and three eighths arpents front to said Lafourche intersection on a depth of . . .' " He stopped reading and turned the page. "It says you also sold your half of the sugar house . . ."

"Yes," said Cecile. "Now, skip down to the end."

Out loud he began again. " 'The present sale is made for and in consideration of the price and sum of Eight Thousand Five Hundred Dollars cash for the purchase of said tract of land.' Cecile! That was a lot of money."

"Can you imagine? I just wish Uncle Charles was still alive. All that time I spent hating, I feel so bad. I bet the reason he gave me that one-dollar bill was so I'd understand that I sold something."

"But, Cecile, where'd your eight thousand go?"

She shook her head. "I don't know. It doesn't matter now. Maybe Uncle Charles used it to raise me."

Laura said, "Or maybe they put it in the bank for you."

"No. Somebody would have told me about it."

Theo pushed the book toward his aunt. "I don't know. One time in high school I went down to the bank and found a hundred eighty dollars in an account somebody had started for me when I was born and had completely forgotten about. Give it a shot, Cecile. Gus has all that precomputer stuff in the back room."

Cecile picked up her purse and stammered. "I can't go. I lent Sister Elizabeth my car. Laura and I walked here."

"It's two blocks," protested Laura.

"Take Gus's truck," said Theo. "Laura and I can walk home."

"The truck?" Cecile glanced back and forth at their

faces. "You're going to force me to be brave, aren't you?" She opened her purse to put on fresh lipstick and walked out the door.

Laura put away the ledger. "Isn't that exciting? She made me read it to her over and over. You should have seen her face."

Theo glanced around the room at the shelves of faded ledgers. "Professor Ireland, if there were land dealings going on in the last couple of months, could we look them up here?"

"Sure. But you need to know the plat or section you're interested in."

"Section?" He walked over to study the huge parish map covering one wall. On the eastern half of the map, thin blue Bayou Lafourche ambled down to the gulf, and along its banks sleepy towns were marked by cross-hatching, like empty games of tic-tac-toe. The western half was missing all signs of population and was printed over with Vs to indicate swamp and marsh. Craning his neck, he examined the far southwest sections where the new state park abutted Atchafaya. "How about sections one hundred thirty-two and one hundred thirty-three?"

Laura scanned the folio-size plat books laid sideways under the counter. "There's nothing here by that name."

"Okay, then, try Second Boudreaux Addition."

"Yes. That's one of them." She pulled out one of the large volumes and turned leaves. "Okay, how about this: 'Certain tracts of land situated in this Parish on the right descending bank of the Atchafalaya River twenty-six and one half miles west of the town of St. Lô . . . at a depth running between parallel lines back to the intersection of the line between the East half and the West half of Section one hundred thirty three . . .' "

"Sounds good to me."

"Okay." She turned back to the first page. "If this is what you want, it's 'Transaction No. 24,332: leasing agreement between State of Louisiana and Armelise Land Company.' "

"Oh, Lord!" Theo pulled the book over to him and read with glazing eyes.

"Theo, what's the matter?"

Without answering, he skimmed the page quickly and turned to the next. Suddenly he blurted, "To and unto Munson W. Pugh, designated signatory of the Armelise Land Company, legal corporation under statutes of the state of Louisiana . . ."

"Who's that?"

He scanned all three pages and pushed the folio back to Laura. "This is a ninety-nine-year lease. It's from the state to Munson Pugh of the Armelise Land Company."

"Is Munson Pugh related to Reba and Dorothy?"

"Not by a long shot. Reba and Dorothy got their name from the fact that the Pughs owned slaves all up and down here before the Civil War. All the white Pughs moved to Baton Rouge and became lawyers after the war. I would read this to mean that Munson Pugh is a front man for the Armelise Land Company."

"And who's that?"

Theo bit his lip. "The last Armelise Land Company I know anything about was put together in the 1930's by my grandfather and his brothers to log off cypress back in the swamps. They named the company Armelise after their mother."

"Your father!"

"I was thinking more about Gus and Meacham. I just heard them talking about building a marina."

"See how much they paid for it."

He turned to the end and read: " 'The present agreement is made in consideration of the price and sum of One Thousand Dollars.' Cheap. 'The Lessor acknowledges to have received from said Lessees and for which they grant them full acquittance and discharge to said Lease . . .' "

"Theo, if this land is supposed to be a state park, maybe Meacham pulled strings to get it leased back."

He closed the oversize ledger with a thump. "Hold that thought."

"What do we do now?"

"I think we need to visit a friend of mine back in the swamp."

"You just gave Cecile the truck."

"Let's go home. We can ask Dorothy to borrow her Pinto."

They went out the front door and Laura started for the highway corner. "Not that way," said Theo. He pointed down the side street. "There's more shade down here."

"I wish you would have told me that earlier."

Under the shade of the live oaks, they walked down root-lifted sidewalks, crunching tiny acorns under their feet. They passed the Dollar Store and the post office and entered the residential district with its crape myrtle hedges and soft tarry streets. Heat pressed in from all sides and perspiration formed in places Laura never knew she had sweat glands.

The shady back street ended at a wide sidewalk leading up to a brick Gothic church. Laura read the sign. "St. Philomena Catholic Church. Is this where your family goes?"

"This is where everybody goes."

"Not Reba and Dorothy."

"Excuse me. I meant everybody white."

They followed the sidewalk almost to the church and veered off left. Opening the cemetery gate, Theo said, "Shortcut home."

Laura blinked in the blinding light. The treeless cemetery lay whitewashed and brilliant, like a miniature Mediterranean town. Domes and pediments rose randomly across the yard and tiny temples clustered at intersections, as if Rome had been shrunk to doll size and the exiled pagan gods had set up housekeeping in cheerful domesticity on the other side of the world.

Beside the temples, on smaller tombs, small marble lambs reclined on stony pallets and chiseled Carrara roses grew mold in the clefts of their petals. An angel poised on green phthisic feet wore a smile of soft stone idiocy and stony italic poems gathered lichens as their praise. Heading homeward, Laura read the now familiar names from the tombs: LeBlanc, Crochet, Hebert, Rodrigue. Halfway across the yard Theo stopped suddenly and said, "Here's ours."

"Our what?"

Before them was a tiny Gothic chapel of polished gray granite. Laura read the frieze. " 'Talbot Brothers.' Which ones are they?"

"My grandfather, Theophile, and his three brothers. They're the ones who formed Armelise. They were supposed to be a pretty wild bunch."

"But there's at least twenty names on the door."

"That's because people from all four families are buried here." Theo's eyes became distant as he read the names and dates engraved in the doors.

Softly Laura asked, "Are your mother and Claiborne here?"

He pointed to names near the bottom: Camille Bergeron Talbot and Henry Claiborne LeBlanc Talbot. Claiborne's dates indicated that he had lived fourteen years.

"We can go if this makes you too sad."

"No. I like to visit."

"Does Claiborne's name mean you're related to Father LeBlanc?"

"Momma had a miscarriage between Honorée and Claiborne, and I think he helped a lot."

Sweat beads dripped down her hairline and Laura scratched behind her knee. "How do they get all the coffins in? It's such a tiny building."

"The coffins are wood. They rot faster than embalmed bodies."

"Ugh."

"Come on, it's too hot to stay here."

At home they climbed the back porch steps and found Cecile prancing stocking-footed around the kitchen, Scotch glass in her hand. Waving a green computer printout, she said, "Look at this. It was right there, under my maiden name: $221,667, that's nearly quarter of a million dollars."

"Cecile! That's wonderful!" Laura hugged her.

"May I see?" asked Theo.

"Of course."

As Theo read the printout, Cecile told the story: "I went into the bank and saw Tina Savoie. I had no idea she worked there but it turns out she's Gus's secretary. I asked her if she could help me and told her I was wondering if maybe I had an account that I didn't know about. She said, no, the IRS would certainly not let that happen, but she ran it up on the computer anyway and said, 'No, ma'am, Mrs. Talbot, I don't see anything here.' And I said, 'Mrs. Talbot? My name was Cecile Bergeron.' She she typed in 'Cecile Bergeron' and the computer starts running, and running, and little Tina's eyes start getting bigger, and bigger. Finally she squeaked, 'This is six figures,' and she pulled it out and gave it to me. I made her promise not to tell anyone, even Gus. She looked offended and said she wasn't allowed to anyway."

"Cecile, that's great." Theo laid the printout on the table. "But there's something really wrong here."

"What?"

"Look at the bottom: '$25,000 on 3/31.' That's a withdrawal. '$10,000 on 5/25.' So is that."

"I don't know what you mean."

"I mean that somebody—obviously not you—has been making withdrawals from your account."

CHAPTER 11

~~~~~~~~~~~~~~~~~~~~~~~~~

They parked the truck where the Canal Road ended on the swampy shores of Lake Velourde. Laura climbed out and looked at the pea green lake. "I feel terrible about leaving Cecile that way."

"There's nothing we can do." Theo pulled up a six-pack of pop and a bag of ice from the back. "She needs to call the bank and see what happens next."

Laura looked at the rows of shabby boat houses tucked between the cypress trees in the water. "Does this place have a name?"

"Chacahoula Landing. Indians used to pull up here."

Theo took a key from his pocket and crunched across the crushed oyster shells to one of the decrepit sheds. The corrugated steel sides were entirely rusted away up to the water line, and the roof was tar-papered over and patched with boards. Securing this precious property was a flotsam blue door taken from the bedroom of a very old house.

Unfastening the outsized Master lock, Theo flung open the door, and Laura entered to find a sparkling blue bass boat with swivel fishing seats, a 140 Evinrude, and a quiet little electric motor for trolling. "What a pretty boat. You'd never guess it was in here by looking at the outside."

Theo pulled down life jackets from the wall. "They keep the boat houses crummy on purpose."

"In anthropology we call that nonstatus consumption," said Laura. "It's when you live on an inconspicuous level so as not to call attention to yourself through your possessions."

"Or maybe it's called 'insurance companies won't write boat houses for a hurricane.' Here, take the soft drinks and ice, there's a cooler under the seat."

Laura took the six-pack. "Why'd we buy this? You hate pop."

"We'll be glad to have it after we've been out in the sun for a few hours." Casting off the shock-cord lines, Theo cautiously backed the boat through the cypress trees. Out past the rippled gray trunks he gunned the Evinrude for the trip across the lake.

Laura breathed in deeply. The muggy day smelled of vegetation and black mud. Warm wind whipped her visor, which she turned backward on her head. Far ahead the shoreline was a fringe of dark cypress trees. She dipped her hand into the glassy water and found it warm. Calling back to Theo, she asked, "How deep is Lake Velourde?"

"Five feet," he shouted.

"You're kidding? You mean I could actually get out and stand up?"

"Be my guest."

They reached the far shore, a shady cypress swamp, and Theo geared down. Laura asked, "What are those knobs sticking out of the water?"

"Cypress knees. It's how the roots get air. Don't go jumping out of the boat around here: some of the knees are submerged." He cut the Evinrude and walked to the front of the boat, where he put the tiny electric motor in the water. "Too shallow?" asked Laura.

"Quieter."

Sitting high in a swivel fishing chair, Theo guided the boat through the cypress swamp with the pedal control. The water was so clear, it was black from the rotting leaves on the bottom. Gray tatters of Spanish moss brushed against their faces and Laura reached up to pull some off an overhanging branch. "Bugs. Careful," said Theo.

She threw it overboard and he said, "Look there," pointing to a knobby log drifting rapidly.

"Why is the log moving so fas—" She halted abruptly. "It's an alligator! Follow him. He's getting away."

"You're out of your mind."

They watched the place where the animal had disappeared but could see only a faint spreading circle.

"I didn't really get to see him," said Laura. "Will there be any more?"

He turned her visor around properly on her head. "You be our lookout."

She settled into a fishing seat and smiled. "Where are we going?"

"Miss Ida's canal, if I can still find it."

"You mean people actually live back here?"

"Laura, this is a good living if you can swing it. How many people do you know who can actually feed themselves by pulling in their crab pots everyday?"

"Who's Miss Ida?"

"An old *traiteur*, kind of like a folk doctor. She cured my warts when I was twelve."

"No she didn't. How'd she do that?"

"Something to do with a green potato and a dead cat."

"Theo, you can't possibly believe that. You're from a rationalist tradition. A folk healer won't work for you."

He held out his hand to show its missing warts.

"Did your warts actually go away after she treated you?"

"I think it took a couple of months. After I gave her the Bull Durham." He steered through the trees into a watery green path edged on both sides by cypress. Moss hung down in their faces and the whirring of the electric motor could not drown out the drone of the cicadas.

After a quarter mile the canal ended at a wooden platform circled by a Cyclone fence. On the platform sat a small oil well, a tangle of pipes and valves, like sculpture by a junkyard welder. Theo steered the boat off into a darker branch canal. Here moss-draped cypresses grew so close, they formed a canopy closing out the sky. Occasionally in the shadows Laura spotted hummocks of damp earth tagged with red plastic ribbons.

"What are the tags for?"

"Trappers," Theo said. "Don't go doing an anti-fur thing at Miss Ida's, okay?"

"Theo, I'm a professional."

They rounded a curve and the canal became even narrower. A hundred yards ahead the water changed colors abruptly from a bottle green to an eerie shade of iridescent lime. Under the canopy the canal looked like a shimmering green tunnel through the woods. "Theo, what's happening to the water? It looks like melted lime sherbet."

"I'll show you when we get there."

When they were entirely surrounded by the lime green liquid, Theo said, "Now, put your hand in."

She dipped into the water and the sherbet surface parted to show dark green underneath. Scooping up a handful of lime covering, she saw it was made up of thousands of tiny two-leafed plants. "What is this?" she asked.

"Duckweed. Nuisance plant."

"It's beautiful."

The luminous green trail ran like a dream path for half a mile under the trees. Enjoying the tunnel from her perch in the bow, Laura sniffed and looked at Theo: the sweet damp air was carrying a foul musky scent. "Nutria," he said.

"Will we see them?" she asked.

He shook his head. "They heard our motor miles ago."

The duckweed trail ended abruptly in a large pond where a dock and shanty sat on the low bank. A green squared-off boat was tied up at the dock and a tiny gray-haired woman watched quizzically from the front porch. "Outstanding," said Theo. "I'm glad she's home. But she doesn't know who we are yet. I don't think she's ever seen this boat."

"Is there a Mr. Ida?"

"Not for years. They called him 'the Pope.' At his funeral the Caillou Indians sat in the cemetery all night with torches."

"Wow. What did he do to deserve that?"

"I'm not really sure, but he was the best fisherman I ever saw. They said the fish would come and jump in his boat."

"Miss Ida and the Pope."

Standing up to dock, Theo said, "She's going to be mad at us for not staying. I'm going to blame you, okay?"

Miss Ida walked to the dock with outstretched arms. She had a hawk nose and a tiny yellow face with quick dark eyes that took in everything. When the motor was cut and the old woman opened her mouth, Laura had to smile: Miss Ida sounded like a parrot, a parrot with a Cajun accent.

"Theophile, You got so big. What Dorothy been feeding you?" she squawked in a high singsong voice and formed her words far up in her nose. "And you brought a pretty girl. She's your wife? But no: you don't look married." Looking back and forth at the two of them, she waggled a finger. "But only not yet, you don't look married."

"Ida, this is Laura. Laura, this is the famous Miss Ida Bourgeois."

Ida took Laura's hand and rubbed it, as if gauging the suppleness of her skin. "How you do, Laura? Such a pretty girl." She turned to Theo. "But, Theophile, something's de matter with you." She reached up to pinch his cheek. "Your eyes aren't breathing."

"I know, Miss Ida. It's been a rough week."

"Come on to the house," she sang. "I make you something nice and you tell me after dinner."

"Miss Ida, I'm afraid we can't stay for dinner, Laura has to get back to Baton Rouge tonight. We sure could use a cup of coffee, though."

Masking her disappointment, Miss Ida waved them onto dry land. "Come on. We can eat de cake from Sunday." She led them through a bare dirt yard separated from the lake by a flotsam fence of broken oars, Styrofoam coolers, fishing nets and corrugated steel. As she opened the wooden gate, feisty black chickens trotted away, out of arm's reach. Miss Ida led Laura and Theo up the unpainted steps to the front porch and touched the chair backs at the wooden outdoor table.

Theo and Laura sat down and Ida brought out glasses of water. Laura took a sip and found the water odd-tasting and warm, like melted snow. Looking at the swamp around her, she set the glass down on the table. Theo caught the expression on her face and called inside to Ida, "Miss Ida, do you still collect rainwater on your roof?"

Ida came out grinding a coffee mill against her abdomen. "Dat's the best water dere is, huh?"

"You bet."

Laura drank from her glass again and watched the chickens scratch around on the hard black earth.

Next Miss Ida brought out a tablecloth and made them lift their glasses while she spread it on the bare wood boards. Then she set out a plate of muffin-size cakes drizzled with penuche icing. As Laura eyed the cakes, the rich scent of French roast coffee wafted out the door. In a minute Miss Ida came out with a spattered enamel drip pot and demitasses. In front of her guests she laid down tiny spoons for the miniature cups. Laura's had an elaborate enameled finial. She picked it up to admire.

"Dat's my Lourdes spoon," chirped Miss Ida.

Laura looked confused.

Theo said, "Lourdes is a pilgrimage site in France. Our Lady of Lourdes."

"Oh, yes."

Miss Ida stood next to the table but would not sit. "My husband, Joseph, had a miracle in Lourdes. His arthritis went clear away. Dat was right before he died."

"I forgot y'all went to Lourdes," said Theo. "That was a nice trip, wasn't it?"

Ida looked to heaven. "I tank the Lord He let Joseph

make dat trip. Joseph wanted all his life to go and finally the Good Lord let him."

Laura straightened the little spoon before her as Miss Ida poured them coffee. Pushing the cake plate toward them, she said, "Eat the cakes or I trow them to the fish."

Oddly, the steaming coffee was the perfect pick-me-up for the hot summer afternoon. As Miss Ida stood vigil by the table, Theo and Laura sipped slowly and ate pecan cakes swathed in burnt sugar icing. When the eating was done, Theo brushed crumbs off the table and dropped them into the chicken yard. The bantams sprinted up and fought for their fair share.

"Miss Ida," Theo said, "we heard there was some construction going on back here someplace. Do you know anything about that?"

Miss Ida's face turned grave and she looked suddenly tired. "You mean that big one down by the end of river? Dat's de one gonna kill us all."

Theo pulled out a chair and beckoned for Ida to sit down. "Why's that?"

She plopped on the wooden seat. "Dey chop down all the trees, dey fill in the marsh, as far as you can see, hot sun. You can't even walk across, it's so big. It's a dead place."

"Whereabouts, Miss Ida?"

"Way down past the levee. You take the other canal at the oil well straight on to Bayou Chêne, you can't miss it."

Theo got up and kissed the old woman on the cheek. "Well, we've got to get moving now, Miss Ida. When are you coming to visit me in town?"

Ida perked up at the joke. "Oh, boy. I can see me driving my boat down the street."

"I told you I'd teach you to drive a car."

"You bet. Dat's all I need." Her black eyes smiled at the thought.

"Offer's still good," he assured her. He looked at Laura. "You about ready?"

Laura unfolded her long body reluctantly. "Miss Ida, Theo said you're a folk healer. I'd really like to come back and talk to you."

"You come anytime," the old woman squawked.

"Would you ever consider doing an oral history? It would be talking into a tape recorder—"

Miss Ida waved away the idea. "I know what dat is. They make me do dat *so* many times. They want the same thing over and over. Last time I said, 'Fifty dollars,' and they gave it to me. Fifty dollars now, I talk into the tape recorder."

Back at the oil well Theo steered the boat straight across and followed the canal south. Unlike the other waterways, this one had been dredged wide and clear through the swamp, like a Roman road. In backwaters off to the sides, oil wells like stovepipe sculptures pumped silently, sucking water and oil from a thousand feet below.

"The wells are everyplace," said Laura.

"Even the cemeteries."

After a half mile the straight canal opened into a glaring hot lake dotted with mud piles and cypress stumps. Spiky oyster grass was the only living plant; the sun beat down mercilessly.

Theo worked his way across the lifeless lake with an eye out for low stumps and deadheads. Laura wiped away sweat in the creases of her elbows and knees and—seeking any kind of relief—she got out drinks from the cooler. They drank pop and in a few minutes spied a long white shore heaped with fill dirt and mounds of broken concrete riprap. Theo headed toward it.

Beaching the boat on the rough man-made shore, they climbed the four-foot rise. Before them was a vast field of freshly graded dirt and oyster shells. Far across the site, two yellow bulldozers sat idle next to a trailer and more piles of concrete riprap.

"Theo, how big is this?"

"I count in football fields. I see eight."

"This is *not* a boat launch."

"I would say."

"Why isn't anyone here? This is a weekday."

"Come on, let's go see what's at the trailer." They set

out across the graded surface in long serious strides. Trudging in silence, they concentrated on their footing, finally reaching the trailer to find it surrounded by a chainlink fence. Theo squinted through the fence at a building permit on a plywood notice board. "I can't tell who it's issued to," he said.

"I'll climb over."

He pulled her down by the shirt. "Laura, I'm only out of jail right now on my PR. The last thing in the world we need is to be caught trespassing."

She sighed.

Walking around the fence, they looked at a sparkling body of water shimmering on the other side of dumped piles of broken concrete. "What's that lake?" asked Laura.

"It's the Atchafalaya River. If this is Gus's marina, he's lying about the location, as well as everything else."

"This whole thing is illegal, isn't it?"

"Hard to say in Louisiana." Theo took off his Cardinals cap and wiped his forehead. "The real problem with this site—whatever it is—is it's worthless out here in the middle of nowhere."

"But they could build roads. And it has access to the gulf."

"Yeah, but if it's an industrial site, which it looks like to me—it has no access upriver. The Atchafalaya is blocked off in Simmesport by the dam." He touched her arm. "Come on, let's get out of the sun."

"You were right," said Laura. "All I can think about is the cold drinks." She picked her way through the piles of concrete riprap, stumbling on rocks. Suddenly an undulating animal slithered across the path.

"Snake!" she shouted.

Theo stepped forward and punted the snake out of their path. They watched its thick gray body fly through the air and hit a pile of concrete. "It's just a hognose."

"Sorry. I don't know my snakes."

He darted over to where the snake landed and called, "Come help me find him and I'll show you something funny."

Cautiously Laura picked her way over and helped search the dark crevasses. "What do we want him for?"

"Boo used to raise these. Hognoses are a panic." Lifting a jagged stone, he said, "Here he is."

They squatted down in front of the mottled gray serpent convulsing spasmodically on the rock. "He's dying," said Laura.

"No. It's an act."

The snake jerked a few more times, then turned over in agony, its pale belly to the sky. Its mouth fell open and a trickle of blood flowed out onto the powdery concrete.

"Theo, this snake is *dead*."

"No, he's not. Watch." Theo picked up a stick and turned the snake right side up. Immediately the serpent convulsed and flipped again on its back.

"Give me that." Laura took his stick and turned the snake over once more. The serpent lay still a few seconds, jerked twice, then flipped over, exposing his belly to the sky. Laura stood up and dropped the stick. "What a phony."

"Hey, I think they're kind of a kick."

"He's a snake. He's supposed to be *courageous*."

"You have to take on Goliath to be brave?"

They trudged across the graded dirt, jagged chunks of shell pressing into their soles. The sun seared Laura's scalp through her hair, and sweat matted her shirt to her back. Halfway across the field she heard an engine start up. Turning around, she said, "Somebody's here."

One of the bulldozers was raising its scoop, moving out from behind the trailer. The driver appeared to be a gorilla.

"Does that man have something on his face?" Laura asked.

Theo squinted. "I can't tell at this distance." His eyes grew wide as he watched the bulldozer fly across the field. "Run!" he cried.

Grabbing her hand, he turned to bound across the soft earth, dragging her along. "Let go," she cried. "I can't run like this!"

He let go and they dashed like sprinters toward piles of

concrete on the far bank. The diesel engine gunned and Laura swung around to look. The gleaming Caterpillar grill was fifty yards away. "He's coming!" she screamed.

She stretched out her stride, trying to match Theo step for step. Heat rose off her cheeks and chest as from a furnace, and clouded her eyes. Her ankle twisted in the soft earth but she caught herself and kept running.

"Faster, Laura!"

The diesel gunned again, very close, and she twisted around. The Cat was twenty yards away, driven by a man wearing a black feathered Mardi Gras mask. When he was close enough to see her face, he lowered the steel scoop and aimed right for her.

Theo veered to the left and Laura followed. "Split up!" he cried, zigzagging to tease the driver.

Dizzy with heat, Laura ran to the right, barely able to make out the piles of concrete just ahead, where she would be safe. Stumbling the last few yards, she ran panting into the piles and collapsed. Suddenly the immense noise of the bulldozer roared behind her and the huge machine pushed off concrete shards, tumbling them down on Laura. She screamed in terror.

Staggering over to a higher pile, Laura stood behind it, desperately sucking in air, barely able to see from the heat. The roaring beast loomed up over the pile, shovel gleaming in the air, and knocked the tip of the pile down on her feet.

"Into the lake," Theo screamed.

Dodging the rolling stones, Laura hobbled down the low bank and splashed into the water, sinking up to her ankles in soft mud. Falling forward in the cool lake, she crawl-stroked a few lengths to stop the fire on her face. Turning over, she looked up to see the driver standing in his cab, cursing in pantomine. Then he backed up his machine and disappeared. Exhausted, Laura stood up to look for Theo.

Suddenly the air exploded and with a great metallic shove, a pile of stones came tumbling down the bank. Laura dove backward into the water and turned over to swim—head down and arms digging—the fastest sprint she'd ever done.

She swam hard twenty yards, combing the bottom ooze with her fingers each stroke. Poking her head up, she saw the driver standing in his cab again, looking for Theo. She and the driver spotted him at the same time. Theo was fifty yards away, shoving their boat off the shore into the safety of the water. The Caterpillar revved its diesel and backed up to go after its prey.

"Theo, look out!" she shouted.

With the beast still a comfortable thirty yards away Theo pushed the boat into the lake with plenty of time to spare. He jumped on the bow and the boat immediately grounded in scant inches of water.

The Caterpillar growled angrily and lowered the shovel, aiming for a pile of riprap directly above the small boat. Laura's heart hammered in her chest. Theo leaped off the back and pulled the stern farther into the lake. The immense machine gunned its engine and tumbled the huge pile of stones down the bank as if they were made of papier maché. Theo frantically struggled through the muck, trying to pull out the boat. Rocks rolled down the bank, bombarding the shiny blue bow.

"Theo!" Laura screamed.

Up on the bank the bulldozer driver stood again in his cab and surveyed his destruction. Then, ponderously, he turned the gleaming yellow beast around and left for good.

Laura slogged three steps toward the boat, losing her shoe in the mud. Lying down to swim, she found there wasn't even enough depth to kick. Muddy, scared, and miserable, she stood up to wait for Theo while far across the field the Caterpillar gunned triumphantly and changed gears.

Theo climbed over the gunnels and jettisoned a hunk of concrete. Laura stood watching as he motored toward her, keeping an eye on the bank. He pulled in close and she struggled over and collapsed breathlessly in the bilge water. "You okay?" he asked.

Laura looked up. Theo was caked with mud and his hair was a matted fleece.

"Talbot, you look awful."

His face relaxed and he smiled. "So do you."

Walking to the bow, he threw two big concrete chunks into the water. The sparkling blue fiberglass was pocked with dents. Gunning the engine, they motored across the lake, downing four cans of pop between them.

Back at the landing Laura helped tie up the boat and stumbled barefoot to the truck, aching and eager for air-conditioning. Under the wiper was tucked a piece of pink mimeo paper. "Theo," she called. "Somebody left us a message." Turning it right side up, she said, "It's from Quatorze."

"What does it say?"

Holding the pink sheet with filthy fingers, she read:

FATHER LEBLANC FOUND BOO'S BODY. WHERE THE HELL ARE YOU?

CHAPTER 12

The priest sat in the last pew reading the daily office from his prayer book. Stained-glass light from the windows spilled red and yellow patterns on his black cassock. In the back of the church Theo dipped his fingers in the holy water font and touched them to his forehead. Walking to the pew, he stood waiting while Father LeBlanc read to an amen and marked his place with a holy card. Without speaking, the priest got up and walked toward the altar. Theo followed.

In the front of the church Father LeBlanc genuflected and slowly pushed himself back up with a hand on his thigh. Theo followed and tagged after him out to the vestry. The priest looked at the wooden key cabinet on the wall and finally spoke. "This is exactly how I found it." Taking a red-tagged key from his pocket, he said, "And this is the one that was out of place. It's from the Sacred

Heart section, here, and I found it because somebody put it in blue St. Judes."

Theo looked at the cabinetful of antique skeleton keys and modern brass ones. "The cabinet doesn't lock."

"There's never been a reason to lock it before." The priest turned on his heel. "Follow me." Leading Theo out the side door, he strode quickly down the broken sidewalks of the cemetery, cassock flying as he righted flower pots and brushed debris off tombs. Pacing to the main intersection, they came to the Dugas family memorial, where life-size statues of sainted women sent up silent cries from beneath a twelve-foot granite crucifix. The priest turned to Theo. "Where's Laura?" he asked.

"I dropped her off at home to see about a problem Cecile has."

"You mean about her money at the bank?"

"How'd you find out?" asked Theo.

"Tina Savoie's mother was at the hospital this morning. She said not to tell anyone."

They turned into a narrow side walkway, strode five more yards, and stopped abruptly. Theo looked up to see the name on the mausoleum: Guidry.

Father LeBlanc pointed to fresh scratch marks below the mausoleum door. "Those are the first things I noticed when I came out. That's what made me try the key." He inserted the old skeleton key into the hole in the granite and twisted two complete circles. Noisily, the bolt disengaged from the jamb.

Pocketing the key, the priest pushed open the massive granite door. The smell of damp earth washed over them. "Right in front," he said.

Inside around the edges of the crypt were skulls, metal coffin parts, old shoes, and rotting tatters of clothing, all gracefully decaying in beautiful shades of nicotine brown. Bones from at least ten skeletons were scattered on the earth and a single leathery brown female was the only identifiable Guidry. Directly at Theo's feet lay a new plastic morgue bag. He knelt down and unzipped a corner, knowing already who was inside.

Pulling back the cover, he gazed at Boo's chalky face

as the former sheriff and sometimes friend slept peacefully through the intrusion. The pungent smell rose thick and warm, like dead rats at the dump. Theo closed the bag and stepped out into the sunlight with the priest.

Squinting down the miniature street, Theo asked, "Any idea how he got here?"

"Not really. But everyone in town knows I deliver the Eucharist at the hospital on Thursday mornings and wouldn't be around. Somebody must have come in then." Hooking the key into the hole, Father LeBlanc pulled the door almost closed. "What do we do with him?"

Theo shaded his eyes against the bright sun. "We get him chilled down, for starters."

"Not the hospital."

"I was thinking about the funeral home."

The priest nodded. "Good plan. Monroe Perrier's a parishioner."

Theo wiped his forehead and looked down the narrow walk. Over in the next row yardmen whitewashed the Boudreaux mausoleum in preparation for Tuffie. Down at the Toupes' a riot of bright flowers beckoned gaily.

"Do you want to borrow the garden cart to move him?" asked the priest.

"Please." Glancing to the far end of the yard, Theo eyed the vine-covered Cyclone fence with its doddering double gate. "And if we're going to do this without attracting attention, I need to back a truck up to that gate. Can you still get it open?"

The late afternoon sun glinted bright gold behind the fig trees at the end of the backyard. Theo pulled up beside Gus's LTD on the grass and climbed out of the pickup. Inside the kitchen he found Cecile and Gus at the table, iced glasses of Scotch before them.

"Where's Laura?" Theo dropped his baseball cap on the counter and made a beeline for the refrigerator.

Cecile looked up from the needlepoint canvas she was working in her lap. "I hope you don't mind but I sent her to the bank. I wasn't feeling well enough myself and she said she'd be glad to run an errand for me."

"Um." In front of the open refrigerator door Theo poured a big glass of iced tea down his gullet, then poured himself another.

"Cecile," said Gus, "I thought your accounts were all on Grand Isle."

Cecile pulled crewel thread elegantly into the air. "You have some nice CDs here. I sent her down to see about rates."

"Well, next time just call me at the bank. I'm always happy to take care of family."

"I know that, Gus. Thank you."

Theo sat down and leaned back to balance the kitchen chair on two legs. "Gus, you out visiting?"

"I'm afraid not." His uncle looked sternly over the tops of his gold-rimmed glasses. "I came here to tell you that Baton Rouge is very upset with you."

Theo placidly crunched ice. "I don't know anybody named Baton Rouge."

"Stop it, Theophile. The attorney general says that the drug money was returned in a different shoebox than it got lost in. He wants *all* the evidence returned *exactly* as it was found."

"Sorry. I don't know anything about it."

"Theophile, don't play games with me."

Theo sighed. "Gus, I'm starting to get a little bent out of shape here. I busted my fanny for you finding that money, and now you want me to find your lost shoe box too. What do I do? Start looking in trash cans?"

"Theophile, this is not funny."

Theo stared flatly at his uncle. "How does the AG know what the drug money looked like in the first place? Was he in on the buy?"

Gus put down his Scotch glass and pushed back his chair. "Please don't think we're finished with this, Theophile."

Theo continued to stare at him, then took a long sip of tea. "Okay, Gus, catch you later."

Cecile sewed quietly until Gus had driven off, then asked, "What was that all about?"

"Who knows. But how about you? Nobody in their right mind would buy CDs at Gus's piddling rates; I take it you sent Laura down to check out the withdrawals on your account."

"That's right. Thank you for not telling Gus; he would have gotten all excited."

"Where's Dorothy?"

"Upstairs mending a dress for Reba. I gave her the evening off."

"What should we do about dinner?"

Cecile put down her sewing and reached for an apron. "You don't think I can cook anymore?"

"I didn't say that."

Opening the refrigerator, she said, "Did you know that Reba sings in a club in Paincourtville?"

"I believe I heard that."

There were footsteps on the back porch and Laura opened the door. Pulling off her sweaty visor, she plopped in the chair and stretched her long legs out before her. "Hi."

Theo poured her a large glass of iced tea and, setting it on the table, watched while she drank.

"Well?" asked Cecile.

"Well." Laura pulled Xeroxed papers from her shorts pocket. "You aren't going to like this." She smoothed the papers and handed them to Cecile.

Cecile peered down her nose. "I'm having a little trouble following this."

"Oh, excuse me." Laura came around the table and stood by Cecile. "This is a receipt for withdrawal of money. It says on May ninth, twenty-five thousand dollars was withdrawn from your account. The signature at the bottom says 'Elizabeth Reilly.' "

"Elizabeth? But that's not right. How would Sister Elizabeth know about my money?"

Theo reached for the receipt. "Let me see that. Is that her handwriting?"

Cecile studied the signature for a second. "I think so."

Looking suddenly old, she sank to chair. "But I thought she was my friend."

Laura touched Cecile's shoulder. "I'm sure there's been some mistake."

Taking Cecile's empty Scotch glass, Theo dropped in a fresh ice cube and set it before her. Pouring amber liquid into the glass, he said, "Cecile, don't take it personally. Just call Cousin Bert and prosecute the hell out of her."

"No. I don't *want* a lawyer. What I want is to know why she'd steal from me." Cecile's face contorted as she held back her tears. "She knows I give her everything I can."

Theo rubbed his aunt's shoulder. "Hey, Cecile, come on now. She just figured you weren't using the money and she wanted to put it to a good cause. Think of all those typewriters you bought."

Cecile pulled a white handkerchief from her sleeve. "It's not the money so much. It's just that, I guess I thought we were working together." She dabbed her eyes. "I bet she thinks I'm pig stupid."

"No way could she think that. I think you're about the craftiest lady in your class. I didn't even know you had dyslexia until Laura told me."

"Laura! How could you?"

Smoothly Theo interrupted, "Hey, I think it's wonderful. I can't believe you've tap-danced through life without anyone so much as guessing. You know what I thought of when she told me? I thought: what would Uncle Bron have done if he'd found out? You know what he would have done?"

"What?"

"Told jokes about it. And since he's not around, I made up some of my own. See how you like these." He picked up a banana for a microphone. "Did you hear about the new organization, DAM? Stands for Mothers Against Dyslexia.

"You know them, those are the people who ride around with bumper stickers on their cars: 'Dyslexics of the World Untie!' And, of course, they're closely allied with a group that spells a little better, the ADI—Agnostic

Dyslexic Insomniacs. And you know what they do, don't you? They're the people who lay awake at night wondering if there's a Dog.

"Thank you. Thank you. You've been a great audience." He bowed twice and peeled his banana.

Cecile smiled and blew her nose. "Thank you, Theophile. That was very kind."

"Hey, kind has nothing to do with it. I expect you to make up some for me now, but not until after you call Cousin Bert."

Cecile stood and smoothed her skirt. "No. I don't think a lawyer is what I want."

"Come on, Cecile!"

"I think what I'd like to do," Cecile said firmly, "is just extract myself from this situation as cleanly as possible. If the woman wants to empire-build, then more power to her. She's just not going to do it at my expense anymore." She looked at her watch. "Good Lord, it's after five and I haven't even started dinner. Theophile, there's no lettuce in the refrigerator."

"Then we must be out."

"Then we'll have to eat our tomatoes on bare plates. I want you and Laura to go lay the table in the dining room, please. We're not going to keep eating in the kitchen like servants."

"Aw, Cecile, it's too much trouble without Dorothy."

"Don't argue with me, child."

"No, ma'am. Come on, Laura. The dictator has spoken."

Theo led Laura out to the hall closet, where snowy tablecloths hung from coat hangers. Pulling an impossibly long cloth off a hanger, he said, "Dorothy's the one who has to iron all this stuff."

In the dining room he threw the cloth down the entire length of the sixteen-foot table. As Laura helped spread the cloth, she whispered, "What happened about Boo's body?"

"We put him in Perrier's Funeral Home. Money Perrier is going to drive the body to Baton Rouge himself tomorrow."

Cecile walked into the room with lilies in a vase. "Money Perrier used to drink with your daddy."

"Cecile, don't sneak up on us like that."

"I wouldn't trust Money Perrier with Boo's body."

"Money's stopped drinking. Daddy hasn't."

"Even so, Money's not very dependable. He's the kind who used to go to a dance with one girl and leave with another." She set the lilies down at one end of the cloth, smoothed an invisible wrinkle, and left the room.

Theo went over to the built-in china cabinet along the wall and Laura asked quietly, "Is the body still in good enough condition for an autopsy? It's been almost two days now."

"You take what you can get." He handed Laura three blue Wedgwood plates and took out silver from a fleece-lined drawer. Rubbing her thumbs over the raised white garland on a plate, Laura said, "Well, at least something is working out. That's too bad about Cecile's money."

"One thing at a time."

Dorothy came down the stairs holding up Reba's red satin dress on a hanger. "I'm finished, Ms. Talbot," she said to Cecile. "Only thing is, I got to get this to Reba now, and she got the car at the club. Can I use the phone to call my friend?"

Cecile waved a cooking spoon. "Oh, don't bother, Dorothy. Theophile can take it over for you, can't you, dear?"

"As a matter of fact, I can't." He looked at his watch. "My lawyer's going to call between five and six, and it's almost five-thirty."

"I can take it," volunteered Laura. "Except I don't quite remember where the club is."

Dorothy looked at the floor. "That's all right. I can call my friend. After the dress I got to get *me* home."

Cecile interjected, "I have an even better idea. Laura, why don't you take Dorothy *and* the dress, and pick up some lettuce for me before the store closes. Could you do all that?"

"Sure."

Cecile turned to Dorothy. "Would that work out for you, Dorothy?"

"Yes, ma'am."

"Keys are in Gus's truck, Laura," said Theo.

"I know," she said sarcastically. She went out to the backyard and drove the truck to the bottom of the steps, while on the porch Cecile helped Dorothy slip a cleaning bag over the slippery satin dress.

As Dorothy climbed in and hung the dress behind the seat, Laura said, "I know we go north up the bayou road, but I've forgotten where to turn."

"It's in Paincourtville. I'll show you."

Laura navigated the big vehicle down the gravel drive. "Does Reba sing every night?" asked Laura.

"Five days a week. She'll be doing *two* shows tomorrow and Saturday."

"Bet that wears her out."

"Uh. Can't get her up for church on Sunday."

The sun was a red ball in the west and the air incrementally cooler, smelling of wet drainage ditches and moist black mud. Cocky dogs roamed the streets, nipping at one another's tails, and on the sidewalks, children held noisy powwows while straddling their bicycles. As Laura and Dorothy passed the courthouse, they glanced at the front lawn, where a crowd of boys on skateboards were scraping white lines into the sidewalk with their boards.

Dorothy rolled her eyes. "Umm-umm! Sheriff ain't been dead two days and they already tearing up the place."

"Guess everyone's going to miss Boo."

"Oh, I don't think anything like that. Everybody I know glad he gone, didn't think he treat anybody with respect."

"That's surprising. You would think that professionally he would have to treat everybody with respect."

"I don't mean that. I was talking about Mr. Boo and the ladies."

Laura looked at Dorothy out of the corner of her eye. "Yeah, I heard he might be sleeping with somebody else."

"Lot of somebodies. *Anybody* thought he was little bit sexy, he'd try to sleep with 'em. He could put terrible pressure on you. After that, he treat you like you ain't there."

"That's too bad."

Dorothy sighed deeply. "I guess I'm most sorry about Miss Sally. She's such a nice lady. Maybe Theophile being in town help her out some."

"Cecile told me Theophile and Sally almost got married once."

"Oh, yeah, Theophile help her out a lot. They *real* tight. This here's Paincourtville. You can turn up there, where that water truck come out."

Laura parked in front of the club and waited in the pickup while Dorothy brought the dress inside. In the fading daylight the tar-papered building looked even shabbier than before, its foundation listing to one side and its fuchsia trim blistered and peeling.

When Dorothy came out, she directed Laura back down the bayou highway to a turnoff south of town, where they cut back into the cane fields and drove for two miles. Crossing a train track, they came into grassy acreage entirely surrounded by walls of cane. In the center of the grass was a rusty railroad water tower, a boarded-over country store, and several newer brick ramblers.

"Which one?" asked Laura.

"We the third house." Dorothy pointed to a tiny shack Laura had not noticed. It had green asbestos siding and was only wide enough for a window and door.

Laura pulled up in front and Dorothy climbed down, "Thank you, Miss Laura. I hope everything works out for you."

"Thank you, Dorothy."

Thirty minutes later Cecile sat them down to a salad of marinated tomatoes on store-bought lettuce, followed by a main course in covered casseroles. Laura raved about the salad and Cecile asked, "What do you like to cook, Laura?"

"I don't know. Usually I just eat whatever's in the refrigerator."

Theo broke in, "Laura has a really good chicken dish she makes with canned soup."

"I see." Cecile took away their salad plates and passed around a fragrant dish of vegetables that looked like jalapeños.

"Are the peppers hot?" asked Laura.

"Peppers?" Cecile stared. "You mean you've never eaten okra before?"

"I guess not."

"Well, isn't that something." And she watched as Laura served herself to make sure she spooned a goodly portion onto her plate.

After dinner Cecile brought out Sally's cake. It was half gone and all the drizzles of cream cheese icing had been scraped carefully off the plate. "Will you look at this? Dorothy must be feeding this to Reba."

Laura's face turned crimson. "That was me."

Cecile laughed. "We were all like that the first time we tasted it. I heard Sally's momma even used to kid her that Theophile wasn't coming to the house to see her, he was coming over to eat her cake. Isn't that right, Theophile?"

Theo ducked his head. "I can't remember. No cake for me, please."

"Laura?"

"Yes, please."

After dinner they cleaned the dishes, and Cecile asked, "Anybody for gin?"

They played for pennies in the dining room, Cecile methodically gathering the money before her. "What are y'all doing tomorrow?" she asked.

Theo discarded. "Trying to keep out of trouble until the autopsy report comes in." He watched as Cecile swooped down on his discard. "How about you, Cecile? What are you going to do?"

"I'd like to go back to the island tomorrow and see what kind of mess Miss Dinah left in my front yard. I'd invite y'all down but we hate letting company see us when we're so ugly."

"I wish you'd do something about the money you lost. You could at least call up Sister Elizabeth and hear her side. I'd like to know how she got into the account in the first place."

Tires crunched on the drive and Theo tilted his chair back to look out the window. "It's Money Perrier." He threw down his cards and went to the back door. Laura and Cecile followed him out to find the undertaker climbing the back steps, his liver-spotted face sweaty and red. Bursting into the kitchen, he said, "Theophile, somebody took that body."

Theo slapped his forehead and Money blurted, "They jimmied my back door. Theophile, I'm sorry. I don't know what to do."

Theo grabbed his baseball cap from the doorknob. "Laura, call Quatorze and tell him what happened. Come on, Money, let's go."

Money backed against the counter. "Theophile—"

"Wait," called Laura. "I'm coming."

Theo blocked the door with his arm. "No, you're not. After you call Quatorze I want you to pack your bags and go down to Grand Isle with Cecile. I'll call you there."

"Theo, but why?"

"Because I can't keep you safe here. I can't even keep a dead body safe here."

"But it's not your fault. The morgue cooler was an accident. I can stay out—"

The phone rang and Theo dashed to the back hall. Money called to his back, "Theophile, I'm not going with you. I don't want to get involved."

Theo picked up the phone as Laura crept out in the hall. "Hello?" he said. She watched his face become grave as he listened to a faint female voice. "I see," he said. He cradled the receiver slowly in its plastic bed.

"Who was it?"

"Reba. There're some ambulance drivers from Baton Rouge in the club and they're telling everybody they have the Redemption Parish sheriff out in the parking lot."

CHAPTER 13

~~~~~~~~~~~~~~~~

Reba opened the back door of the lounge. She was wearing her red dress, this time with a red knit turban. Ignoring Laura, she burst out, "Theophile, they be out here in a minute. Willie had to give them drinks to make them stay."

Theo stared at Reba's silver eye shadow. "Y'all can't stall 'em, get somebody to flirt with 'em?"

"That's the problem. They looking for women and nobody wants to go."

"Damn."

"They ain't very nice. They already making fun, we from Diddletown." Two boys came behind the building to smoke and Reba shouted, "Y'all go away!" Turning to Theo, she said, "What you want me to do?"

He looked at the low-slung ambulance station wagon

with its curtained back windows and knobby door locks. "I need a coat hanger."

"Fine." She disappeared into the club and came back with a black hanger.

Theo quickly untwisted the wire corkscrew, spattering his hands with enamel specks. Measuring the distance between the top of the ambulance window and the door lock, he made two bends in the straightened hanger and fashioned a loop at the end. "Reba, how long could you keep 'em if you went in and sang?" He pushed the loop past the black rubber gasket around the window, slid in three feet of bent hanger, and fished around for the lock cap.

"I already tried. They told Willie Diana Ross is an ol' grandma. I'm doing Aretha next set."

He pulled out the hanger and minutely adjusted the bends. "Then what would happen if Laura went inside and sat down?"

"No," snapped Laura.

"Laura, all you'd have to do is sit there." He inserted the hanger again and trolled for the lock. "You wouldn't have to say anything, or even look at them. By the time they figure out you're not very interesting, I can have the body out and ready to go to Baton Rouge." The wire loop hooked the lock and he pulled it up. "Outstanding."

"Theo, I am not going in there."

Reba added, "It *would* make them stay."

Fiercely, Laura lashed, "Great plan, Talbot. And what am I supposed to do if they ask me to come outside with them?"

"Just say no. Come on, Laura, please. I need about twenty minutes."

"It'd be okay," said Reba kindly. "Willie won't let nothing happen."

"And how do I get myself out of there?"

"That's what we need to talk about. If you don't mind, I'd like you to drive the truck to Baton Rouge with the body in the back."

"Me?"

"Yeah, I'm going to run interference for you. Don't worry, I'll have everything all set up."

"What do you want me to do?"

"First of all, go inside and watch Reba's set. Don't talk to the drivers, but when they start to leave, you leave too. Come back here and you'll find Gus's pickup with the body in the back packed in ice. Let the drivers see what you've got and then drive straight to the pathology lab in Baton Rouge. Stick out your hand; I'll draw the directions for you."

"They'll kill me!"

"They can't touch you and they know it. All they're going to do is follow. Give me your hand." He pulled out his pen.

"That's right," agreed Reba. "You're white."

Laura watched as Theo drew the Airline Highway on her palm and wrote down an address. "Why aren't *you* doing this?"

"Because I'm going to borrow the Pinto from Reba and tag along behind. Do you mind, Reba?"

"I guess."

"What for?" Laura demanded.

"Because at some point those guys are going to realize they're in trouble and they're going to go somewhere to tell somebody, and I'm going to be right behind." He clicked the pen and turned to ask Reba, "Those guys bigger than me?"

"One of them's real big." She slipped back inside.

Laura gritted her teeth and turned to go.

"Wait, don't go in yet. Give Reba time to set it up inside."

"Talbot, I hope you know what you're doing."

"You'll be fine. And don't sweat all over that map."

She growled and walked to the front of the building, stepping inside to face the same bald-headed bouncer. Gawking at the bills in his hand, she said, "I don't have any money."

The bouncer nodded and waved her over to an empty table in the center next to two white-coated men who sat ever-so-casually with their chairs pushed back and bottles of beer on their thighs. Laura sat down and a Coke instantly appeared on the table. She looked up to see Willie, who said loudly, "How are you this evening, Miss Laura?"

"Fine, Willie. Is Reba singing tonight?"

"Yes, ma'am. In just a minute."

Laura scooted in her chair and noisily caught it on the curling linoleum as Willie and several other men positioned themselves casually around the black-painted plywood room. Most of the patrons—dressed in bright tank tops and jeans—talked in low tones and ignored her, but from the corner of her eye she watched the drivers scoot around in their chairs to stare at her and whisper.

Ewell, the guitarist, emerged from the back door to fuss with an electronic keyboard onstage, then left. Reba poked her head out the door, then came onto the platform to scattered applause. Laura clapped noisily as Reba sat down at the keyboard and pulled a microphone up to her mouth. "I'd like to start my second set with some old Aretha Franklin favorites."

The drivers clapped appreciatively, evidently not caring that Aretha was old enough to have grandchildren too.

Reba laid down trembling chords in G, tinkled her way up to C, and settled back down where she started. Lifting her face to the microphone, she poured out the liquid velvet of "Doctor Feelgood." The crowd listened to her lover's lament in the prologue and was so moved that by the time she had set up for the steamy chorus, they were calling for her to "tell it" and "sing it."

After the last moaning line, when Reba explained how truly good the doctor made her feel, the audience applauded vigorously while the ambulance drivers stamped their feet and called for "Respect." Reba immediately laid down the clomping chords of "Chain of Fools" and then moved into "Natural Woman." Laura finished her Coke, and another appeared on the table.

The drivers again asked for "Respect" and this time Reba explained she had no backup. As an appeasement she put down the lilting lovely chords of "Say a Little Prayer" but as the song progressed the drivers lost interest. When it ended, they pushed back their chairs and stood. Laura leaped up and ran to the door.

Walking around back, she found the bouncer and two other men leaning on a tree next to the ambulance. The bouncer nodded almost imperceptibly and she glanced in the back of Gus's truck to see a long white morgue bag covered with crushed ice. Climbing into the truck, she found the keys in the ignition. The drivers appeared around the corner so she started the truck and idled in reverse.

The taller driver looked into her truck bed and back-pedaled a step. "Hey!"

Laura screeched out of the lot onto the back streets of Paincourtville. Reaching the highway, she stopped to turn north as looming yellow headlights filled her windshield mirror. She locked her doors and squinted into the mirror, barely able to make out the white hood of the ambulance. Pulling onto the highway, she smiled with satisfaction as they followed. She grabbed the steering wheel with two hands and drove up the bayou, teasing the ambulance along behind.

The two vehicles sped up the bayou road, past elegant suburban homes and tiny tar-paper shanties with rickety porches. Beyond the tangled undergrowth on the right side of the road, white moonlight glanced off the black water of Bayou Lafourche. Laura concentrated on her driving until, suddenly, five miles north of Paincourtville, the ambulance pulled out to pass.

Slowing down, Laura watched the red lights disappear into the night. Unclenching the steering wheel, she let out a sigh of relief. "Home free," she said out loud. Turning on the radio, she listened to the honeyed tones of a big band announcer as she drove north to Baton Rouge.

The empty road stretched out predictably before her. On the left were cane fields as far as she could see; on the right, a grassy shoulder sloping down into Bayou Lafourche. A few miles down the road a green road sign indicated that to get to Baton Rouge, she needed to turn right and cross a bayou bridge. Putting on her blinker, she slowed for the turn and suddenly slammed on the brakes.

Out her windshield, on the bridge to the right, the white ambulance station wagon was parked sideways blocking the road, the two drivers leaning against the door with their arms crossed. Spotting her headlights, they walked forward to flag her down. Laura hit the gas and sped straight ahead, up the bayou road, leaving them shouting and waving behind her. Remembering the smaller bayou bridge back in St. Lô, she turned around on a wide shoulder and passed the ambulance just as it pulled out to follow her.

Speeding south down the empty road, Laura watched as the ambulance fell in close behind. Pressing heavily on the gas, she found the ambulance had no problem keeping an even ten yards from her rear.

Oncoming headlights blinked from low to high and back, blinding her and making her swerve. The vehicle shot past and honked. "Theo!" she shouted. He was in a dark full-size pickup and she wondered why he wasn't in the Pinto as he said he would be.

Behind her the pickup crossed the center stripe and boldly skidded to a stop right in front of the ambulance. Cautiously the ambulance crept forward onto the shoulder, pulling up to the pickup's window for a parley with the driver. After brief negotiations, the ambulance turned around and sped north toward Baton Rouge.

"Thank goodness." Laura jumped out of the truck to greet Theo. The dark pickup turned around and drove toward her. As she squinted to make out Theo's face, she watched in horror as the face behind the wheel became a head masked by the white peaked pillowcase of the Ku Klux Klan.

Shrieking with fright, she stumbled back to her truck and banged down the door locks.

The Klansman pulled up beside her, angling his truck hood in front of hers. Jumping out, he strode stoop-shouldered toward her, his ragged eyeholes outlining weird pink shapes under his eyes. Laura reversed, then took off down the road.

"Wait!" Hopping on her tailgate, he hitched a bumpy ride before jumping off.

Laura sped south to the safety of St. Lô. She passed a car going the other direction and was astonished by how quickly she zipped by. She passed another and it honked, trying to tell her to slow down. Tearing along furiously, she honked and flashed her lights, hoping to attract police. Peering again in the mirror, she saw with sinking hopes that the only vehicle she had attracted was the dark pickup. It climbed swiftly up her tail and nudged her on the bumper.

Pressing the accelerator to the floor, she careened down the winding two-lane road, the Klansman's headlights right on her tail. Suddenly, the pickup shot past and pulled directly in front of her. Slowing to a crawl, he rolled ahead, swerving back and forth across the road, forcing her down to ten miles an hour. She jerked to the left to pass and he veered adroitly to block her. "Stop it!" she screamed. Like a cat with prey, he watched her in his mirror.

Suddenly Laura hit the brakes and slid to a stop in the middle of the road. Her thumping heart jerked her breath out in spasms. Cautiously the Klansman backed up. Laura did nothing, pretending to be waiting to talk. He backed up more and Laura cheerfully waved. Finally, when he was only five yards ahead of her, stretching to get out of the cab, she gunned the engine and took off past him down the road.

The Klansman honked angrily and fell in behind. Laura put both hands on the wheel and drove frantically toward St. Lô. She sped through Vertrandville, swerving to avoid movie patrons streaming from a storefront after the Thursday night feature. In her side mirror, she watched the Klansman inch up beside her, trying to drive abreast. She pushed the gas pedal to the floor and he fell behind, staying there a moment while they waited for an oncoming car.

The car swooshed past in a rush of headlights, swirling the cane next to the road. When its taillights were pinpoints in the dark, the pickup once again appeared in her mirror, very close and ready to pass. Concentrating on the road, Laura drove down the center line, determined not to let him by. The truck inched up beside her in the oncoming lane and tapped her door with its bumper. She veered slightly to the right, and the Klansman moved abreast, slamming this time into her front fender. Her wheel jerked right and she ricocheted onto the shoulder. Bumping forward a few yards, she steered back onto the road next to the pickup.

Steadying the wheel with all her strength, Laura pressed the gas, determined not to give up her lane. Once again the pickup cozied alongside, trying to nudge her off the road. Refusing to move, she held the steering straight and watched from the corner of her eye as her side mirror slowly crumbled under the strain. The Klansman continued to steer right, pressing his fender against hers and, with no further difficulty, bumped her emphatically onto the shoulder, where she rattled down a slope.

Laura screamed. High stalks of sugar cane slapped against the windshield and the truck jounced over furrows, pounding her head into the ceiling. Abruptly she bounced to a halt.

Unbuckling her seat belt, Laura turned to see the Klansman pull up behind her. She started the truck again but the wheels spun helplessly in the soft furrows. Turning around, she saw the Klansman walk down the slope.

She pressed on the horn. "Help!"

The Klansman stopped at her tailgate and opened it, letting ice fall onto the ground. "Stop it!" she cried. "You can't take that." Again she pressed the horn.

The Klansman pulled the body bag out with both hands and stooped to slide it on his shoulders. Instantly he straightened and shouted an obscenity. "Where's the body?" he barked. He glared through his mask and tramped past the cane to Laura's window.

Laura looked at the open tailgate. "Isn't that it?"

"Open the door."

Laura stared at the door locks as if the magic of her vision would keep them down. The Klansman banged on the window. "Where's the damn body?"

"I thought that was it!" She leaned on the horn. "Help!"

The Klansman crunched back through the cane and she turned around to watch him take a tool from the back of his truck. Shoulders hunched forward as he walked down the slope, he waved a crowbar at her.

Laura started the engine and pressed the gas again, only to find herself spinning in ruts. The Klansman slammed the crowbar into the passenger-side window. "Stop!" Laura demanded. Cocking the crowbar over his head again, the Klansman pounded the window with all his might, this time etching a spiderweb into the glass. Laura screamed and mashed the horn.

Taking the crowbar in both hands, the Klansman began poking a hole directly over the passenger door lock. Desperately she honked the horn and spun the truck wheels once more. Jamming the stick into reverse, she pressed on the gas again and the truck jolted backward but was blocked by the Klansman's pickup. He shouted, "Stop right there, Missy!"

She jerked the truck into drive and cut left, where the tires gripped solid ground as she drove parallel to the furrows. Breaking a trail through fresh cane, she cut back up to the road, spun out on the gravel, and once again sped south toward St. Lô, driving wildly down the bayou.

Half a mile on, the pickup's lights appeared again. Laura punched the gas and drove down the center line, swerving only for honking oncoming cars. On her left the dark pickup began to pull up close, to once again play his deadly game of nudge.

Up ahead, past a little subdivision under the trees, Laura spied a gravel road running off into the cane. She spun the wheel right, leaving her stalker on the highway. Down the dirt road a sign announced, Talbot Brothers Sugar Refinery.

"Talbot!" she cried.

Ahead, in the sugar mill, a light glimmered in the upper window. Laura sped toward the hulking metal building, stopping at an unlighted door.

Jumping out of the truck, she twisted the doorknob. Locked. She knocked loudly and turned around to see the Klansman pulling up in his truck. "Mr. Talbot!" she screamed, hoping to alert Theo's father. She banged on the door and ran around the corner to find a large open entrance, wide enough for farm vehicles. "Help!" The sound echoed off machinery in the dark mill as the Klansman rounded the corner.

Dashing into the darkness, Laura struck her hip on a conveyor belt. Groping with hands and feet, she felt dead air beneath the belt; she threw her body under it.

Seconds later the Klansman stood in the doorway, peaked hood silhouetted against the moonlight outside. Raising his crowbar, he stalked into the darkness. Laura held her breath and sat very still.

Slowly the great door rumbled closed, leaving her in blackness. She heard the Klansman shuffle across the concrete floor, and suddenly the lights blazed above. Down the conveyor belt three massive cogged wheels rasped against one another; inches above her head the black belt jolted into motion. Spotting a stairway in the shadows, Laura darted out. "Mr. Talbot, Mr. Talbot!" she screamed.

The Klansman leaped out to block her path. Over the noise of the conveyor he shouted, "Where's the body?"

"I swear it was in the truck." Laura stepped slowly backward to a wall where shovels and axes hung on nails. "Why didn't you take it?"

The Klansman loped forward, wielding his crowbar in tiny circles. "The sandbags didn't fool anybody, honey."

"I didn't know they were sandbags."

"Where's the body?"

"I don't know. Mr. Talbot!" Grabbing a heavy axe from the wall, she tried to hold it as the Klansman did his crowbar. Chuckling deeply in his throat, he lunged forward, easily knocking the axe out of her hand. It thudded on the floor and she leaped to avoid the vicious blade. "Mr. Talbot!" The Klansman stalked closer.

"What do you want?"

"I already told you; I want that body."

"I don't know where it is."

"Let's see if we can make you remember." Waving the crowbar menacingly, he lunged toward her and swung, missing her on purpose and grabbing her wrist as she ducked.

"Let me go! *Mr. Talbot!*"

"Unless you've got a case of Budweiser, honey, Valmont's not gonna budge." His Cajun brogue was as smooth as Southern Comfort.

"Let me go!" she screamed.

His fingers were a vise around her wrist. Up close the pillowcase smelled of starch and had neat ironing creases. The ragged eyeholes showed mostly pale skin, focusing her attention on the pink half-moon of his lower lids. As he blinked behind the hood, Laura brought his hand up to her mouth to bite and he thumped her on the head with the crowbar. "Unh-unh. You be good, honey."

The blow vibrated her head. "I don't *know* where the body is."

"I'm getting a little tired of this, and I don't want to listen to it anymore." He grabbed her hair and pulled her across the floor. "We can't let you run around with bodies that don't belong to you." He stopped in front of the conveyor and Laura twisted around to see the gleaming rollers meshing perfectly as they turned. "No!" she screamed. She sat on the floor, jerking his hand with her.

"Damn you." The Klansman pulled her up by the hair and thwacked her back with the crowbar. Pain shot down the back of her legs.

"I don't want to hurt you, honey," he crooned, "but you're going to tell me where the body is."

"I don't know!"

"Then I guess we'll start with your hand."

Hooking the crowbar on his belt, he turned his back to her and pressed her forearm between his arm and his body. Dragging her forward, he held her hand inches from the grinding rollers. "Don't worry," he drawled softly, "I know a guy in New Orleans who does a great job on reconstruction."

Laura bit her lip and strained mightily against his back with steady pressure, using her other hand on his curving spine. Still he drew her hand forward. Next she tried short kicks and clawing, but all he did was pull her closer and closer to the rollers. Holding her hand inches away from the grinding cogs, he asked, "Where's the body, honey?"

"I don't know." With her free hand she tore at his hood.

"Hey!" Without releasing her wrist, he turned and swung his arm like a bat, smashing her jaw so hard, her eyes teared. He righted his hood and stared at her with angry, familiar eyes. A wet spot had formed over his mouth and through the pillowcase he seethed, "Do that again and I'll beat you to a pulp." Once more he twisted her arm against his body and dragged her up to the rollers.

"I swear I don't know where the body is! I swear!"

"It's your left hand. Hope you don't need it."

Laura screamed and kicked him behind the knee. His shoulder dropped against the roller, ripping his shirt and skin. A streak of blood welled up to the surface and angrily, he unhooked his crowbar from his belt. "I think it's about time somebody taught you how to act like a la—"

Suddenly the rollers stopped, leaving a roar of silence. Both Laura and the Klansman looked over to see a shaggy old man steadying himself by the fuse box.

"I never heard myself give permission to start the line." The old man's voice echoed through the mill.

The Klansman dropped Laura's arm and stumbled backward toward the exit. Pushing frantically on the huge sliding door, he grunted, straining with all his might.

Across the floor the old man called disgustedly, "Hypo Hebert, what are you doing with that damn pillowcase on your head?"

CHAPTER 14

Hypo pushed back the mill door and slipped into the night. Laura stared at the black space where he disappeared and then looked at Theo's awful father. He was a wild man with a bony, shrunken skull and unkempt gray hair. His cheeks and eyelids were burned bright red and he looked at her with a ravaged pair of Theo's own dark eyes. "You're Laura," Valmont said.

"Yes."

"You all right?"

She rubbed the welt on her head where Hypo had used the crowbar. "I think so."

"Sorry I couldn't get to you faster. I'm a little slow on my feet these days." He put a hand on the fuse box. "Mind if I turn off the lights? They attract bugs."

He threw switches and the air went dark, leaving only

dim light from the loft and door. "Where's Theophile?" he asked.

"He said he was going to ride interference in another car but I think he took Boo's body up to Baton Rouge and gave me sandbags."

Valmont chuckled. "Quarterback sneak. He didn't want you to know so you'd make a better decoy."

"He almost got me *killed*!"

Valmont laughed again. "Think we ought to whup him?"

Laura felt a weight lift from her shoulders. "I'd be happy just to yell."

Still chuckling, Valmont shuffled slowly across the floor. "What you need to do is go back to the house and call the sheriff—can't call the sheriff. Okay, go back to the house and call Quatorze; tell him what Hypo's up to and make sure Quatorze knows Theophile's on his way to Baton Rouge with the body. Quatorze'll take care of it. If you'll excuse me now, I think I'd like to go upstairs."

"Wait—I can't go with Hypo still out there."

"Naw, Hypo won't bother you now. He knows what I'd do to him." Valmont stumbled on the first step. "Lord-a-mercy."

Laura rushed over to help him up. His clothes stank and through his shirt she felt his bony arm, as fragile as a chicken wing. "Are you okay?"

Breathing fetid air into her face, he said, "Darlin', don't you worry about me." He bent over to crawl up the stairs, grunting as he lifted himself on each step. "You just take care of Theophile, you hear?" On the back of his head was a bald spot with a bandage.

Laura watched for a moment before turning away. "Good-bye," she called.

"Bye, darlin'. You take care."

In the kitchen Cecile and Sister Elizabeth sat at the table with their hands in a sincere pile. Cecile's mascara was pooled in teary bags under her eyes and the nun sat forward in a posture of intense listening. Laura stood in the doorway, afraid to interrupt.

Cecile looked up. "Laura, what happened to you?"

Laura brushed her shirt. "Hypo Hebert tried to put my hand through the sugar mill. Or maybe he just wanted to scare me."

"Hypo? Are you all right?"

"I might have a bump."

Cecile motioned for Laura to sit and examined her scalp. "Why would Hypo want to hurt you?"

"I think it means he killed the sheriff. Theo said whoever was trying to keep Boo from autopsy is probably the one who killed him because an autopsy would end up showing who did it by showing how."

"Well, if that doesn't beat all. Is the body being autopsied now?"

"Theo's taking it. I think." Laura looked at the black-stained hollows under Cecile's eyes. "What are you two doing?"

Cecile went to the sink and wet a napkin. "I must look like last week's roux." Carefully wiping the skin under her eyes, she said, "Elizabeth and I have been straightening things out. I should have talked to her in the first place; it would have saved us both so much grief."

The nun nodded, biting her lip. Holding up a Xeroxed bank slip, she said, "This isn't my signature, Laura. My name has been forged."

"Forged? Who would do that?"

"We're calling a bank examiner first thing in the morning."

Laura leaped up. "Oh, dear. I'm supposed to call Quatorze about Hypo." She went to the back hall and telephoned a night police dispatcher, who said she was up in Assumption Parish, working both Redemption and Assumption, and that she would relay the message to Quatorze as fast as possible. When Laura returned to the kitchen, the older women looked at her with set faces, already having decided her fate. Cecile crossed her arms. "If Hypo's still out there, you're not safe, Laura."

"Yes, I am. Theo's father said Hypo wouldn't touch me now."

"Laura, please go look at that door."

Laura walked to the kitchen door and examined the aging lock. Rust blooms covered its surface and the bolt was permanently stuck inside the door casing. "Oops."

Cecile said, "It's been like that since I got married in 1945. I don't know about you, but I'm not prepared to sleep tonight in a house protected by the eye hook of a screen door." She turned to the nun. "Sister, we'd feel much better if you could come with us to Grand Isle. Could you? Safety in numbers."

Sister Elizabeth nodded grimly. "I think so. The program only runs half days on Friday. I do need to go by the convent, though, and tell them where I'm going."

"Fine. Laura, dear, please, go pack a bag."

In the darkness they followed Bayou Lafourche south to the gulf. As Cecile drove down her familiar stretch of road, she gave Laura a running commentary to keep their minds off Hypo. Without taking her eyes from the road, she directed their attention to the site of Bronier's first Texaco station and Valmont's cane field that always took high yield award. Passing the activity center, she pointed out the water tower where Theo had once painted "Bring on the Nubiles," and nobody knew what nubiles were.

They drove past minimarkets and empty-lotted shopping centers, all the way down to Cut Off and Galliano, where the cane fields stopped and marsh began. In Golden Meadow the bayou widened and shrimp boats docked right up next to the highway, while across the way noisy juke joints spilled life out on the road.

Finally, down in the marshy blackness, where the air was thick with salt, they climbed a high arching bridge and looked over the top to see the pulsing red lights of the oil rigs out in the gulf. Cecile scanned the horizon. "I'm glad you're coming at night so you can't see how ugly a hurricane makes it."

Down a sandy highway they passed fishing shacks,

trailers, and beach houses on stilts. When the neighborhood became scented with jasmine, Cecile slowed and turned at a driveway with a white hurricane light. They pulled into the sandy front yard of a screened beach cottage on pilings.

Cecile climbed out and opened the ground floor garage. After they had stowed the car, she locked the garage and pointed to an inside stair. "Up there, Laura. I don't have air-conditioning, so run over and open the porch doors as soon as you get in."

Laura brought her canvas duffle upstairs and found herself in a big L-shaped room with sand-scratched oak floors. A tiled kitchen took up one end and in the sitting area rag rugs and floral chintzes made a homey scene.

Cecile walked past her and unlocked the double doors to the porch. "I said open the doors. We've got to get this place cooled down."

Laura followed her out on the screen porch, where a zephyr from the gulf felt like the wind from paradise. She took a deep breath and felt that the sea, at least, was on her side. "What a spot."

Cecile inhaled too. "Bronier used to say if they could bottle this and sell it, nobody'd drink alcohol anymore." She turned to the nun, who had just joined them. "Sister, do you mind sleeping on the couch? Laura, we can set you up with a rollaway bed either in the living room with Elizabeth or out here."

"Here. Just point me in the right direction and I can do everything."

"What lovely company." Cecile led her back inside and opened a walk-in closet off the kitchen. "There's your bed; watch the door threshold when you roll it out. And here's your sheets. Don't worry about being outside, dear; no one can get in without breaking down the garage door first."

Laura made the bed and waited her turn for the bathroom. Climbing under the stiff sheet, she listened to the lapping surf, trying to imagine the height of the waves. Turning over once, she thought of Theo, then dropped into the sleep of the dead.

•   •   •

The sun was hot and the painted porch smelled of linseed oil. Laura sat up and looked at the beach. The hurricane had left enough flotsam to stock a junkyard but directly beyond the wreckage, the pristine scallops of surf beckoned for miles in either direction. She went inside and found Elizabeth and Cecile at the table over coffee. Cecile looked pretty and rested, wearing a wide turquoise hairband in her silver hair and matching slacks. "What would you like for breakfast, dear?"

Laura asked, "Do you mind if I run first?"

"On the beach? You've got to be kidding. The usual trash from the rigs and boats are bad enough, but this place looks like D day after a hurricane."

"I've been on dirty beaches before."

"Don't say you haven't been warned."

Laura changed into shorts and bounced down the stairs. Picking her way through driftwood, plywood, Styrofoam ice chests, lumber, tampon inserters, clear plastic sheeting, and half a dingy, she stopped at the thin, smooth strip of hard sand by the surf. Washing her bare feet in the warm water, she faked some stretching and ran down the sand.

Wild wind sang in her ears and her hair blew back from her face. She strode past houses one by one, leaping over beer cans, shredded tires, bleach jugs, tobacco tins, and a multitude of plastic pop bottles filled with a suspicious-looking yellow liquid.

She ran three miles and finally, seeing no natural end to the run, turned and ran back. Pacing past the beach houses, she realized she didn't know what Cecile's looked like from the beach. As she approached the three-mile mark, she scanned each house anxiously for familiar signs. Finally she came to a place where the driftwood was deep and a squat man sat on the hull of half a broken dingy. Closing in, she recognized Gus.

When she was close enough to see his eyes, Theo's uncle lifted himself off the hull and brushed his hands. "Well, hello, gal."

"Hi, Gus. When'd you get here?"

"Ten minutes ago. When I heard you went running, I came outside just in case you couldn't remember what the house looked like."

"You were right. I forgot to look before I left. Did Theo come with you?"

"I'm afraid not. I haven't seen him. Gad, this beach is awful. I'm embarrassed for you to see it." He gestured for her to lead the way and then spoke to her back. "A friend and I came down because we heard about your run-in with Hypo Hebert. But it appears that you're all right."

"Did they catch him?"

"Last I heard he bought a ticket to Jamaica at the New Orleans airport. Customs is waiting for him in Kingston."

Gus's LTD was parked in the sandy grass before the house and they climbed the stairs to find Cecile and Elizabeth making awkward conversation with a short gray-haired man in an expensive polo shirt. Laura glanced at Cecile for an explanation of the visitors and Cecile slowly blinked in a gesture of extreme contempt.

Genially Gus waddled over to the man and said, "Laura, I'd like you to meet my good friend, former Governor T-Harry Meacham. T-Harry, this is Miss Laura Ireland. Laura's an anthropologist."

Meacham walked over, extending a hand, keen appreciation in his bright blue eyes. "Shame on you, Gus. You didn't tell me the young lady was so pretty." He cupped both hands over hers and smiled warmly. "I'm so glad Dr. Hebert didn't harm you last night."

"It wasn't for lack of trying."

Laughing genially, Meacham sat down on the couch, patting to a place beside him. "You'll have to tell me about it. Did Dr. Hebert actually believe you had the sheriff's body tucked away in the back of your pickup?"

"Yes. My friend Theo took the real body himself and left a decoy without telling me."

Meacham nodded sympathetically, knitting his silver brow. Looking at Cecile, the former governor said, "Mrs. Talbot, could you find something for this young lady to drink? I bet she'd like a Bloody Mary, and I'll take straight tomato juice."

Laura shook her head. "Nothing alcoholic, please. I just ran."

"Then two tomato juices, please, ma'am. Laura, you have to tell me about yourself. Where do you teach?" Meacham stretched an arm across the back of the couch and looked at her with interested eyes.

Laura folded her arms across her chest. "I teach in Bellingham, Washington. It's on Puget Sound, just south of the Canadian border."

"Washington. When I was governor, I had occasion to meet your Governor Evans. He was a fine politician, if you can ever call any of us fine. Are you interested in politics?"

"I don't keep up with it as much as I'd like."

Meacham moved closer on the couch. "I'll have to tell you some of my stories. I bet an anthropologist could find something to study in the American political process."

Cecile came over with two tomato juices on a tray. "Or it could be, Mr. Meacham, that Laura doesn't want to hear your life history so early in the morning."

Amid dead-still silence Laura gulped tomato juice while Meacham slowly sipped from his glass. Gus got up to pour himself a demitasse of coffee behind the kitchen counter and, stirring noisily with the tiny spoon, he tasted his coffee and said, "Well, Laura, we're so glad to see that everything turned out all right. All I can say is I'm sorry you had to meet up with Hypo the local weirdo."

In an overstuffed chair Cecile curled her feet up under her and said, "Hypo's problem is he thinks the world revolves around him because he's a doctor."

"Balderdash," said Gus. "Hypo's been like that since he was born. That dingy mother of his used to peel his shrimp for him 'til he was twelve. She still irons his underwear."

"Hush," said Cecile.

Sister Elizabeth, who had been sitting quietly on a dining room chair, fixed her gaze on Gus. "If, as Laura indicates, Hypo has killed a man, I would suspect there is a more immediate cause than the actions of his mother."

"I'm sure you're right, Sister," said Meacham. "No telling what kind of mess he's gotten himself into. Or," he stretched a hand out again to Laura, "maybe he already told you?"

Laura shook her head. "He didn't say a thing."

"That's too bad." The former governor leaned forward to put his juice glass on the tray. "Gus, did you have a chance on the beach to ask her about the other matter?"

"No. I hadn't come to that yet." Gus beamed at her brightly. "Laura, our good friend the attorney general is looking for a shoe box that was used to hold drug money. Theophile returned the money yesterday but did so in another box. You can imagine what they're thinking—that he's withholding evidence and all—and it really doesn't look very good for the boy. Is there a way you can help him out on this?"

Laura clutched her glass. "If they think Theo's in on a drug deal, they're nuts. We just got here Tuesday."

"Yes, but you see how bad this looks. You'd be doing Theophile a real favor by returning the box if he gave it to you for safekeeping."

"I don't have it."

"And you don't know where it is?"

"No."

Meacham stood up. "Gus, see if you agree with me on this, but don't you think the best idea would be for this young lady to come with us to Baton Rouge?"

"Now?" Gus's eyes watered behind his glasses. "W-why, yes, I suppose." He glanced quickly at Laura.

Meacham put a hand out to help Laura off the couch. "Then we need to get on the road. We've got a lot to do today."

From across the room Sister Elizabeth said firmly, "Laura's staying here."

Everyone turned to look at the nun's steely eyes.

"Why, Sister," said Gus. "We're only asking Laura a little favor. Maybe we can even help her look for Theophile. Wouldn't that be nice, Laura?"

Laura leaped up. "You mean Theo might still be in Baton Rouge?"

"Why, there's a good possibility if that's where he was last night." Gus beamed at her.

She waved her hand. "Let's try the pathology lab. I still have the address on my palm."

"Laura, you'll be staying here, dear."

Meacham shoved his hands in his pockets. "I think this young lady has a right to go anywhere she pleases, Sister."

The nun sat with hands in her lap. "Mr. Meacham, I hate to be so emphatic about this, but Laura is not leaving. I feel very strongly and will not hesitate to call the archbishop if necessary. He is, as you know, a close friend of Governor Ramsey's."

Meacham pivoted to look at the gulf, and then turned back, composed and smiling. "Well, then, Gus, I think our business is done here, don't you?"

Gus clattered his demitasse noisily on the saucer. "Of course." Waddling to the stairway door, he waited for his cue.

Meacham walked over to join Gus and turned, smiling like a man with an auspicious Merrill Lynch statement. "Ladies, it's been a pleasure meeting y'all. No need to see us out. Mrs. Talbot, thank you for your kind hospitality."

The men disappeared down the stairs and the three women listened to the car drive out on the road. Cecile picked up her cigarettes and walked to the porch. "Now, wasn't that a performance," she said thoughtfully.

"What did they come *here* for?" asked Laura.

Sister Elizabeth got up and pushed back the curtain. "We don't know. But it's obvious you know something disturbing to Gus and Meacham."

"But I can't imagine what it is. And anyway, Hypo's the one who tried to kill me."

Cecile said, "Yes, but something's very wrong. Did you see the look on Meacham's face when Elizabeth told him you weren't going to Baton Rouge? I thought his eyebrows were going to fly off. What do they want you for? Think, Laura. You must know something."

Laura walked to the refrigerator and poured herself a

refill of tomato juice. "The only information I have about Gus and Meacham is that they might be building a huge industrial complex back on the Atchafalaya."

"Might be?"

"That's all we know so far. Yesterday morning Theo and I found records in the courthouse saying that this great big construction site at the end of the river is being leased from the state by the Armelise Land Company."

"Armelise?" said Cecile. "But that's that old logging company. It's been defunct for years."

"That's what Theo said too."

The nun walked over to Cecile's desk for paper and a pencil. "So you don't actually know if Gus and Meacham are connected to Armelise?"

Laura sighed. "All I know for sure is that there's a lawyer in Armelise named Munson Pugh."

The nun nodded, writing down the name. "Then I think the best thing to do is call our convent in Baton Rouge and have somebody run over to the capital to look up the Armelise incorporation papers."

Laura groaned. "That could take forever."

Elizabeth sat at the desk. "Not necessarily. Some of the sisters have lots of experience over there from tracking down slumlords. Cecile, may I use your phone?"

"Of course."

The nun punched numbers. "They may be able to fax the information to the convent in St. Lô. Which means we'd have to go back this afternoon. Do you mind, Cecile?"

"Sister," interrupted Laura, "before you call, may I call St. Lô to see if Theo's back yet?"

"Certainly."

Cecile said, "The number's on my phone list, Laura, under 'Camille.' "

Laura dialed and listened to the ringing at Theo's house. Nobody answered. "Cecile, may I try the pathology lab in Baton Rouge?"

"Of course."

Laura called Baton Rouge information and asked for

the number of the East Baton Rouge Pathology Laboratory. A male voice answered. "Hello?"

Laura's words caught in her throat. "I'm trying to find Theophile Talbot. He might have brought in the body of the Redemption Parish sheriff last night."

"Oh, yeah, we're working on that one right now. Somebody said a doc might have killed him. Makes it a little hairy."

"Is the man who brought the body in still there?"

"Hold on, let me ask." The man put a hand over the receiver and held a muffled conversation with someone in the room. "Hello?" he said again.

"Yes?"

"Somebody saw your man leave early this morning with a pretty little gal with black hair. He said he was coming right back, but hasn't yet."

CHAPTER 15

Laura worked the fishing lure out from the frayed nylon rope and hooked it on the Styrofoam board with the rest of her collection. Down the beach a fat man in a blue jumpsuit walked toward her. His shoes were off and his pants legs rolled up, showing shapely, almost feminine, white calves. Laura picked up her trophy board and walked the surf to meet him.

When she was close enough, she eyed him cautiously. "What are you doing back, Gus?"

"I never left. I just took T-Harry to the gas station to rent a car; he had to get back to Baton Rouge. Whatcha got there?"

She held up her row of fishing lures. "There were so many of these, I started a collection."

"Theophile'll like those."

"I know. But I don't know whether to give them to him or stick them in him."

Gus laughed softly. "What's the boy done now?"

"I called the pathology lab in Baton Rouge and they said he drove off with a pretty woman with black hair, so I keep imagining him in a convertible with this woman with long black hair flying in the wind."

"Oh, no. That'd be Sally. She's in Baton Rouge at her mother's."

"Oh." She squinted down the beach to Cecile's shadowy screen porch. "Does Cecile know you're back?"

"I was just going to see her." He started walking up the beach. "I parked down the road so as not to disturb the ladies too much." They walked a few more steps in the warm surf. "Laura, I hope T-Harry didn't upset you too much this morning. He gets a little impulsive at times. He was so wound up about Hypo, he got on the phone at the gas station and set up a press conference for this afternoon."

"Why would T-Harry Meacham have a press conference about Hypo?"

Gus sucked in a breath of air. "Well, he's been in the parish a lot lately and both Boo and Hypo were good friends. I think he'd like to get to the bottom of this as much as anybody."

"Oh."

Gus stopped to pick up a stick and throw it sidearm across the water. "The other reason I came back is that T-Harry reminded me there's a big reward for the return of the shoe box. Five thousand dollars, as I remember, but it could be more."

"That's a lot of money." The foam washed over her feet, undermining the sand beneath her.

"That wouldn't help jog your memory, would it?"

"Gus, I don't have the shoe box. I honestly don't know anything about it."

"But if you find it, you'll be sure to tell me right away?"

"I don't know." She watched sharp-eyed as he brushed off his hands.

"Well, I hope you will. T-Harry and I want to be sure the powers in Baton Rouge are kept happy so they won't put any impediments on this little marina we're putting together back on the Atchafalaya."

Looking directly in his eyes, Laura said, "If you're talking about the construction site, Gus, don't bother lying anymore. Theo and I have seen it and we know it's for something structural."

"You've talked to the Corps?" Gus's voice was high and thin.

Laura looked confused and his face relaxed. "Never mind, then. That's another matter." Leading the way to Cecile's sandy grass lot, he added, "I suppose our little secret had to get out sometime. But I want you to know, we're very proud of what we're accomplishing back there and the longer we have to prepare it, the better it's going to be."

"What *is* it going to be?"

"Well, the specifics are strictly confidential, but I don't mind telling you we're negotiating with both a well-known chemical company and a very aggressive Japanese port-building consortium. Either one would make an acceptable client, in my opinion."

"Port building? Your site docsn't even have access upriver. Theo said there's a dam at Simmesport."

Gus leaned against the pilings of Cecile's house to brush his sandy feet. "Why, yes. That does appear to be a problem."

A noise sounded on the stairs and Cecile and Sister Elizabeth rushed into the garage. "Laura," asked Cecile, "is everything all right?"

"Sure."

"Why don't you come upstairs now, dear?"

"Cecile," snapped Gus, "I want you to stop making out like I'm some kind of ogre. This gal's old enough to do as she pleases."

Icily Cecile asked, "Where's your car, Gus?"

"Down the road; I went for a walk on the beach. Do you mind?"

Ignoring Gus, Sister Elizabeth asked, "Laura, do come

up, won't you? Cecile and I need another person for cards."

Gus raised a hand in retreat. "All right, ladies. Have it your way. I know when I'm licked."

They watched him trudge heavily out to the road and Sister Elizabeth asked, "What did he want, Laura?"

"He said T-Harry Meacham is holding a press conference about Hypo and Boo this afternoon. And, Cecile, I tricked him. He told me that he and Meacham are Armelise." They climbed the stairs to the breezy cabin.

"*Are* they? Who do you suppose they paid off to get building rights back there?" Cecile sat down at the table and shuffled cards. "But I want to hear more about this press conference. What in the world is Meacham holding that for? It makes no sense."

"I didn't think so either." Laura pulled up a chair.

"Did Gus tell you what time?"

"Only that it's sometime this afternoon."

Glancing at the nun, Cecile said, "Elizabeth and I decided something when we saw you on the beach with Gus. We don't want you to leave our sight until this whole thing is cleared up. Or at least until Hypo is caught."

"But I feel perfectly safe—"

The nun fixed her gray eyes on Laura. "This isn't a negotiable point. Cecile," she continued, "Laura and I've been in Louisiana long enough; it's time for us to learn *bourrée*."

Cecile dealt out five cards apiece and turned over her last one as trump. Discarding low cards and nontrumps, they built hands to take tricks, trying to take at least one each hand so they wouldn't *bourrée* and have to match the pot. At noon they turned on the television and watched stories on Eastern Europe, the New Orleans sewers, and the devastation Hurricane Dinah had left in Florida. Not a word was said about Meacham's press conference.

At two o'clock they closed the cabin and drove up the bayou to St. Lô, where Sister Elizabeth directed them to a two-story house across from the church. The nun led them inside the convent and dropped her overnight bag in the front hall. Sorting through mail on the table, she said, "Oh, good. Sister Grace left a note." She read it and handed it to Cecile. Laura instantly positioned herself to read over Cecile's shoulder: "Sister E, a man from the Comptroller of Currency wants you to meet him at the bank."

"It's the bank examiner," said the nun. "I'll go down there now if you two will turn on the TV."

"Sister, may I use the phone?" asked Laura.

The nun smiled sympathetically. "Of course. It's back in the office."

"Give him my love, dear," said Cecile.

Laura called Theo's house and listened to the phone ring twelve times. Sister Elizabeth slipped out quietly and Cecile pulled out a deck of cards, coaxing Laura into a game of gin. They played in the living room while monitoring the TV. At three-thirty the news team blond from a Baton Rouge station interrupted the soap opera commercials to say that the body of the Redemption Parish sheriff was being autopsied in Baton Rouge and that T-Harry Meachan would be appearing live at six.

At four-thirty two nuns—Sister Grace and Sister Claire—came in from their jobs at the mental health clinic in town and started dinner. Sister Grace was a bouncy little woman with ears that stuck out through her short gray curls. Sister Claire was a somber thirty-year-old who looked as if she was in perpetual turmoil about her spiritual journey. Laura went back to the kitchen to help peel shrimp for dinner and when the phone rang, Sister Grace darted out to answer it.

"It's for you, Laura," Grace called.

Laura dropped shrimp into the bowl. "Finally!" Dashing into the office, she picked up the receiver. "Theo, where are you?"

"Hello, Laura? This is Hypo Hebert. I'm sorry about last night. I wasn't really going to hurt you."

"Hypo."

"Listen, I want to make a deal with Theophile. I know a whole lot about a certain politician, and I want to talk to Theophile, or somebody, fast. Tell him I can make a tape for him if he'll meet me with a cassette recorder in a place I choose and I don't want—"

"Theo's not here."

Cecile came into the office and stood quietly by the phone. Laura said, "Just a minute, Hypo." She put a hand over the receiver. "Cecile, it's Hypo. What do I do?"

Cecile turned up her palms and shrugged.

"Hello, Hypo? We think you should turn yourself in to the police."

Hypo muttered an obscenity and hung up.

After the call Laura paced the floor until Sister Elizabeth came in shortly before six o'clock.

"What happened at the bank?" asked Cecile.

The nun's cheeks were flushed and she waved a thick document. "Nothing yet with the bank examiner but I convinced Tina Savoie to let me look at Gus's files. I think I might have found something we'd all like to read."

Elizabeth handed the document to Laura and walked into the living room. "Take a look while I warm up the TV."

"What is this?" Laura asked, scanning the Xeroxed pages.

"An incorporation agreement for Armelise."

Laura riffled pages. "Isn't that what they're looking up in Baton Rouge?"

"Those will be articles of incorporation. We'll need them to find out who the principals are, but what you have in your hand should be full of interesting particulars."

A TV commercial blared in the living room and all five women gathered around the set. The Baton Rouge station flashed its blue-and-red logo, announcing that regular programming was being preempted for a live press conference.

Next the station's token blond came on. She said that former Governor T-Harry Meacham was at the Fairfax Hotel and they would go live to him immediately. Laura found herself staring at an obscenely handsome young aide who waited patiently for his cue behind a decorated rostrum as the twenty-odd reporters in the audience talked shop. Half a second later the aide turned on and sincerely welcomed everyone, announcing that "the governor" was very grateful the press had taken time to attend on such short notice.

Glancing at his notes, he explained that "the governor" had some new information on a case that was tearing at the very fabric of southern Louisiana and he wanted to share it with the people who deserved to know. The aide looked off to the side and the cameras followed, focusing on a distinguished-looking T-Harry Meacham, somehow mysteriously taller than the people around him.

Meacham strode out into the light, smiling distractedly, as if weighed with a serious matter. He was groomed to perfection, his rolled shirt collar framing his face as if it had grown there. He wore a razor-sharp navy blazer, and his red paisley tie hung on his chest like an advertisement for Italian silk. On camera he looked much younger than his sixty years.

Cecile sat down on the cushions. "I can't wait. What do you think he's going to say, Laura?"

Before Laura had a chance to reply Meacham cleared his throat and methodically arranged papers on the rostrum. "Thank you all for coming. I wish that this occasion were a happier one, but unfortunately the subject involves a tragedy concerning close personal friends of mine. I wish to give y'all as much information as I have at this time so the people of Louisiana can judge for themselves the events that will soon be coming to light."

He took one step back and touched his heavy tie as if it were a talisman. "By now many of you have already heard about the lamentable death of my good friend Sheriff Boo Guidry of Redemption Parish. Boo was found Wednesday morning on a cane field road, ostensibly the victim of a hit-and-run accident. This matter came to my attention while I was in Redemption Parish on business and, after inquiring into the circumstances, I did not feel Boo Guidry's death was as clear-cut as it first appeared. It was for that reason I asked for further investigation by the Louisiana State Patrol."

"You did not," said Laura. Cecile hushed her.

Raising his earnest brow, Meacham looked candidly into the eye of the camera. "Because I am close personal friends with many of the good people of Redemption and because the budget of the parish could not accommodate the expense of an investigation, my office, working in conjunction with our state patrol, agreed to have Sheriff Guidry's body transported up to Baton Rouge for autopsy."

"You lie!" The color flared in Laura's cheeks.

Meacham dipped his head slightly. "Happily, Louisiana has some of the finest medical professionals in the country. The East Baton Rouge Pathology Laboratory has been most cooperative in this case and, because of a collaborative effort of its three pathologists, they have completed a very extensive workup in a very short time on the deceased's remains." He opened a manila envelope and pulled out a multipage document.

"It is only within the last hour that the good doctors have given us autopsy results and these are—as they are explained to me by the professionals—most revealing."

Meacham folded back the first page of the document theatrically. "Dr. Wayne Mauvis and his staff have detailed for us two interesting findings on the sheriff's body. The first is that the blood alcohol reading of the deceased was .15, substantially higher than what is considered legally drunk—even in Louisiana." The press tittered. "And secondly, a fluid sample—I will try to get this straight—taken from the vitreous humor of Sheriff Guidry's *eye* showed a—and I quote—'a nine-milligram-per-deciliter concentration of potassium chloride.' "

Putting the document on the rostrum, Meacham again stroked his tie. "Because this finding meant very little to me as a layperson, Dr. Mauvis kindly explained that potassium chloride is an emergency room drug used to restore regular heartbeat. In large doses, however, such as the amount found in the body of Sheriff Guidry, it will cause instant death." Meacham looked at the pages. "The doctor reports: 'Death was caused by cardiac arrest secondary to the heart stopping.'

"Some of you may be asking, as I did, how the sheriff received such a large dose of potassium chloride. Dr. Mauvis explains that the only way to deliver that much potassium chloride quickly is with a hypodermic. He suggests that *somebody* with a professional knowledge of the pharmacopeia obtained the potassium from a legitimate source and used it to inject Sheriff Guidry. Again, you may be asking: Who in Redemption Parish would have—"

The commotion at the back of the press room was ignored at first. Then a loud noise rang out—like the dropping of heavy books—and Meacham's handsome face contorted with pain. The camera quickly panned to the back of the room to show the blurred image of a lanky balding man—three peninsulas of receding hair jutting down onto a smooth white forehead. Men in suits wrestled him to the ground and twisted a handgun from his grasp. The room was in chaos.

"It's Hypo!" screamed Laura.

"It couldn't be!" Cecile leaped up to look closer.

The camera flashed again to the rostrum. Meacham had fallen back and was supported by aides. Then the camera panned quickly to the men pressing the gunman to the floor.

"I can't see him!" cried Laura.

Abruptly the video was cut and for a few seconds they heard only confused shouting. The station logo came on and a buttery baritone announced that they would be returning to regular programming. The next sound was "Girl from Ipanema" in Muzak. The five women stared in horror at the screen.

"What happened?" Grace cried.

"Hypo shot the governor." Laura's words sounded hollow in her ears.

From the back of the house came a low beeping noise. "The fax," said Elizabeth. They rushed to the office, where a printer dutifully extruded pages.

Standing over the machine, they watched curling pages being squeezed out like pasta. The pile of paper grew higher and higher. "Long," said Laura, and the pages just kept coming.

Finally the printer left them with forty slick pages of legal fine print. Picking them up to tap into a pile, Sister Elizabeth said, "Why don't you all sit down and eat. I can read through this."

"I should help," said Laura. "At least let me read through the one you brought home from the bank."

Elizabeth hugged the document to her chest. "I hate to admit this, but I've had quite a lot of experience reading legalese. I'll do the articles of incorporation first and that will make the incorporation agreement much easier. Why not go eat, dear? You can monitor the radio."

"If you insist," Laura said.

"I do. And turn on the radio while you eat so you can find out what happened to Meacham." Sister Elizabeth sat down on the desk chair, back erect, and began reading with a pencil in her hand. Laura closed the door and followed her nose to the fragrant shrimp in the kitchen. Already the radio was broadcasting an onscene account of Meacham's shooting. He was still alive and was being transported to Our Lady of the Lake Medical Center.

After dinner Laura peeked in on Sister Elizabeth so often that Cecile grabbed Laura's arm and brought her to the kitchen table. "Let's see if we can win some money off the nuns."

Dragooning Sister Grace into a gin game, they played until eight o'clock, when Sister Elizabeth came in, fatigue wells under her eyes. "How's Meacham?" she asked.

"They're saying shoulder injury." Cecile watched Sister Grace modestly lay down yet another winning hand. "Just serious enough for the sympathy vote. I bet you money he runs in the next election."

"Sister E, what do the agreements say?" asked Laura.

The nun smiled weakly. "Sorry. Only half finished." She turned on the kettle for tea. "But I think we're getting to the bottom of this." Silently she made tea and went back into the office.

At nine o'clock Sister Grace scraped her generous winnings off the table and pleaded early bedtime. Dealing for two, Cecile said, "They've opened a bedroom for us, Laura. Elizabeth wants us to sleep here tonight."

"How will Theo find me?"

"You don't know much about small towns, do you?"

At ten o'clock Elizabeth came in and Laura jumped up. "Well?"

The nun dropped wearily into a chair at the kitchen table.

"Sit, Laura. You'll be very interested in these. They go a long way toward explaining the extraordinary event we saw on television this evening."

"Really?"

Riffling through pages in the faxed document, the nun began, "It seems that Armelise Land Company is a corporation designed to garner contracts from the state to 'provide improvements and accessibility' to state and national parklands. Furthermore, Armelise contracts itself out to do 'auxiliary logging necessary for the enhancement and improvement of sites.' I can imagine that's quite lucrative." She checked her notes and turned two more pages. "But the most interesting part, as far as I'm concerned, are the parties who have shares in Armelise."

"Who?"

Folding back the page, the nun pointed to an indented list. Laura read: " 'Augustin Talbot, two hundred shares; Harry L. Meacham, two hundred shares; Valmont Talbot,' Oh no, '*four* hundred shares; and Hippolyte Herbert, two hundred shares.' Hippolyte Herbert? Hypo?"

"Yes, dear." said Cecile.

Laura sat with her mouth open. "But why would Hypo try to shoot one of his partners?"

"Because Meacham betrayed him. The press conference this evening was designed to distance Meacham from Hypo after Meacham knew the autopsy would be done. They both knew an autopsy would implicate Hypo."

"But I don't understand. Why does Meacham even care? Wait a minute. Do you think *Meacham* helped Hypo murder Boo?"

"That's an interesting question. If he did, I'm sure it wouldn't be in any way that could be proven. Did you hear what Meacham said about the method used? A professional with knowledge of the pharmacopeia."

Cecile added, "Don't worry. Meacham's too smart to get his pretty face involved in a murder. But I imagine he certainly didn't take any pains to stop Hypo. Especially if he thought Hypo could get away with it."

"He almost did." Laura nodded. "I see now. Meacham held his press conference to run damage control when it became public knowledge that his partner killed a sheriff. This is great. I wonder how Gus, Meacham, and Theo's father are going to like having Hypo as a business partner now?"

The nun straightened her shoulders and picked up the document. "Actually, there's a very interesting clause in the articles here that makes more sense now that you ask it that way. I noticed it because it's not something one usually finds in these kinds of contracts. Ah, yes. Here it is:

" 'In the event that any of the heretofore named parties is found guilty of a felony which brings disrepute in any manner upon the integrity, assets, or operation of the corporation, unless the court finds the defendant in any such action to be criminally insane sufficient to constitute an affirmative defense, that party shall forfeit all rights under the terms of this Agreement, including specifically the right to any compensation from the proceeds of the Enterprise. Furthermore, the Corporation shall be entitled to purchase the shares owned by such convicted felon at par, the sum of twenty dollars per share.' "

"You'll have to read it again," said Laura. "I didn't understand."

"What it says is that Gus, Meacham, and Valmont can buy Hypo's shares if he's convicted of a felony, which at this point seems likely, don't you think?"

"Wow. How sneaky! Poor Hypo. I wonder if he even knew what he was signing?"

"In my mind the interesting question is, What part did those men have in planning Boo's death if they were clairvoyant enough to include a clause like this in the first place?"

Cecile shook her head. "Hypo never had a chance against those three, did he?"

Laura sighed. "Theo's going to be so upset about his father being the biggest shareholder. Well, at least we know that if Hypo set off the pipe bomb at the mill, Valmont is safe now."

"No," said the nun. "I don't think so. There was another clause some place that seems very applicable." She pressed her lips together and scanned the pages. "Yes. Here it is:

" 'Upon the death of a shareholder in said corporation, any or all remaining shareholders shall have the right of first refusal to purchase, buy, or redeem from the estate of the deceased any portion up to one hundred percent of aforementioned shareholder's corporate shares.' "

"That sounds reasonable to me," said Laura.

The nun put the document down and folded her hands on top of it. "Yes, it does. But if you take the two clauses I read together, it's easy to foresee a situation in which Valmont, Gus, and Meacham buy out Hypo—the felon— only to have Valmont die"—she raised her eyebrows— "*unexpectedly* and have the two remaining men buy *his* shares." She squared the document on the table. "And given the nastiness we've already seen connected with this little piece of cleared swamp, I would say the prognosis for Valmont's health is still not very good."

CHAPTER 16

SATURDAY MORNING

The caller rang again, and knocked. Laura padded down the convent stairs in her nightshirt and spied Gus through the glass. As she swung open the door, he glanced at the UCLA bruin on her chest and modestly looked away. "Good morning, gal. May I come in?"

Laura moved aside and he said, "I heard y'all slept over here last night."

"Sister E thought it would be safer."

Gus looked around the foyer. "Where're the others?"

"Cecile and Sister Elizabeth went downtown."

"Did they?" He smacked his belly and said, "Well, how about some of that coffee I smell?"

Laura led him back to the kitchen, where the Mr. Coffee light was on. Searching cabinets for mugs, she poured

Gus a cup and made coffeemilk for herself in the microwave.

Gus sipped from the mug and made a face. "Damned Yankee coffee." He dumped in two spoons of sugar and stirred, watching Laura punch buttons on the microwave. "I don't suppose you've seen that shoe box this morning, have you, gal?"

Laura watched the cup revolve inside the microwave. "I haven't even thought about it since yesterday."

"You know, after you told me about Theophile's running off with Sally, I was thinking, and realized that nobody here probably has the heart to break it to you."

Casually Laura said, "Break what?"

"Well, I would say there's a ninety-nine-percent chance that Theophile won't be coming back. He and Sally, they've always been very close. They even planned to get married at one time."

"I know. Theo told me."

"Well, you can be sure the boy glossed over the particulars. In any case, there's not much left for you to do here. I came over to say that if you wanted a ride up to the airport, I'd be glad to provide."

Laura glared. "We read the Armelise incorporation papers last night, Gus. We know all about you and Meacham. Everything was so transparent, all we could think about was when Theo's father would get bumped off for good."

"You what?" Gus raised his pudgy hands and shook his head in bafflement. "Where did—? How could y'all get things so entirely turned around? Laura, T-Harry and I are working very hard to make an honest go of that land company. As for Valmont, he is very soon going to be in the best position he's been in for a long time. Yesterday I started legal proceedings to take power of attorney for him. Once we get that in place, Valmont will be safe from everything except his own sick mind."

"Theo's the one who should have something to say about that."

"Theo," Gus said pointedly, "is not here."

Laura bit her lip. "We know about the clause where

you can buy each other's stock if somebody commits a felony. The only thing we couldn't figure out is whether you just goaded Hypo into killing Boo or whether you actually helped him."

Gus shook his head again. "You poor girl. It's starting to look like boogey men are all over the place, isn't it? Miss Laura, one of the reasons we inserted that clause in our contract is because we knew that Hypo was a very hot-headed individual and we hoped it might tend to bring him under control. Personally I have never believed in violence and I will not have any dealings with anyone who does. In my opinion, there's not a conflict in the world that can't be negotiated peacefully."

Laura's hands shook as she took her coffeemilk from the microwave. "I don't believe you for a minute. My only consolation is that your ridiculous construction site is almost worthless."

Gus laughed softly and his big belly shook. "Oh, you are a pistol, aren't you? I tell you what: if you will go out and get something from my car for me, I'll show you why everyone's making such a big deal out of our little project. Go look under the seat and you'll find a blue-covered booklet from the Corps of Engineers."

"I'm not dressed."

"Well, go put some clothes on."

Laura dashed upstairs and pulled on Bermudas, into which she tucked her nightshirt. Out on the street she groped around under Gus's car seat and pulled out the blue booklet. On the cover were the twin crenellated towers of the Army Corps of Engineers. The title read: "Displacement Proposal #3, Mississippi-Atchafalaya Drainage Basin." Laura flipped pages and found it plentifully supplied with charts, hydraulic tables, and graphs. Immense amounts of water were being talked about, all measured in kilotons per second. Walking back to the convent kitchen, she laid the booklet on the table. "What's it about?"

Gus pulled it toward him. "This is about a problem we have here with the Mississippi. Have you ever seen the river from the air?"

"Some of it."

"Did you notice all those big loopy bends and bows? Winds around like a snake, doesn't it? Well, those bends and bows mean the river's old and it's looking for a new bed. The Atchafalaya, on the other hand, is brand spanking new, as those things go, one hundred forty-five miles shorter than the Mississippi from the same place at Simmesport. The river knows that, and the Corps of Engineers knows that. The Corps also knows that either we can wait for nature to move the river or they can do it themselves." He pushed the booklet over. "This report addresses itself to that. It's in two parts, a feasibility study about dismantling the control structure at Simmesport and a suggested schedule for the diversion of flow into the Atchafalaya."

"You mean they're actually going to reroute the entire river?"

"Well, not all of it. The most desirable objective, especially to folks upriver, is to turn the Atchafalaya into the main shipping channel. But they'll be sure to leave plenty of water for New Orleans and Baton Rouge."

"Nobody's going to let you do that!"

"On the contrary. In the long run it will happen whether the human race wants it or not. And I don't know about you, but I'd much rather have an orderly transition by the Corps than get stuck with the horribly messy way Mother Nature handles those things."

Laura crossed her arms. "And you and T-Harry Meacham will already own frontage, won't you?"

"I should say we will. Not only the parcel you've seen, but if things work out, we'll have all kinds of parcels up and down the basin. If we play this right, both T-Harry and I will go into retirement riding some of the most valuable industrial real estate in the world." Gus sipped his coffee.

Footsteps sounded in the front hall and Laura looked out to see Quatorze, Cecile, Sister Elizabeth, and an unknown man in a yellow shirt and tie. At the same moment two uniformed deputies mounted the kitchen stairs and came inside. Looking apologetically at Gus, they stood in the corner, arms by their sides.

Gus was baffled. "Brew? Andy? What are you doing on *this* side of the parish?" Neither answered.

The group from the front of the house walked noisily to the kitchen. As Quatorze entered, he too looked sheepishly at Gus and positioned himself by the hallway door.

Sister Elizabeth scanned the people in the room and her face became suddenly grave. Introducing the stranger, she said to Gus, "Mr. Talbot, I'd like you to meet Mr. Tiny Breaux, from the state Comptroller of Currency." Tiny was a big man with a pocket protector for pens and the only tie Laura had seen so far in Redemption Parish. He put out a hand to Gus. "Actually," he said, "I'm not from the state; I work out of Donaldsonville."

Gus stood up and shook hands cautiously. "Foots Thibault runs your office, doesn't he?"

"I replaced Foots six months ago."

"I see."

Quatorze reached into his back uniform pocket and unfolded papers. "Gus, you know I don't want to do this, but I got a warrant for your arrest. Four counts of grand larceny, seven counts of petty larceny, and twelve counts of forgery."

Gus opened his mouth like a fish on dry land. "But that's not so. Larceny is stealing; I would never steal."

Cecile snapped, "Stop it, Gus. You've been stealing from me for the last two years. Mr. Breaux tracked it all down. Stealing my money, I don't mind so much. If you needed it, I'd have been glad to give it to you. The part I *do* mind is that you forged Elizabeth's name. "What did you think? You could send her to jail? Gus, she's a *nun!*"

Gus's eyes watered. "I want to make a phone call. My lawyer is T-Harry Meacham."

Tiny Breaux touched his pens and cleared his throat. "Actually, Mr. Talbot, I don't think I'd do that if I were you. About a month ago somebody called our office and said that a party at your bank was improperly channeling funds for land development projects, and we're fairly certain that call came from Governor Meacham's law office. We didn't act on it because we don't have time to track down every little rumor we hear." He gestured to the nun.

"But when Sister here called Thursday, we thought: 'That's one time too many.' "

Gus sank into a chair, his eyes as empty as a lot back of town. Quatorze took a plastic Miranda card from his breast pocket and read: "You have the right to remain silent and do not have to say anything at all. Anything you say can and will be used against you in a court of law. You have the right to talk to a lawyer . . ."

SUNDAY AFTERNOON

Laura brought her bags down the carpeted front stairs and shoved them into a corner with her foot. From the back of the house Dorothy came out tying on an apron and smiling kindly.

"I thought Mr. Quatorze isn't taking you up to the airport 'til four o'clock."

"He's not, but Father LeBlanc asked Cecile and me over for coffee at two and I wanted to be packed before we left." Laura looked at her watch. "Cecile was supposed to be back from her Sunday dinner to pick me up by now."

"She meet a friend at church?"

"A cousin, I think. They invited me too, but I think they really just wanted to talk by themselves."

"I'm sorry I didn't have no Sunday dinner for you. I just got back from picking up my car in Baton Rouge. Theophile left it at that laboratory *all* a mess."

"Figures. When he screws up, he really does it in spades, doesn't he?"

Dorothy looked at Laura with kind eyes. "Sorry about what he did to *you*. I think you much better for him than Ms. Sally, but you can't tell men nothing."

Laura rolled her eyes. "Don't you know it."

The housekeeper flashed her teeth, showing two cuspids that didn't quite meet the gumline. "Had me thinking about the Christmas he came in from helping Ms. Sally when Mr. Boo beat on her. He was so jangled, he drove the old station wagon right into the back wall of the garage."

"When was that?"

"He didn't tell you 'bout that?"

Laura shook her head.

"Maybe he don't want you to know."

"It doesn't matter now. I'll never speak to him again anyway."

Dorothy laughed slyly. "Okay. See, Mr. Boo used to beat up on Ms. Sally when they first got married. Sometimes it got so bad, she'd run outside and hide in the cane. Reba and me, we'd be looking out the window, we didn't know what to do. Well, Christmas she was pregnant with Gumby, Theophile's home, and when Boo got to beating up on her, Ms. Sally called Theophile, he came out and beat the huss out of Mr. Boo." She shrugged. "Least that's what I *think* he did. After that we never heard nothing over there. 'Cept maybe Gumby crying."

"I didn't know that."

"Yeah." Dorothy scratched the scaly skin of her elbow. "Theophile be real nice when he's trying."

Tires sounded on the crushed shell drive and Laura looked out to see Cecile's Mercury. The horn sounded and Laura glanced back at Dorothy. "Will you be here when I get back? I want to say good-bye."

Dorothy flashed her million-dollar smile. "Sure. You have a nice time at the priest's."

"Thank you." Laura ran out to the car and climbed in. After profuse apologies for being late, Cecile drove over to the rectory, raving about the precocious grandchildren of her second cousin, Mimmie, who was also an old high school friend.

At the rectory Father LeBlanc graciously settled them into the old armchairs in the living room and waited while the housekeeper set a tea tray on the table. "Cecile," said the priest, "I want you to know you're being honored. Those are Mrs. Gaudet's grasshopper cookies there on the tray."

"Are they?" Cecile slid forward, reaching for the plate. "I never get to buy these at bazaars. You're always sold out, Mrs. Gaudet." The housekeeper smiled and disappeared.

Father LeBlanc poured coffee into a demitasse and

handed it to Cecile. Turning to Laura, he asked, "Coffee, Laura?"

"Yes, please." Following Cecile's lead, Laura popped a chocolate-and-green layered confection into her mouth and, as the mint layer melted on her tongue, calculated how many more she could eat politely.

Cecile stirred her demitasse and looked at the worn patterned carpets and the dreary bookcases of Inspirational Literature that had not been taken down in at least twenty years. "Father, that was nice this morning at Mass, the way you asked everyone to pray for Gus."

"Nice, nothing. I just didn't want everybody out front afterward cutting that poor man to the ground. You got to figure that's all they've been talking about since he was arrested yesterday."

"I'm afraid I would have been the worst," said Cecile tartly. "Laura, there was no message from Theophile when you got back to the house?"

"No, ma'am."

"You would think he'd at least have the decency to call you. Men can be such cowards sometimes."

"I thought I would write him a note before I left this afternoon, just in case he did come back."

"What time are you leaving, dear?"

"Quatorze is taking me up to the airport at four."

Cecile sipped coffee. "Did you hear what Theophile did to Dorothy's car yesterday?"

"Dorothy said he left it a mess at the pathology lab."

"I'll say. My cousin has a nephew on the Baton Rouge police and he told her they found it abandoned at the pathology lab. By the time poor Dorothy got up there to claim it, someone had stolen the battery. She spent last night in Baton Rouge and had to borrow money for a new battery."

Laura reached for a cookie and came back with two. "I'd be furious. Theo ought to pay for the new battery."

Cecile shook her head philosophically and reached for a cookie. "Sometimes I think the Talbot men all have rocks for brains."

The priest sipped his demitasse, watching the chocolate

delicacies disappear from the plate. "I haven't had time to see the *Picayune* today. How is Meacham's shoulder?"

Cecile swallowed. "I saw him on the news last night leaving the hospital. He had on this body cast and was smiling like the Cheshire cat. You know what he said to the press? It was scandalous. He said: 'And to think, I don't even *know* Dr. Hebert's wife.' They were just eating it up."

"Will we ever learn?" muttered the priest.

Laura reached for another cookie. "Did they say anything about Hypo on the news?"

"Only that he's being held for both attempted murder and suspicion of murder, the first being for Meacham and the second for Boo, I assume." Cecile put the delicate coffee cup to her lips. "It all seems so stupid. I don't even understand why he thought he had to kill Boo in the first place."

Laura wiped chocolate from her mouth with a napkin. "All I can put together is that the whole bunch of them must have given Boo a shoe box of money for some reason and then Hypo, or maybe all of them, wanted the money back. No, wait, I know: Boo must have asked them for even *more* money—the million dollars—and that's when they decided they had to kill him."

"Why would they give Boo money to begin with? If you want police protection in this parish, it's your legal right."

The priest covered the tiny cup with his hand. "Cecile, usually you give the sheriff money to get him to look the other way."

"For what reason?"

"Maybe to plant a pipe bomb on your partner?"

"Oh." Cecile's forehead furrowed. "But I can't imagine Gus tiptoeing up the sugar house stairs. Or Meacham, for that matter."

Sadly Father LeBlanc said, "I can plenty imagine Hypo." He looked out the window at the bright umbrellas of okra in the garden. Sighing deeply, he readjusted himself in the chair. "And poor Valmont. If Gus gets convicted on those larceny charges, that makes Valmont the sole surviving partner of T-Harry Meacham. How long you think he's going to last with Meacham? That's like swimming with the sharks, that is."

Cecile raised her chin. "And the problem is nobody will mourn Valmont's passing."

Laura's voice caught in her throat. "Theo will."

Cecile reached over to pat her hand. "You poor dear. I'm *so* sorry he's left you like this. I expected much better of the boy."

"Will you send me clippings, Cecile, about the trial and everything? I'd love to find out if Hypo implicates Meacham and Gus in Boo's death."

Cecile snorted. "Don't hold your breath expecting anything to stick to T-Harry Meacham. He's a lawyer and when he was governor, the only thing we really learned about him was that he never left a trail on himself when he committed crimes. All kinds of people tried to get him in front of a grand jury and nobody could make *anything* stick. That man's turned felony into an art form. When he dies, his epitaph ought to read," she blocked out letters in the air, " ' 'He raised unindictability to new heights.' ' "

"Not in my cemetery," said the priest.

Cecile brushed crumbs off her lap and put her demitasse on the high table. "Father, today at lunch Mimmie told me that Mr. Phil was in the hospital. He was Bronier's old foreman and I really should go visit. How do you feel about riding out there with an old lady?"

The priest too put his cup on the tray. "I don't ride with old ladies, but I'd love to ride with you. Could we stop by the nursing home first?"

"Certainly. Laura, can we give you a lift back to the Talbots'?"

"No, thanks. I think I'd like to walk." Laura reached for a last cookie.

"She still hasn't learned." Cecile pulled her purse to her side. "Are you *sure* you don't want a ride in the air-conditioning? Sunday afternoon is always the hottest time of the week."

"No, thank you, really."

"If you get heat stroke, dear, don't say you weren't warned."

The priest stood and called to the back of the house. "Mrs. Gaudet? I'm going to the nursing home with Cecile. Thank you for the coffee."

"Thank you, Mrs. Gaudet," called Cecile.

"Yes, ma'am," came the reply from the kitchen.

All three walked down the front porch steps and paused at the bottom. Extending a hand, Laura said, "Father LeBlanc, thank you for everything. It was very nice meeting you." She turned to Cecile. "I guess I'll see you back at the house before I leave."

"I'll hurry."

Putting on her visor, Laura watched the priest and Cecile walk to the silver Mercury out past the vegetable garden. As the priest scooped his cassock in and closed the passenger door, Laura turned to walk down the fissured concrete path to the cemetery. Opening the gate, she entered the silent white domain.

Sharp shadows lay in black triangles on the brilliant tombs while in the spaces between, crushed shells gleamed as bright as sunshine. A chiseled Virgin radiated mossy grace from her fingertips and a Paschal Lamb collected algae. Once again Laura read the friezes: Landry, Folse, Naquin, Arsenault. Turning at the main intersection, she paddled down the walk to see the Talbot mausoleum one last time. She approached the granite tomb and spied a dirty piece of pink paper under the door. Picking it up, she read:

FATHER LEBLANC FOUND BOO'S BODY. WHERE THE HELL ARE YOU?

The note had been poked out from inside.

"Theo!"

She pushed on the door. "Theo!" Banging with her fists, she yelled, "Theo, don't worry. I'll get you out." She leaned her weight against the door and shoved. It didn't budge. "Theo," she sobbed, "I'll be right back."

Down the baking sidewalks she ran as fast as the beating sun would allow. Instantly she broke into a sweat, the heat demanding that she stop. Ignoring the warning, she sucked in air and stretched out her stride, making a beeline for the rectory.

Reaching the house, she ran around the corner to see the Mercury down the street at a stop sign. Two women on the sidewalk were carrying on an animated conversation with Father LeBlanc through the open window.

"Father!" Laura cried.

The women said good-bye and the car pulled away.

"Stop!" yelled Laura. She ran down the middle of the street, melted tar sticking to her shoes.

The Mercury pulled up to the end of the next block and stopped again as Cecile looked down all three sides of the intersection.

"Cecile!" screamed Laura. "Stop!"

The car started up and Laura let out an ear-piercing scream. The Mercury jerked to halt in the middle of the intersection.

Running down the tarry street, Laura ignored the two women gaping at her on the corner. Bits of gravel stuck to her soles, digging into the balls of her feet. She approached the driver's side and the dark window of the silvery car hummed down. Cecile looked out in bafflement.

Shoving the pink paper in Cecile's face, Laura said, "Theo's in the mausoleum. He put this under the door."

"But that can't be."

Laura rattled the dirty paper. "This is a note we got Thursday. He must have put it in his pocket."

Cecile stared. "Get in."

Laura climbed in back and Cecile turned the Detroit boat around in a driveway. As they reached the churchyard, Father LeBlanc barked, "Pull around front. We need the key." He grabbed the dashboard with white fingers. "But it's going to be gone. You watch."

As Cecile slowed to park in front of the church, the priest said, "Don't stop. Drive right up on the sidewalk."

Without hesitation Cecile bumped onto the wide walkway and drove all the way to the church doors.

Father LeBlanc got out. "This way."

The women followed his furious pace, Cecile clipping along behind in patent pumps. Pushing open the heavy wooden doors, they dashed into the chilled church and jogged down the aisle to the vestry. Opening a flat wooden cabinet on the wall, Father LeBlanc ran his finger across the hooks. "I knew it."

Cecile ran breathless into the room. "It's in the St. Jude section, Father."

"The keys are gone, Cecile, both of them. Go get Manny Préjean. Tell him to bring his tools."

As Cecile rushed off to the house, Laura ran with the priest outside, dashing full speed down the cemetery sidewalks. The lifeless tombs radiated heat like a wood stove and the air was heavy with the smell of stagnant vase water. The priest ran down the blocks so fast that Laura lost him at the Wailing Women under the crucifix. As she stared at their anguished stone faces, she called, "Father?"

"Back here."

She found him kneeling down by the crack under the door of the Talbot tomb. "Theophile, are you there?" he called.

Laura ran up and joined the priest. "He's there. I promise." She lay down on the hot step and tried to peer under the door. "Theo," she called, "we're getting a man to let you out. Hold on." The step was so hot, she stood up again.

Twenty interminable minutes went by and finally Cecile's car appeared at the side gate. Out of the passenger side slowly climbed a man in a Sunday shirt and pants, carrying a battered red toolbox.

"Manny, over here," shouted the priest.

The locksmith called across the tombs. "I wish you coulda told me what kind it was." He reached the Talbots' mausoleum and eyed the tumbler lock. "Good." His toolbox clattered on the step. "I don't have to make a key." Pulling out a tiny leather kit from his pocket, he inserted a featherweight tension wrench into the tumblers with his left hand and probed with a lock pick in his right. "How long's he been in here?"

Laura sat on the step across the walk and swatted gnats. "I don't know. I *do* know he was in Baton Rouge Friday morning."

Troubled, Manny looked at the priest. "Honey," he said to Laura. "This is Sunday."

An ambulance pulled up behind Cecile's Mercury, crimson light spiraling, and neighbors from across the street came out from their dinners. Quatorze arrived in a squad car and in a few minutes the cemetery was buzzing with people. The paramedics listened to the static on their radios and neighbors took turns holding a golf umbrella over Manny.

Ignoring the hubbub, Manny Préjean worked with his eyes closed, leaning against the polished granite. Laura sat in the shadow of a tomb, watching the subtle movements of the locksmith's arm as he teased the hidden springs. Father LeBlanc came over and sat beside her, offering a cup of water. "Miss Laura, I want to tell you, Theophile's been in there a long time. You hear what I'm saying?"

"I know."

"All I'm saying is, don't be getting your hopes up."

"I know."

They watched the muscles of Manny's back relax and flex as he worked the unseen lock pins. Refusing an offer of water, he held his tongue between his lips, biting in concentration. He struggled a few more minutes, when all of a sudden his face relaxed and he pulled away from the door. "There you go." He pushed the door in half an inch and stepped back for the paramedics.

"Theo!" Laura jumped up and the priest caught her by the shoulders.

A paramedic pushed on the door and met resistance. "Theophile," he called. "Move away from the door." He waited a moment and pushed again. "He's still there," he said to his colleague.

"He's dead," whispered a neighbor.

Laura walked over, dragging the priest with her. "Theo, move away from that door."

With no other solution in sight, the paramedics pushed the door slowly open, exposing brown skulls and rotting boards to the light. Gingerly, one of them stepped inside and at that moment an arm fell out from behind the door. Laura screamed.

The paramedic disappeared in the blackness and seconds later came out, pulling Theo across the polished stone. Laura dashed over as they slid him onto a gurney. Into his ear she called, "Theo, I'm right here."

A low moan rose from his throat.

CHAPTER 17

The ceiling fan circled slowly as Laura offered yet another glass of water. Shaking his head, Theo ripped off the bandage covering the IV punctures on the back of his hand.

"Theo, they said to keep drinking."

He balled up the bandages and dropped them on the coffee table. "Laura, if you don't cut it out, I'll make you come with me to the toilet next time and watch."

Father LeBlanc finished his yam-pecan cake. "That was almost as good as the cake Camille used to make." He put his plate on the coffee table. "Theophile, you remember your mother's spice cake?"

"Vaguely."

"Umm. Nothing vague about it."

Cecile pulled the twisted wool of her crewelwork into the air with a cocked wrist. "I'd offer you more but there's just enough left for Quatorze and Tutoo. We *are* still waiting for them, aren't we?"

"Yes." Theo looked at his watch and rearranged his feet on the couch. "I hope they're not getting too much flak at the post office. I should have addressed the package to Tutoo instead of you, Laura."

The priest wiped his mouth and sat back in his chair. "Theophile, they don't gossip enough at the hospital. All I heard was that you were extremely dehydrated and had a mild concussion. I assume that means you were hit over the head."

Theo rubbed his hair. "I feel like such a pud."

"How'd you let that happen?"

"Friday morning Sally was driving me around trying to track down where the shoe box came from. After we found the store and put the box in the mail, she dropped me off back at the lab. I walked across the lot and saw the hood of Dorothy's Pinto was up. When I looked in, the battery was gone, and whonk, right on the back of the head. I had no idea where I was when I woke up. I thought maybe I was dead, it was so black."

"Only sleeping with them," murmured the priest.

"After I realized I was alive, I thought I must be locked up in Baton Rouge somewhere. Then I felt around and realized it was my brother Claiborne beside me. I think I must have messed him up pretty bad. I felt some bones break."

Laura cringed. "Theo, that gives me the creeps."

"Yeah. He was a pretty creepy kid sometimes."

"Did you see who hit you?"

"No. But they had to be Meacham's flunkies, don't you think? After the shoe box."

"Cecile," said Laura, "you were right about Meacham and his unindictability. There's not a way in the world to prove he had anything to do with trying to kill Theo."

Theo picked up the water glass and sipped. "That doesn't concern me right now. The only two things I care about are Boo's homicide and keeping my daddy alive.

The autopsy took care of the first and I'm hoping Laura's package will take care of the second."

"I know the autopsy was pretty damning, but will the DA really be able to convict Hypo of killing Boo?"

"Tutoo says it's all circumstantial at this point but he wants to give it a stab. What he'd really like to do is find witnesses who at least *saw* Hypo with potassium chloride on his person. Tutoo doesn't have much to go on right now and he's going up to Baton Rouge tomorrow to take a statement from Sally to see if that helps."

Laura searched Theo's face. "How is Sally?"

He met her eyes, unflinching. "In her own private pain. You and I should send flowers." Laura looked away but Theo kept staring at her, as if suddenly realizing something.

Footsteps sounded on the front porch and Cecile went to answer the door. She reentered the living room with Quatorze and a slim, balding man with a large brown-wrapped package under his arm. As Quatorze stayed shyly in the foyer, the balding man greeted everyone in the room. Without getting up from the couch, Theo said, "Laura, this is Tutoo Landry, the district attorney. Tutoo, Laura Ireland."

Tutoo had a shining, tapered skull and thin, sloping shoulders. He wore a tight starched collar and bow tie and reminded Laura vaguely of a bowling pin. Extending his free hand, he said, "I wished we would have had you with us at the post office, Laura. It would have made it a lot easier to pick up the package." He sat down across from Theo and put the box on the table. "Well?"

"It's addressed to Laura. Why don't we let her open it."

Laura sat down on the edge of a chair. "And it isn't even my birthday."

Quatorze crept forward from the foyer and stood behind the chair as Laura ripped off the brown paper. Pulling a pocketknife from his pants, he handed it to Laura for the tape. She slipped the blade between the flaps, opened the corrugated carton, and pulled out a feather-light red package wrapped in a dry cleaning bag. Styrofoam peanuts tinkled to the floor.

"Can I open it?" asked Laura. "Or is it evidence?"

"I don't know yet," said Tutoo. "Why don't you let Quatorze do that?"

Quatorze moved to the table and peeled back the gossamer plastic, setting a red Ferragamo shoe box down on the coffee table. "There she be," he said.

"Is this the one Reba gave you with thirty-two thousand dollars in it, Theo?"

"The very same."

"But you can't actually trace this to T-Harry Meacham can you? There must be hundreds of men who wear Ferragamo shoes."

"Laura, this is Louisiana. Quatorze, how many people you know wear gray suede Ferragamo Loafers?"

"Never heard of them before."

"Wimp shoes," Theo assured her.

"Lawyer shoes," said Quatorze.

Tutoo crossed his legs, displaying a heavy black wing tip. "Careful with your name-calling, Quatorze."

Theo twisted around to put his feet on the floor. Gently picking up the box through the cleaning bag, he showed Laura one of the ends. "See that price sticker? That's how we tracked it."

Laura sat forward and squinted. " '$219 reduced to $179. Graham & Dunn Shoes.' "

"That's his favorite shoe store, their July sale. Sally drove me over there and we found the clerk who sold these to Meacham. See that: 'Size 9-D Loafers, gray suede.' The clerk even had it written down on a file card. Meacham was wearing them at the courthouse the other day."

Tutoo took the shoe box and re-covered it in plastic. "Theophile, I'll grant you that this shoe box was probably Meacham's and I believe you when you say he wants it back very badly, but this ain't enough to convict him with. This don't prove he helped pay off the sheriff thirty-two thousand dollars to let them kill your daddy."

"I know that. And I think underneath it all, Meacham

knows that. But considering how hard he worked trying to get this back, if you keep this shoe box in your office safe, I don't think my daddy'll have any more 'accidents' over at the sugar house. The press would love something like this and Meacham knows it: unmarked cash in a shoe box from a style that's the exact size Meacham wears from the store he shops at. And the worst part is the price sticker: that's a week's salary for most people."

Swathing the shoe box in its wrapping, Tutoo sighed. "Now, if we just had something this red and pretty on Hypo."

Laura watched him cover the box without touching it. "Do you think you can really convict Hypo? Theo says the evidence is all circumstantial."

"That's right so far. What I'd really like are some witnesses who can connect Hypo with the potassium chloride. I need to canvas the hospital staff."

"I bet Hypo's too smart to have let anyone see him." Laura bolted upright. "Wait a minute! *I* saw him. He took a little drug bottle out of the emergency room cabinet the other night, Theo. When we went to see your father. I can be a witness."

"Did you see that it was potassium chloride, Laura?" asked Tutoo.

"No." She looked at his sincere blue bow tie. "But I could show you where it came from on the shelf. It was a clear bottle with a gray label. There were about a dozen just like it."

"Sounds promising. What do you think, Theophile?"

Theo shrugged. "Worth a shot."

"Maybe y'all'd like to come on out to the hospital with me later this afternoon."

"We'd be glad to, wouldn't we, Theo?"

Theo clicked his tongue. "Now it makes sense. *Hypo* locked you in the morgue, Laura. He was afraid you'd realize what you had seen."

"Of course. Wow. Hypo must have thought I was pretty clever. I never would have realized that."

"Yes, you would have. Especially after things calmed down and you had time to think about what you had seen."

"In fact, here you are realizing it now, Laura." Cecile put aside her crewel and peeked into the coffeepot. "Gentlemen, we've saved some of Sally Guidry's Yamboree Cake for you, but I'm afraid I'll have to make more coffee."

Laura jumped up. "I can do that." She took the pot back to the kitchen and emptied the grounds into the trash. Putting water on to boil, she took down the battered blue recipe box from the cabinet and looked under "Cakes." On a brittle yellowed card she found the recipe for Buttermilk Spice Cake written in a graceful sloping hand. Using an empty card from the back of the box, she copied ingredients as the water hissed on the stove.

Theo came into the kitchen. "What are you doing back here? You don't make coffee."

She tried to hide her work. "Copying a recipe."

He moved her arm and laughed loudly. "You get the strangest ideas sometimes."

"Don't worry about it, okay?"

"Laura, listen to me. I can cook. Maybe I like it that your only recipe is Chicken Legs in Campbell's Sauce."

"Well, what if *I* liked Sally's Yamboree Cake and want to learn how to make something like it?"

He leaned over and put his face in the crown of her hair. "You thought I was with Sally this weekend, didn't you?"

"Yes."

"You know I could never do that to anybody, don't you? Not just to you, to *anybody.*"

"I know. But all the evidence pointed the other way. Gus said . . . never mind. I let him do a number on me."

He planted a kiss in her hair. "What do you want to do with the rest of the afternoon?"

"We said we'd go to the hospital with Tutoo."

"Want to stop by and see my father after that?"

Laura spun around in her chair. "Why? I mean, I don't have anything to say to him. Do you?"

"No. Just checking. How about the River Road? Want to go see the plantations?"

"I don't think so. I think I need to clear my head. How about let's go fishing?"

About The Author

Born in New Orleans and raised in Atlanta, Linda Mariz lives in Bellingham, Washington. She has degrees in history from the University of Missouri at Columbia, and Western Washington University. Her first Laura Ireland-Theo Talbot mystery, *Body English*, is available through Bantam Crime Line.